A Witch in Notting Hill

By Alexandra Paige

An Irish Summer

Weekends with You

A Witch in Notting Hill

A Novel

ALEXANDRA PAIGE

An Imprint of HarperCollins*Publishers*

 For information, address HarperCollins Publishers, 195 Broadway, New York, NY 10007. In Europe, HarperCollins Publishers, Macken House, 39/40 Mayor Street Upper, Dublin 1, D01 C9W8, Ireland.

HarperCollins books may be purchased for educational, business, or sales promotional use. For information, please email the Special Markets Department at SPsales@harpercollins.com.

hc.com

FIRST EDITION

Interior text design by Diahann Sturge-Campbell

Cat illustration © md/Stock.Adobe.com
Magic spirals illustration © Orange Sky/Stock.Adobe.com

Library of Congress Cataloging-in-Publication Data

Names: Paige, Alexandra (Novelist), author
Title: A witch in Notting Hill : a novel / Alexandra Paige.
Description: First edition. | New York, NY : HarperCollins, 2026.
Identifiers: LCCN 2025032549 | ISBN 9780063482401 (trade paperback) | ISBN 9780063482395 (ebook)
Subjects: LCGFT: Fiction | Romance fiction | Witch fiction | Novels
Classification: LCC PS3616.A337815 W58 2026
LC record available at https://lccn.loc.gov/2025032549

ISBN 978-0-06-348240-1

Printed in the United Kingdom

26 27 28 29 CPI 10 9 8 7 6 5 4 3 2

To London, bookstores, wise old women, and everywhere else magic is undeniable.

CHAPTER 1
Willow

Shit. Shit, shit, shit. This was bad. Not like the time I accidentally made my elementary school disappear bad, or the time I accidentally teleported my sister to Montreal bad, but it was bad.

But it was fixable, right? It had to be fixable. I was sure it was fixable.

"Just hang on, Vera," I muttered, mostly to myself, because I was no longer sure whether my manager understood English. Did cats understand English? *God, what have I done?* "I'm going to fix this, Vera, I promise. Just, uh, hang in there."

I scrambled around my trailer, looking for what, I wasn't entirely sure. I didn't even know how I turned her into a cat in the first place. How the hell was I supposed to know how to turn her back?

Being a witch was hard.

Being a bad witch was even harder. Way harder than being an actor.

In the books and the movies, everyone makes being a witch seem so easy. A flick of the wrist, a Latin chant, a flying broom, *et voilà*.

You're having the time of your life. No disappearing schools, no sisters in Canada, no seemingly irreversible spells.

Meanwhile, in reality, you refuse one measly romance contract, then somehow turn your manager into a cat right before the summer solstice party. Which happens to be the party of the year. And also the party where she was apparently going to introduce you to your would-be co-star after she convinced you to sign the contract.

Only there was no contract, and now no Vera, either. Only me, already sweating through this gown, and Vera in cat form blinking at me with a panicked expression I was certain wasn't far from my own.

Okay. *Think, Willow.* How did we get here?

Vera suggested I do a romance, for what felt like the millionth time lately, and I declined, for what also felt like the millionth time, because she already knew I'd never do a romance. Romance made my powers a little wonkier than usual, even when it wasn't real, and I never thought it translated well to the big screen, anyway. Maybe that was because I didn't have a ton of experience off-screen, which was yet another reason not to try to make it work. When catastrophe follows seemingly every time you get close to someone, you tend to avoid romantic encounters altogether.

So I declined, but Vera pressed the issue because the money would be good and my powers had been pretty stable lately, so it might not be a bad time, and then I tried to put my foot down and firmly refuse, so I reached out to touch her forearm to make sure she was really listening, and before I knew it . . . she was a cat.

That part, however, was exactly like the movies. A flash of light, a puff of smoke, a soft meow, and here we were.

Was it something I said? The way I touched her arm? Did it have something to do with the solstice? I ripped the colossal headband off my head and tossed it across my trailer, raking my hands through my hair and no longer caring about the hours it took to tame my unruly waves into a bouncy blowout.

"Vera, what the hell happened?" I moaned without lifting my head from my hands. All she did was meow in response. Which I suppose made sense, since it was all she *could* do.

This obviously wasn't the first time my powers had gone haywire. As a kid, they would short-circuit during heightened states of emotion: when I was fighting with my sister, failing math, trying to play sports. Honestly, this predicament was how I'd gotten into acting in the first place. I'd auditioned for the school play after my magic had interfered with every other club or activity I tried, and something clicked. I could be someone else onstage. Someone who was finally good at something. Someone who could keep her magic more or less under control.

Until eighth grade, that is. When I had my first real crush and immediately lost it.

Before that, spells would fail when I was actively trying to cast them, which made them relatively easy to reverse, since I knew what they were in the first place. But where Fletcher Cohen was concerned, spells would happen seemingly out of nowhere. I'd be in class, minding my business and trying desperately not to stare at the side of his head, and before I knew it, the power would go out or snow would fall from the ceiling or everyone in class would be floating around like Mylar balloons. Needless to say, I didn't have a crush again for a long, long time. And needless to say, it was a blessing I went to a magic school or I don't think I'd have had a single friend.

So when I started acting professionally, I made sure my contract had a no-romance clause. Acting was supposed to be the one thing I knew I could do right. The one thing I was good at, where I didn't have to second-guess myself or compare myself to my family. I couldn't risk malfunctioning on set and ruining a movie, or outing myself in the first place, so I steered clear entirely, and up until now Vera had been cool with that.

And as far as relationships went, I steered clear of those, too. It was hard enough to date with my busy filming schedules, not to mention learning to balance my rising fame with my easily overstimulated personality and my desire to keep my powers under wraps. It was all a lot.

My hope was that I'd figure out how to gain control sooner rather than later and be able to risk a chance at a normal relationship someday, but honestly, that was at the bottom of my priority list. Especially now, as I stared at Vera where she sat on the floor, pinning me with her marble-eyed gaze.

"I'm going to get us out of this," I said, and if I wasn't mistaken, she furrowed her brows. "*You* out of this," I corrected myself. "I'm going to get *you* out of this. Just as soon as I, uh, figure out how the hell I got you into this."

Remembering I'd tossed my journal in the bottom of my bag before I left the house, I dug it out and riffled through page after page of notes about spells. Some I'd mastered in childhood, like making plants grow and mending holes in clothes and fixing broken household items and replacing stolen desserts before my sister and I got in trouble. Others I was still learning—because being a witch essentially meant a lifetime of learning—like how to heal a broken limb or break up LA traffic.

If only I had a spell for finding a spell.

But I didn't, and no matter how many pages I flipped, I found not a single note about turning your manager into a cat. Or back into a person. Or shape-shifting at all, frankly. I hadn't even known it was something I could do until ten minutes ago.

And just as I was about to scream at the top of my lungs, there was a knock on my trailer door.

"Willow?" A man's voice. Deep, rumbling, instantly recognizable. "It's Kit Hayes."

Kit Hayes. Presumably coming here because I was now late for the party, where he thought we were going to connect ahead of the movie we would be starring in together. We hadn't met face-to-face before, but we'd been in each other's orbits long enough for Vera to get in his ear, apparently.

"Hi!" I shouted through the door, my voice unnaturally high in my state of panic.

"Are you ready?"

"Ready?" I asked, looking at cat Vera with wide eyes. "Ready for what, exactly?"

"The party?" He laughed, but only because he was confused and not because any of this was funny. "Vera mentioned we might walk in together, you know, to drop a hint about the film." *Are you serious?* I mouthed to Vera. If cats could shrug, she would have. "She said to drop by at nine, but I can come back if it's a bad time."

"What is wrong with you?" I whisper-yelled at her, trying to keep my hands from flailing around and casting any other spells.

"What was that?" Kit asked through the door.

"Oh, not you! Sorry, just, uh, finishing up a phone call. Just a second." In an effort to appear normal, I flung the door open, which I immediately realized was a mistake. I hadn't seen Kit this up close before, and he was even hotter in real life than he was on the screen. Tall, angular, impeccably dressed, leaning against the doorjamb of the trailer with his hand high above my head. For a fraction of a second, I understood Vera's vision.

Until my stomach jumped and the lights flickered and I felt a familiar, dangerous sizzling in my fingertips. At least this time I had a warning.

"Hi, I'm so sorry, I'm going to have to meet you there," I sputtered, trying to keep my smile from wavering despite the increasing terror at whatever was about to happen. When I started to close the door and he slapped his big hand against it before it shut in his face, I felt my hair stand on end. *Stay calm, Willow. Come on.*

Normally, I could come face-to-face with a hot guy and not have to worry the sky was falling. But since I was already in a state, and the currents were still racing through my veins and this trailer and the air between us, I was fighting an uphill battle.

"Are you okay?" he asked. "I can wait if you want, or I can—"

"I'm fine!" More shaking. A dull buzzing sound. A warning meow from Vera. "I'll meet you there!" I pushed the door back against his hand, and he let it slam, the sound ricocheting obnoxiously between us. I knew I was being rude, but what was the alternative?

With my back against the door and the atmosphere seeming to settle now that Kit was out of sight, my breathing returned to normal. Well, normal was relative. My breathing returned to what it had been before, which still wasn't great. I needed to make some moves.

"All right, Vera, you're going to hate this, but we have to go." I unzipped my gown and dropped it in a heap on the floor, and I could have sworn she gasped. "I can't go out there and leave you in here like this, can I?" Silence. "Exactly. And the solution to this isn't in this trailer, so we need to get the hell out of Dodge before I turn anyone else into a household pet."

I changed back into my street clothes, relieved to trade my stilettos for my well-loved Sambas and the gown for sweatpants and a crewneck, and called my driver. He was in front of the trailer before I even knew where we were going, but I knew it needed to be far from here.

With Vera in my arms and my hat pulled low in the hopes that no one (especially the vicious paparazzi) saw me sneaking away from the party, I slipped into the back of the car and took out my phone to do what I always did in moments when I needed guidance or comfort: listen to an old voicemail from my grandmother.

It took only a minute of scrolling to find the one I was looking for. May 1, 2009. The one I listened to every time something went wrong. Really wrong. I clicked Play and immediately relaxed into the sound of her voice, turning the volume up in case somehow Vera could hear it, too.

Hi, Wills. It's me, Granny Annie. I heard what happened at school today. Being magic is hard, isn't it? Even at my age, I still lose control sometimes. Remember last Thanksgiving? Boy, was that a scene.

The memory made me laugh every time. Granny accidentally had a few too many, and before any of us knew it, the turkey was climbing out of the roasting pan and threatening my mother with a steak knife.

You don't have to call me back or anything, she continued, *but I wanted you to hear this, so listen close. Your powers are a gift, my girl. Even when they feel like a curse. And ultimately, your magic has nothing to do with what spells you can and cannot conjure at all. You are the magic, Wills. The spells will work themselves out. And even if they don't, we'll always have something to laugh about, and there are far worse things than that.*

And if you find yourself really in a bind, you know I'm always here, darling. Our magic might not be transferable, but I'll always find a way to help you. And if I can't—

I knew the voicemail by heart, which meant I knew the exact words that were coming next. Why hadn't I thought of this sooner?

—Coven and Codex can. I know, I know, London is a long way from California. But trust me. If I can't sort you out, the bookshop can. Come to think of it, bookshops are always the answer, aren't they? Oh, listen to me, rambling away like an old bat. I love you, honey. And I don't want what happened today, or in the past, or whatever happens in the future to make you doubt your magic. Okay? Give me a call if you need me. Okay, I love you. Bye-bye.

Of all the times I'd listened to the voicemail, I'd never once internalized the bit about the bookstore. I'd never thought Gran wouldn't be around to answer my questions, so I never bothered to make a Plan B. But in classic Granny Annie fashion, *she* made the Plan B. It had been sitting in my voicemail this whole time.

And with sudden, crushing clarity, I knew exactly where we needed to go.

CHAPTER 2
Willow

Admittedly, I was spoiled. Or at least I *had* been, where travel was concerned. Between TSA PreCheck, Global Entry, and a manager who handled most of the logistics, travel was easier for me than most. And it wasn't that I took it for granted—trust me, I knew how good I had it—but there was nothing that could have prepared me for traveling with a cat for the first time. Especially a cat who used to be a person. A very bossy, detail-oriented, type A person.

I scrambled to get her registered as an emotional support animal on the ride to the airport, paid the exorbitant fee for same-day approval, and tried hard not to panic about how ill-prepared I was for a last-minute trip to London. This wasn't about me; it was about turning Vera back into a person. So if I had to wear the same outfit for however long it took, so be it.

I'd forgone my security team in favor of Vera's privacy, though upon arrival at the airport, I wasn't so sure it had been the best idea. No one knew she was a cat, and I wasn't exactly keen on tipping off the whole team, so I hadn't done more than send an email from her account saying she was going on a silent retreat in the UK on short notice and not to reach out until she returned, but the teeming crowds at the terminal made me wish I wasn't alone.

Armed with a baseball hat, the largest sunglasses I could find, and my unassuming gray sweat set, I grabbed my tote and Vera in the cat carrier—the nicest one I could find on the way there—and made my way to security. The heat in LA was becoming unbearable, and since it was the height of summer, it was no surprise everyone was racing to leave the city. Families and older couples and glamorous twentysomethings waited in security lines, checking and rechecking their bags for passports, wallets, designer sunglasses, heaps of technology, and beauty products poised to set off the security scanners.

And I stood paralyzed in the doorway, barely far enough into the airport to stop triggering the doors' automatic sensor.

Before she was a cat, Vera used to assuage so many of my fears. That was one of the myriad reasons she was such a good manager. She helped me navigate crowds, helped me manage my fear of flying, helped me still my racing heart rate as we went through TSA because I did not, in fact, accidentally somehow have a weapon in my bag.

Only now, when I looked at her sparkling yellow-green eyes peering back at me through the mesh of her carrier, I felt more anxious than ever. *I'm so sorry*, I mouthed for what must have been the billionth time in the last two hours. *I'm going to get you out of this.*

She nodded sagely, which I took as a sign she understood me. A small victory in the depths of this mess I'd created.

I had no idea what I was doing, but just that gentle nod strengthened my resolve. If there was ever a time to beat my anxiety, it was now. I took a deep breath and slipped into the PreCheck line, my boarding pass pulled up on my phone and my passport in my hand long before anyone would ask for either. The quicker I could make it through, the better. Especially if the TSA agents didn't say anything about who I was as they scanned my documents.

I shuffled up to the kiosk when it was my turn, sliding my passport through the opening in the plexiglass and hovering my boarding pass over the electronic scanner. *Please don't say anything, please don't say anything.*

"And for the cat, ma'am?"

This was . . . not what I expected him to say.

"For the cat?" I repeated. "I, um, oh, here," I said, pulling up the last-minute Emotional Support Animal certificate in my email. Was this what he meant?

"Her veterinary documents," he prompted, sounding so bored I wondered how he was even awake.

"Veterinary documents?" Apparently my confusion had rendered me unable to do anything but repeat his every word.

"Vaccination records, et cetera," he droned, waving his hand like he couldn't even be bothered to finish his sentence.

How could I not have thought of this? Surely I didn't have veterinary documents, since Vera had never been to the vet, since she wasn't even a real cat. Except in the eyes of this TSA agent, she was as real as could be, and I was standing there like an idiot, unmoving.

"Ma'am, if you don't have the documentation, please step to the side," he said with a sigh. "One of our agents will sort it out with you. Next." He was already waving the family behind us up to the kiosk, and they were jostling me and Vera out of the way before we could even figure out where to go.

"Shit," I whispered, trying to ignore the disapproving look in

Vera's eyes. At that moment, I was glad she was a cat. I wasn't sure I'd be able to handle the wrath of human Vera at my having made such an idiotic mistake.

"Right this way, please," another agent was saying, guiding me roughly by the elbow out of the PreCheck line and to a small room behind the ropes. "What seems to be the problem?" she asked once we were uncomfortably seated on plastic chairs under fluorescent lights that rivaled the sun.

As I explained my dilemma, letting her hear my voice quivering in the hope of garnering some sympathy, her face remained stone-cold. She nodded but said nothing. By the time I finished my sob story about needing to get to my sick grandmother in London and being unable to travel without my emotional support cat (semantics, creative liberties, whatever), I thought her eyes might have softened. Or, at the very least, she was no longer frowning.

With a heaving sigh, she jiggled the mouse on a desktop computer and said, "Let me see what I can do."

After a few excruciating minutes of clicking around and mumbling to herself, she clapped her hands together. "Well, then," she said. "All settled. You'll just need to remove your hat and sunglasses for the photo for your temporary permit. Once it's printed, you're free to go. And I trust you won't make this mistake again."

"No, ma'am," I said, eagerly removing my disguise for the photo and not even bothering to care about her scolding. I was so relieved to be able to travel with Vera, I forgot anything else that might have mattered.

Like putting my disguise back on when I returned to the security line with my permit in hand.

The whispers started low, like always, before gaining traction and snowballing into shouts of my name and camera clicks.

"Is that Willow James?"

"Willow!"

"Miss James, can we have a photo?"

"I wonder where she's going."

"Where's her security?"

"When did she get a cat?"

"Do you think she's going to a new film site?"

"Willow!"

With nowhere to hide and my anxiety knotting itself in the base of my throat, I turned back to the TSA agent, relieved she was still standing in the doorway of the small room we'd been in only seconds before. She heaved yet another frustrated sigh and swung her arm wide, motioning for me to come back in.

This was going to be harder than I thought. And if I couldn't even manage the airport, how the hell was I going to manage London?

Before I could overthink it, I heard my grandmother's voice in the back of my mind: *Don't be afraid to use your gift, Wills.*

If only she were here. And if only I was half as confident in what I could actually do. But I knew I'd be letting her down if I didn't try, and even though I rarely used magic in public, especially after I'd been recognized, I didn't have much of a choice.

"Thank you," I said to the agent as I slipped back into the room. She tutted under her breath and shook her head but said nothing. "If I could just have a minute to collect myself, maybe come up with a plan to avoid the crowd, I'll be out of your hair. I promise." I looked around the room, trying to clock anything that might be useful to me: desktop computer, ancient printer, stained wall calendar, stapler, file cabinet, a wilted fern. Bingo.

"In private, please," I added, my pleading genuine. At this she scoffed, and if I wasn't mistaken, I definitely caught an eye roll, but still, she said nothing. An angel.

The second she closed the door behind her, I unzipped Vera's carrier and stared directly into her gorgeous feline face. "I'm going to do it," I whispered. "I'm going to try to use magic to get us out of this. Just this one time, I swear. Once we're in London, I'm going to be better about hiding and I won't get us into a mess like this." She narrowed her eyes. "I know, I know, it was a mistake to do this without security. But I did that for your benefit, too, remember? So now we have to make do." She made a small sound, which I took as permission.

"Right," I continued, reaching for the fern. I rubbed its waxy leaves between my fingers, trying to remember how my grandmother taught me to channel the earth, to breathe with the pattern of the veins, to turn faces toward the sun. "If I can get everyone to just face the sunset long enough for me to get through security," I mumbled to Vera, trying to remember exactly how my grandmother had done it all those years ago.

Ivy, my sister, had broken her leg playing in the yard, and my grandmother hadn't wanted me to see her pain. Before I knew it, I was watching the setting sun streak across the sky and counting its colors while she was carrying Ivy inside, and I was none the wiser. Just a kid enamored by the sunset.

I let the memory well in the front of my mind, sharp and rich and palpable. I closed my eyes, smelling the wet grass, listening to the chirping crickets that signaled the start of summer, feeling the warm breeze on my skin. *Come on.* My grandmother materialized in my memory, pressing her hands into the earth for a prolonged moment just before she scooped Ivy into her arms and I lost sight of them both.

I squeezed the leaves of the fern tighter between my fingers, watching the memory like it was an old movie. As it flicked across the backs of my eyelids, I felt the familiar hum of electricity in my fingertips. *Come on.* I saw her yard, the swings still in motion, the faded fence, the tomato plant. Pins and needles moved from my fingers to my toes, then my chest, then the tip of my tongue.

Then the door flung open.

And all eyes were on the sky.

"Holy shit," I whispered to Vera. "I've done it." Her eyebrows were raised, like, *We better get the hell out of here before the spell short-circuits and we're both cats*, and she was right. I grabbed the carrier and raced out the door, holding my breath as I slipped into the line.

I shuffled forward, with every step braced for the inevitable failure. Back through the ropes, back to the TSA agent—with the proper paperwork this time—back to praying he didn't say anything out loud when he scanned my ID, and wanting to kiss him when he was kind enough not to.

By the time I made it through the body scanner and had my hands "randomly" dusted for bomb residue (probably on account of the suspicious cat, who was glaring pointedly at every person we passed), I exhaled for what felt like the first time since I touched the fern.

And all at once, all eyes were focused on me again.

If I was going to change Vera back, I was going to have to get a lot better at this.

CHAPTER 3

Willow

When we finally made it to Heathrow, we were both exhausted. Not just red-eye exhausted, but the kind of exhausted that comes with overstimulation and a general sense of panic that even the usual daily dose of antianxiety medication can't fix.

Okay, maybe that was just me. Vera was asleep in her carrier, and I felt my jealousy like hunger pangs.

Or maybe those *were* hunger pangs. When was the last time we'd eaten? I'd been too stressed to eat on the flight and Vera had been sound asleep, so we missed every meal they'd tried to serve. And there was no way I was actually going to feed Vera cat food, was I?

I was contemplating whether that was appropriate or degrading when I saw the Pret A Manger logo in the distance, calling to me like an oasis in the desert. This really *was* the Queen's Terminal.

By the time we were armed with sandwiches (cheddar and pickle for me, tuna for Vera) and cold brew (just me—I had to draw the line somewhere), I was ready to get my ass to Coven & Codex and find some answers.

Though the more I looked at Vera, who seemed to be getting cozier in the carrier by the minute, the more I was beginning to wonder whether she was equally desperate. I couldn't even remember the last time she went on vacation (despite my insistence), so I had to imagine there was *something* positive about getting the chance to lie down and do nothing for the foreseeable. Or that was just something I was telling myself to feel better about the whole thing. Hard to say.

With my suitcase in one hand and Vera in the other, I made my way to the Underground. The anonymity of a crowded train platform was so satisfying that I allowed myself to take a deep breath for the first time since LA, but I learned my lesson and remembered not to remove my hat or sunglasses, no matter how desperate I was to have a break from the disguise.

The last thing I needed on this adventure was for someone to recognize me.

Scratch that.

The last thing I needed on this adventure was for someone to recognize me *and* realize I was a witch.

And not even a good one.

Society's response to witchcraft was disbelieving at best and degrading at worst, so the headlines would likely have been more about how I "thought" I was a witch, and that might have been even worse.

There was no upside to this mess. Perhaps I needed a better disguise.

The famous disembodied voice reminded us to "mind the gap" as the Piccadilly line train pulled to a stop, and I felt farther from home than ever. I'd traveled to dozens of countries over the years for work, England included on multiple occasions, and yet, as I shuffled with the masses onto the subway, I might as well have been on another planet entirely.

"Let's hope this is quick," I whispered to Vera. "Hotel, then bookstore, then back to LA before we know it."

Drowsy as she was, she shot me a look that said, *Stop talking to your cat on the Tube*, and as always, she was right. I didn't need to draw any more attention to myself, and I was certain I looked insane. So we both settled in for the ride, listening for our change at Hammersmith, counting the minutes until Notting Hill revealed herself.

And reveal herself she did. After a frenzied change at Hammersmith, we made it to Ladbroke Grove in one piece, and we were treated to quintessential London views on the short walk to the hotel: rows upon rows of pastel Victorian homes, red double-decker buses, cobbled sidewalks, expanses of heavy gray sky.

I couldn't deny the magic of the city, even under this kind of stress. And not my chaotic kind of magic, either. The magnetic kind. The kind that made it impossible to believe life existed anywhere else.

We'd made it.

It was time for Operation Spell Reversal.

CHAPTER 1

Oliver

When I'd inherited Coven & Codex from my granduncle, I'd been informed I'd be inheriting more than just an occult bookstore in Notting Hill (that I wasn't allowed to sell, under any circumstances, no matter how prime the real estate was). His barrister apparently subscribed to the same belief system he did, and she believed his stories of spirits between these walls. Informed me that this was a place where "things happened."

As far as I was concerned, the only "things" that "happened" were hordes of tourists wandering in, running their fingers over spines without reading titles, picking up candles by the lids and dropping them on the floor, and asking me questions about *Harry Potter*.

Anything else was a result of Uncle Arthur's old age and lack of upkeep of the place: flickering lights, drafty windows, groaning floorboards, whistling pipes. All to be expected in an old build that hadn't been properly cared for in years.

Otherwise, nothing else "happened." Day in and out, I stood behind the mahogany desk, manually conducting transactions with a two-hundred-year-old till despite the computer that sat on the desktop, or I wandered through the stacks reorganizing the books that seemed to move themselves around the store, or I managed inventory and hunted down unique selections that customers requested and were willing to pay a lot of money for.

Which is exactly what I was doing this morning when I first noticed her.

A petite woman with auburn hair, a baseball cap pulled low over her eyes, and a floor-length trench coat in the middle of the summer, whispering to what looked like a designer picnic basket hooked over her arm. Between the basket and the wide-eyed look she was trying to hide, it was all very *We're not in Kansas anymore*, and I had no interest in being her Glinda.

I tried to look away, to refocus on the archives I had pulled up on the computer, but her whispering was painfully distracting. Soft but frantic. Melodic. Familiar.

"I'm trying," she was saying. "It's going to take time. Just hang on."

Who was she talking to? And had I actually heard her voice before?

Realizing immediately that would have been impossible and that I likely needed to get out more, I shook my head and returned to my work. Just another tourist. And whatever the whispering was about, I didn't want to know.

I clicked through the digital archives of A Witch in Time and Hexed, two other local shops, trying to find a first-edition copy of *UnHearthed: Tea, Herbs, and Natural Mysticism* for Mr. Blackburn. He was a repeat customer, and most of the time his books were easy to find—I suspected he just didn't have the energy to try to find them. Though if I had the amount of money he did, I'd be paying someone else to do it, too.

I'd only made it through a few more pages before my attention was once again ripped from my desk—this time by a loud crack in the Fables and Folklore room. While it wasn't exactly a library, you'd think in a bookstore you'd at least be able to find a single moment of peace.

Suppressing the melodramatic sigh climbing up my throat, I made my way through the maze of shelves to the back. Uncle Arthur's last wishes also specified that I did not rearrange the store, no matter how little sense the layout made to me. He'd insisted the books were organized in a way that they would find their owners, as opposed to the other way around. *The store speaks to people*, he'd always said. *So long as they are willing to listen.*

I'd tried to be willing to listen. Really, I had. For the sake of the business, if nothing else. But I was either terrible at it or Uncle Arthur was messing with me, because I hadn't been able to find a bloody thing in here since I was a kid.

The Fables and Folklore room was at the back of the shop, behind Celestial Craft, around the corner from a display of incense and tarot cards and lunar calendars, and through a warped archway so low I had to duck underneath it (a lesson I learned the hard way). It only took a second of fumbling for the light switch and a crunching under my feet to realize what the sound had been—an exploded lightbulb. They flickered often, but exploded? Never. Even if they were from some long-forgotten era that left them hanging exposed from the cracking ceiling.

The only light left in the room came from a small stained-glass window, painting the space in jewel-toned shards. It would have been beautiful had I not had a massive safety concern on my hands. And just as I was thanking some higher power that the lightbulb hadn't exploded on a customer, her voice cut through the silence.

"I'm sorry," she said, a little too loud for the quiet of the shop. "I have no idea what happened."

"Are you hurt?" I asked, following the sound of her voice with my eyes until I spotted her clutching her basket with one hand and clutching imaginary pearls with the other.

"No, no, just surprised." She dropped her hand and exhaled, but she kept her eyes cast toward the floor. "Let me clean this up. Do you have a broom around here somewhere?"

So she was American, which I suppose I could have guessed from the baseball cap before I heard the accent. We got a lot of Americans in the shop, but that didn't account for the familiarity of her voice.

She cleared her throat, alerting me to the fact I had yet to respond.

"No, please, it's fine," I said, waving her away. "I'll take care of it." I was already shaking out the antique rug to gather the glass in the center of the room, keeping an eye on her to make sure she didn't get any closer. One sideways piece of glass could go right through her little white trainers, and the last thing this shop needed was an injury on the premises. And the last thing *I* needed was any more interaction with this woman. I couldn't place her and I didn't want to.

"Really, I'd like to help."

"No need. Not like it was your fault the lightbulb exploded, there, was it?"

She laughed, but nothing was funny. It had a kind of self-deprecating tone that made the hair on the back of my neck stand on end. "With the way my life has been going lately, I'm sure it was," she said, and sighed.

I didn't want to ask. I didn't want to know. Or rather, I didn't *want* to want to know. And yet, I heard my voice before the thoughts passed through my brain. "Streak of bad luck, then?"

"You could call it that."

"What would *you* call it?"

Another long exhale. "Bad genetics, maybe. I'm not sick or anything. That sounded foreboding. Sorry. I just . . . You know when you're supposed to be one thing, like it's in your blood and your family is good at it, but then you're terrible? It's one of those. Not that that's a common experience for everyone, I guess. It actually might be oddly specific? Not that you care either way. Now I'm just—"

"I know exactly what you mean." What the hell was I doing? I hadn't wanted to know anything about this woman, and now I was on the verge of confessing my life story to her? I didn't believe in witchcraft, but I would have been lying if I said I didn't feel like I was under some kind of spell.

"You do?"

I looked up from the rug just in time to see her eyes widen, two huge marbles in her perfectly round face. She chewed on her thumbnail, her hand obscuring the lower half of her face, but I didn't need to see any more than her eyes to know she was beautiful. The live wire swinging from the ceiling sparked once more, but even that made it hard to look away.

"Why do you look so surprised?" I asked, trying to ignore the inherent danger sparking above our heads. And maybe also in the space between us.

"I . . . have no idea." She laughed, for real this time. I was nearly tempted to do the same. "I don't know you at all, obviously."

"Obviously."

"But I'm surprised at the thought of you being bad at something. You don't have that kind of vibe."

"And what vibe is that?"

"The sloppy kind that makes people bad at things."

"Ah, like whispering to your picnic basket while you shop?"

She gasped, but I could hear her smile, even if I didn't dare risk another look. I could also hear a rustling in the basket, at which I dared look even less.

"Aren't British people supposed to be polite?"

"Only the posh ones."

"You run a bookshop in Notting Hill," she said. "Feels pretty posh to me. Maybe you are capable of being bad at things."

"It's a good job there aren't rumors about Americans being polite," I said, finally letting my lips contort into something that resembled a smile. I might not have been friendly, but I wasn't a monster.

"Add the American rumor mill to this list of things I'm bad at," she said, returning my smile, though hers didn't light up the rest of her face like I'd expected it to.

"Hiding out in London, then?"

"Looking for something, actually. But can't say hiding isn't also on my agenda."

In the moment I was trying to decide whether I was going to ask what she was looking for, or what she was hiding from, the bell on the checkout desk rang through the shop, letting me know someone wanted to pay and I needed to hustle back to the till before they changed their mind.

The sound was more of a relief than I was willing to admit. If something tangible hadn't pulled me from this conversation, I wasn't sure how I would have gotten myself out. For what might have been the first time in my life, I wasn't faking interest in a chat with a customer. And I wasn't prepared to unpack how I felt about it.

"I have to get that," I said, gesturing toward the till like an idiot. "Please be careful around the glass. And please close the door behind you so no one else goes in."

"Are you sure I can't clean this up?"

"Certain," I said. "Just try not to explode anything else, will you?" I shot a glance at her over my shoulder, and she nodded.

"I'll try my best."

All at once, the heater rattled, the shelves creaked, and the door swung shut between us. Just like that, the spell was broken, and I was pulled from the trance back into reality. A harsh one. One with incessant dinging and a floor covered in glass. And a strange, beautiful woman on the other side of the door.

CHAPTER 5

Willow

Life as an actor and a witch was unpredictable. I'd gotten used to that. I learned never to settle, never to get too comfortable, never to think life couldn't turn around and shock me at any moment. So you'd think I'd have been prepared for the man working at Coven & Codex to be so gorgeous that I exploded a damn lightbulb just by being in his shop, but alas. Somehow, I was still surprised.

I mean, seriously, what the *hell* happened in there? Had it really been so long since I'd been with anyone that just the sight of an attractive man had me short-circuiting the electricity and slamming doors, for god's sake? Though I wasn't even sure "attractive" did him justice. Heart-stopping, more like. Jaw-dropping. The kind of good-looking that made you wonder if you were dreaming, or hallucinating, or if that tingle low in your stomach was real, and if so, it was highly inappropriate for a bookshop at this hour.

Had I not caused a scene almost immediately after I walked in, I probably could have done a better job searching the place. Instead, I panicked that I was going to be recognized, then panicked at the sight of the man—his rolled sleeves, his corded forearms—then panicked at the explosion and my embarrassment and the undeniable electricity racing through my veins, then ran out of the shop before I could make things worse. Crushed it, honestly.

Since I woke up this morning, his deep voice had been rumbling in my chest, and his dark curls and the freckles high on his cheeks made me almost forget the reason I had been in the shop in the first place. They weren't quite enough to soften the blow of not having found a single thing about accidental spells that turned people into cats, but they did slightly soften the blow of having to go back and try again.

Only this time, I hoped to be less embarrassing. And I hoped to actually find what I'd been looking for.

Maybe I hadn't had any luck the first time because I didn't have a clear head. I'd gone straight from a transatlantic flight to a bookshop in a foreign country recommended by my late grandmother, so it wasn't surprising I didn't find anything. I barely had any idea what I was looking for. No plan, no ideas, just vibes. And not even good ones.

Tomorrow, I'd have a plan.

Which meant today I had to make said plan. And clear my head. And not necessarily in that order.

At home in California, I always did my best thinking outside. The sun was always shining, the temperature comfortably in the seventies, the light breeze from the ocean just enough to cut through the humidity and ruffle my hair in a way that made me grateful to be alive. Like most of the population of SoCal, I subscribed to the belief system that the answers to most of life's questions could be found in the fresh air.

"All right, Vera. Time to seize the day." I nestled her into her carrier, tossed the essentials into a canvas tote, slipped on my standard-issue Hollywood actor sunglasses, and left the hotel room in favor of Hyde Park.

What we were met with the second we stepped out of the hotel, however, was not the fresh air I'd been so desperately hoping for. It was a wall of rain. Sideways, lashing rain that instantly soaked you through to the bone.

Having been living in California for so long, I'd forgotten the importance of checking the Weather app before leaving the house. A fact that now made me feel painfully naive, in addition to disappointed. So much for my thinking.

"Forgetting something, are you?" the doorman asked, watching me watch the rain and holding out a flimsy umbrella. "Proper bucketing down out there."

"I was hoping to spend the day in Hyde Park," I said with a laugh, though it wasn't really funny. "Should have checked the forecast."

"Ah, yes, won't be enjoying much of a park day, I'm afraid. Won't be needing those, either." He tapped the arm of my sunglasses, and I tried not to be mortified at how stupid I probably looked. It was doubtful this older English gentleman would recognize me, but I couldn't be too careful.

"Old habits," I said, knowing it didn't actually mean anything and hoping he didn't press it.

"Well, if you need a recommendation for a Plan B, might I suggest the Princeton Arms down the road, there? Quite a short walk and the tea is lovely. Would be a nice place to hide out from the weather."

I stared down the road, considering his suggestion. I didn't have a Plan B, and hiding out in a pub did sound nice. It wasn't exactly soaking in the sun, but I *was* in London, so it was time to adjust my expectations. People had been doing some of their best thinking in pubs since the dawn of time—weren't all the best poets and writers doing all their work in places like these?

"That sounds perfect," I said, trying not to sound resigned. "Thank you."

"Right, then. Off you go." He smiled, handing me the umbrella and ushering me into the elements before I could change my mind. Which was for the best, since I definitely would have, had I watched the rain a second longer.

I hustled down the cobbled sidewalk, trying to keep both Vera and myself under the cheap umbrella and out of the direct path of the screaming wind. Fortunately, the Princeton Arms really was only a short walk away, and we were stumbling through the door and into the warmth before I knew it.

"Oi, hello there," the bartender said, likely shocked by the force with which we crashed through the door.

"Hello, hi, sorry for all of that," I said, gesturing vaguely in the direction of my entrance.

"That's quite all right." She offered a warm smile. "What can I do for you . . . two?" She peered over the bar and into Vera's carrier, cocking her head to the side. "Who do we have here?"

"Oh, that's Vera," I said. "Is that okay that she's here? Sorry, she's my, uh, emotional support cat. But I can—"

"Nonsense," she said. "Welcome in, Vera. Nice name for a cat, that. Bit regal, isn't it?"

That would be because it's a name for a person.

"And you are?" she continued.

"Willow," I said without thinking. "Willow Jones." *Terrible save.*

"Well, welcome in to you, too, Willow Jones. Do make yourself at home." Another weird look at the sunglasses. "Have a browse at our menu here and let me know what you'd like. I'm Gloria."

"Thank you, Gloria."

I looked around the pub as she busied herself cleaning glassware. It seemed to be a safe place to shed my disguise. Or at the very least the ridiculous sunglasses. I'd colored my hair a deeper shade of red in the hotel bathroom as soon as we arrived in a desperate attempt to further hide my identity, and I could only hope it would work the way I'd imagined it would when I was elbow deep in the drugstore dye I'd grabbed on the way to the hotel.

The only other patrons were an elderly man and a young couple, who were far too busy feeding each other fries and sharing a pint they likely weren't old enough to drink to pay attention to the soggy American at the bar.

After storing my sunglasses in my bag, I opened the menu in front of my face and tried to keep my gaze low, but I was relieved to be able to finally see. The pub was dimly lit in a way that was cozy instead of depressing, with sconces lining the walls and candles flickering on the high-top tables. The pattern on the carpet clashed with that of the wallpaper so badly it somehow circled back to charming, and it made me think of my grandmother. She would have loved it here. Hell, maybe she'd even been here. After all, it wasn't far from Coven & Codex, and she did love a good pint.

"What'll it be, love?"

"A cheese toastie, please. And an English breakfast tea," I said, closing the menu and glancing down at Vera. "And a small piece of fish? If that's possible. Just one is fine, whatever you have."

"Coming right up." She smiled and collected the menu, leaving me to my afternoon.

I unpacked my journal and my iPad from my tote, determined to search the virtual stacks before I searched the physical ones so that I wouldn't be so lost when I mustered the courage to go back.

The only problem was I hardly knew where to begin.

I tried vague phrases like "shape-shifting reversal" and "how to undo a shape-shifting spell," bookmarking tabs for books titled *The Challenging Art of Changing Forms* and *There and Back Again*. Though if they were anything like my initial internet search, they would more than likely tell me I would need to know how I did the spell in the first place in order to reverse it.

There was a tab on the Coven & Codex website titled Special Requests, and a quick scan of the page informed me that the owner, Oliver Hadley, would help customers "locate and procure unique titles, antique volumes, and any additional curiosities."

Oliver Hadley. Did he count as additional curiosities?

Before I could dive any deeper down that dangerous, highly unnecessary rabbit hole, the bartender returned with the most beautiful, decadent sandwich I'd ever seen. Cheese oozed from all sides of the thick-cut bread, and a pile of French fries—*chips*—overtook every spare inch of the plate. *Yes.* This was perfect. What better than melted cheese and greasy fries to get my mind off a man?

And since Vera was a cat at the moment, that meant she couldn't give me a hard time about not eating enough protein. So far, it was the only upside to this whole debacle, and I felt guilty for even thinking it. But I thought it nonetheless.

As she delicately tore through a flaky piece of white fish from the comfort of her carrier, I continued scrolling my iPad with greasy fingers, studying the sections of the bookshop, the featured titles, and the bottomless depths of the internet for guidance, before finding the first thing that actually seemed to hold some promise: a section on Coven & Codex's website called Reversals, Retractions, and Revocations.

Maybe there was hope after all.

I wiped my hands clean, prepared to do a deep dive of the section's contents in the hope of not having to do it in the store. The less time I spent in there the better, for more reasons than one.

Only my research was quickly interrupted by the sound of the bells over the door, followed by a low voice with a posh English accent I was certain I'd heard before.

"All right, Gloria?"

"Ah, Oliver, dear. A pleasant surprise. Do come in." Gloria gestured to a seat beside me at the bar, and the last bite of my toastie lodged itself in my throat. This couldn't be happening.

"I'll just be a minute there," he said. "Going to pop 'round back and find Greg for a smoke."

She nodded, and I thanked whatever higher power was out there for granting me a few precious minutes to get myself together and get the hell out before he saw me.

Why does this matter so much to me? Perhaps because I didn't want to draw any attention to myself. Perhaps because I had grease dripping down my wrists and bags under my eyes the size of Texas. Perhaps because the last time I saw him I exploded a lightbulb and I wasn't exactly keen on making another scene. It didn't matter. What did matter was that I knew I wasn't ready for another run-in. It was time to go.

Once he was safely out of earshot, I dropped more pounds than were necessary on the bar, thanked Gloria, assured her I didn't need the change, and headed for the door.

"Have you been in before, love?" she asked before I was safely over the threshold. *Damn it.* "Sorry to stop you there, it's just you seem so familiar, and I hadn't noticed it before."

She'd been so kind, I hated to lie, but I wasn't interested in being recognized by anyone else, especially with Oliver headed back into the pub any minute, so I did what I always did in these scenarios: kept it vague and extricated myself, pronto.

"I get that a lot." I smiled. "Must just have one of those faces. Thanks again." I didn't leave her time to say anything else, though I could tell she wanted to. If I was almost outed by the bartender in a hole-in-the-wall pub, I feared removing my disguise completely was going to be even harder than I thought.

Despite the unexpected intrusion, I'd still managed to mark a few titles and to learn a little more about Coven & Codex and its services, not to mention the impossibly delicious sandwich and the fish for Vera, so this was still a productive afternoon. And when I went back into Coven & Codex tomorrow, I would do it with a little more optimism and refreshed resolve.

CHAPTER 6
Oliver

Sunday slipped by in the rhythm of every other day of my life: work, run, read, repeat. There were errands, sure, and dinner plans with my friends, but the rest of my time revolved around an easy, predictable schedule. One that made sense to me and had little room for chaos.

So when that gorgeous, peculiar American walked back into my shop the next day, the impending chaos turned my stomach over. What was she doing back here? Was it possible I might have what she's looking for? It couldn't be. She didn't seem like the type. Quirky, maybe. But not *witchy*. When she'd first come in, I'd suspected it was just for a browse, not a purpose.

Though what the hell did I know? I'd spoken to her for all of five minutes. For all I knew, she could have thought herself to be the Grand High Witch of North America. And if that was the case, I would need even more distance than I'd thought.

I tried and failed not to study her as she moved through the shop. Same low baseball cap, same basket held tight to her side, this time both paired with oversize sunglasses and a linen dress that hung loosely from her curves. She trailed her manicured fingers over the volumes stacked in Ceremonies and Customs, squinting at the spines, strolled distractedly through the aisles of Elements and Crystals, stalled briefly in Divinations, before ducking around a tight corner and stopping in Reversals, Retractions, and Revocations.

It was never a good sign when anyone stopped in Reversals, Retractions, and Revocations. It meant they'd mucked something up, didn't want to take ownership, so instead blamed powers that didn't exist, then demanded answers from Coven & Codex to fix their problems.

Still, I watched. Captivated.

She pulled book after book from the shelves, *Undone* followed by *Turn Back Time: The Art of Reversing Spells*, flipping through them in vain before gently sliding them back into their respective places. What the hell was she looking for?

I only had another second to wonder before two young women crowded her from both sides of the aisle, phones in hand and crazed smiles painted on their nervous faces. Did they know her?

I took a few steps closer, if only to mitigate anything suspicious that might be going on in the shop. I wasn't close enough to hear their conversation, but I was close enough to see the woman's soft, placating smile as the three of them posed for a selfie. For what purpose, I hadn't the foggiest idea.

Just as they seemingly thanked her and shuffled away, heads bent, giggling over the photo, a few more customers began to make their way toward the back of the shop. What was I missing?

Fortunately, no one else approached her, only stood on the periphery and whispered while nodding in her direction, like she was some kind of museum exhibit. She pulled the hat lower over her eyes and slipped into the Celtic section, taking refuge behind a fairy tree while she waited for the small crowd to dissipate.

Deciding it was finally time for me to follow suit and look away, I slipped my phone from my back pocket to text Minho and Lola: the only two people I'd ever tell about an intriguing woman in my shop, even if I might regret it in the same breath.

Me: Something's going on in the shop today. Second time this American woman has been in, and two girls stopped to take a photo. Small crowd formed.

They both replied almost instantly. Minho worked in a cushy corner office as an architect and had his texts linked to his computer, and Lola worked from home as a video game designer, so the two were usually accessible during the day. Which was often a blessing and a curse.

Lola: Is she a celeb??

Minho: Must be. What's she look like?

Me: Hard to tell. Baseball cap and sunglasses on.

Minho: Definitely famous.

Lola: Anything else?

Undone, curly hair that makes me want to run my hands through it. A body with curves I will get on my knees for a chance to see without the oversize clothes.

Me: Long auburn hair. Short, curvy

Lola: Can you sneak a pic?

Me: No, because I'm not a creep.

Minho: Says who?

Me: Never mind.

Minho: Relax, I'm only taking the piss. CCTV footage?

Me: Is that better or worse?

Lola: Definitely better. Everyone at least knows they're on CCTV.

Minho: She has a point.

Me: Fine. Give me a few.

Really, I needed more than a few. A few to weigh the morality of the situation, and a few more to make a decision. Lola was right. Everyone did technically know they were always on CCTV footage.

But was taking a picture of said footage and sending it to the group chat to identify a customer unethical? Though I couldn't expect them to identify her from my description alone, and it wasn't like they could just camp out in the shop until she eventually did or did not come back, so what choice did I have?

With a glance over my shoulder to confirm she was once again safe from an audience and also not looking anywhere near my computer screen, I switched to the camera view and snapped the clearest picture I could find.

Within seconds of sending it to my friends, my phone was ringing with an incoming call from Lola.

Me: Did we not just establish I'm very obviously working and cannot answer because there are customers in here?

Lola: That was before we established Willow fucking James is in your shop!!!

Willow James. *Willow James.*

Minho: Bloody hell. The actor? The one from French 75? And that sad film Lo is obsessed with?

Lola: Red Garden! And The Truth About Holly!

That Willow James? Was *this* Willow James? The more film titles Minho and Lola volleyed back and forth, the faster my head spun. It couldn't be. This shy, clumsy woman in my shop was the same woman apparently racing to the top of Hollywood's A-list? I recognized her name more from the tabloids and Lola's unnecessary recaps of award shows than from any of the films she'd been in, but I'd seen enough to know her voice, apparently. And to know she was a pretty big deal. And to know there was no denying the truth. It was the same Willow James.

And I supposed it would explain the hat, the sunglasses, the shapeless clothes. A disguise.

What it didn't explain, however, was the basket.

Or what the hell she was doing here.

I looked up from my phone just in time to see her slip through the doorway, bells chiming in her wake, their sound feeling like the only indication she was ever really here. And while I knew it was against everything in my best interest, I couldn't stop myself from hoping she'd come back.

CHAPTER 7
Willow

Well, that was a bust. Not only was I recognized almost immediately, but I was faced with the grim realization that once again, it seemed I'd have to know the spell in order to reverse the spell. Dumbass logic if you asked me.

What I really needed was more time. I needed to be able to comb the shelves without being recognized, needed to pull books out and sit with them for more than a minute or two to figure out what could be useful without having to buy every book in the shop. Not that I didn't want to give Coven & Codex my business, but I couldn't exactly be lugging the entire Reversals, Retractions, and Revocations section around Notting Hill, could I?

So I did what any sane person would do. I sat in a pub across the street all afternoon, staring at the entrance, waiting until five minutes before closing time to make my move. If I could just slip in after the last customer left, ask nicely to browse while Oliver and his assistant were preparing to close, I might have a chance at finding what I was looking for. I would also run the risk of exposing myself, but since Oliver hadn't seemed to recognize me the first time we met, I hoped I was in the clear. And if he did, well, it was better than fans asking for selfies in the stacks.

Not that I didn't love selfies with fans. I just didn't love them when I was trying to reverse a spell, when my manager was a cat, et cetera. Knowing I was an actor was fine. Knowing I was a witch was *not*.

So, I waited.

The pub across the street was much like the others in Notting Hill: charming, classic, but just a touch more upscale. I'd been to pubs all over the city throughout the years, but the Notting Hill ones didn't have the same sticky floors, jaded bartenders, and watery drinks so many of the others were famous for. This particular one was also literary in theme, with deep bookcases and wing-back chairs lining the back wall and coasters that looked like library cards. It was the perfect place to camp out.

The cider was pleasantly dry but unpleasantly warm, and since apparently all bets were off with how I typically chose to conduct magic in my day-to-day, I figured it wouldn't hurt if I chilled the cider by just a few degrees. (At least I *hoped* it wouldn't hurt . . . but lately, who could tell?)

With a quick, deep visualization of glaciers, tile bathroom floors, winter mornings on the East Coast, my high school ex-boyfriend, all things good and freezing, I tapped the glass in a pattern my sister and I had practiced endlessly as children to keep our ice cream from melting. To my relief, frost began to collect on the outside of the glass and nothing exploded in the process.

At the very least, I could still conduct a basic chilling spell, and I was prouder than I should have been. But a win was a win.

After a short, eye-to-eye conversation with Vera, we agreed (or at least I think we agreed) to leave her in the room before I settled in the pub, and I thought (hoped) it was for the best. There was no real reason for me to be schlepping her back and forth, and since we weren't doing anything particularly exciting that I thought she might want to see, even through her cat eyes, I figured she could relax in the room while I tried to take care of this mess.

If only she could tell me what she was thinking.

Holy shit.

If only she could tell me what she was thinking. Was I an idiot? (Yes.) Why hadn't I thought of this before? If I could at least figure out how to make it so Vera could communicate, I could buy myself more time to sort out the spell. If she could at least speak, maybe I wouldn't have to be in such a mad rush and could take my time doing it right. It was such an obvious idea, I couldn't believe I hadn't thought of it sooner.

Though with all the chaos of the last few days, I suppose it wasn't such a surprise that rational thinking had slipped my mind.

So my first stop when I went back to Coven & Codex wouldn't be Reversals, Retractions, and Revocations. It would be Anthropomorphism.

✧

AT 4:56, I signaled the bartender for the tab, mildly alarmed at the total. And then I stood up, and it all made sense. It wasn't just the inflated price of pints on this side of the city. It was the three I'd managed to drink during my stakeout.

I'd been so wrapped up in my plan that I'd completely lost track of the afternoon as it slipped by in a haze of crisp cider and a bottomless bowl of salted peanuts. Classic. Now not only was I the chaotic American who'd been drawing a crowd and talking to her cat, but I was also the tipsy American who would crash through the door right before closing time. Really doing my people justice here on this side of the pond.

Either way, it was now or never.

It took me nearly twice as long as it should have to cross the street, given my vaguely warped depth perception and the unfamiliar traffic patterns, but I made it to the door in one piece with two minutes to spare. I straightened my dress and shook out my shoulders, then did my best impression of a sober person and pushed open the door.

"Sorry, love, we're about to—oh," Oliver said as he turned around and caught my eye. "It's you."

Mortifying. "It's me," I said, forcing a laugh. "But I'm not here to explode anything. I promise." I held up my palms to demonstrate my innocence, but he only looked more confused.

"Hardly your fault," he said. *If he only knew.* "But we are about to close in a minute or so—"

"Please," I said, embarrassed by how desperate it sounded. I cleared my throat before I spoke again. "I, uh, I know it's late. I was just hoping for a minute to browse, maybe while you locked up?"

"You had a minute to browse earlier, no? Reckon I saw you taking selfies in the stacks there." He stood from the box he was unpacking and brushed his hands off on the back of his jeans, and I was surprised by how long it took him to get to his full height. I'd seen him a few times already, but I didn't remember him being this tall.

I did, however, remember him being this handsome. All long limbs and dark waves, flushed cheeks and the kind of indiscernible green-gray eyes that looked like the sky before a storm. He wore a simple pale blue button-down and a pair of dark jeans, but somehow he looked like he'd stepped out of a spread in *GQ*.

And despite the fact I knew I was staring, I couldn't look away from his hands. Veins stretched across the back, and long fingers with short, square nails held a stack of books I wasn't sure I could hold with my arms.

It wasn't until he cleared his throat that I remembered he was waiting for me to respond. I blamed the ciders.

"Sorry about that," I said. "That's kind of why I couldn't browse earlier? It's stupid, and you don't care, so I'll spare us both. But I was hoping to maybe have a minute without anyone else in here?"

He laughed, but I couldn't tell if it was because he thought something was funny. "Always the Americans, isn't it?"

"Excuse me?"

"Wanting special treatment and that."

"This was a mistake," I said, already resigning myself to failure and turning toward the door. "Sorry to bother you. I'll just—"

"I'm kidding," he said. "You can shop. On one condition." I raised an eyebrow. "Tell me who you are. And what it is you're looking for in here."

"That's two conditions."

"Semantics."

"You run a bookshop. You, of all people, should care about semantics."

"And you shouldn't if you want me to let you in." He raised an eyebrow back, and I realized he had a point.

"I'll answer one question," I said.

"That wasn't the deal."

"Ever heard of a compromise?"

"The British don't do compromises."

"Pick a question," I said. "I'm not answering both, but I might be prepared to give you some decent business, so I suggest you find it in yourself to go against your customs for the sake of your shop."

"What kind of business are we talking?"

"Ah, so that's how to get you to compromise."

"One question, five books."

"Three books."

"Nothing on sale. And you answer honestly. None of that talking in circles you Americans love so much."

"Done," I said, hoping he picked question number two but relieved he didn't want to do a lot of talking either way.

"What are you looking for?" *Thank god.*

I was about to confess, but the look in his eyes gave me pause. There was a certain depth behind the gray that hadn't been there a minute ago. An arrogant, challenging shade that made me dizzy.

"You're asking because you already know the answer behind door number one, don't you?"

"Just wanted to hear you say it," he said over his shoulder as he motioned for me to follow him farther into the store. *What the hell?* "Willow James, yeah?"

"Have you known this whole time?"

"Not when you made a mess of my Fables and Folklore room, no. But after the selfie incident, my friends may have, er, confirmed your identity. But only because I wanted to be made aware of what was going on in my shop. I didn't like the way people were looking at you"—he coughed into his fist—"and I wanted to have all the information. Just in case."

He didn't seem like the kind of person who ever talked that much at once, and I had a feeling it was only because his back was to me. "Just in case what?"

"In case I had to, I don't know, intervene." He waved his hand like it didn't matter. "Which leaves us with door number two. What are you looking for, Willow James?"

That's it? He had nothing else to say about who I was? Usually, when people identified me in public, even if they weren't fans, they still had more to offer on the subject. Had I met their favorite actor? Who was I dating? Did I know who did so-and-so's hair at the Met Gala? *Something*. But apparently not Oliver.

Okay, then. Door number two.

"Well, Oliver Hadley," I started, and he turned to face me at the sound of his name. "It's on the website," I said with a shrug. "Can I trust you?"

"To be fair, would I say no if you couldn't?"

"Do you want me to answer honestly?"

"I thought I made that obvious."

Okay, so he was infuriating. Maybe I could get away with a half-truth. He didn't know me, and I was literally an actor for a living. I could sell a half-truth better than anyone.

"I'm looking for something for my grandmother," I said. "She's turned her home nurse into a cat. And now she needs to figure out how to reverse the spell and turn her back." Not bad.

Or so I thought, until what felt like an eternity went by and Oliver hadn't so much as blinked.

"Hello?" I asked, reaching up and waving a hand in front of his eyes. "Anybody home?"

"You can't be serious," he said. Still no blinking.

"I'm sorry?"

"Your grandmother," he said, so slowly it sounded like he was talking to a toddler, "turned her nurse . . . into a cat?"

"Is that not what I just said?"

"Willow, you can*not* be serious."

"Did we not just establish I was serious? What's happening here, exactly?"

He shook his head, and now it was my turn not to blink. "I just . . . I didn't realize you believed in all this stuff."

"This *stuff*?" I asked. He gestured around the shop. "You mean the *stuff* your entire shop is built for? You don't believe in it?"

"You do?"

"Don't sound so surprised," I said. "In case you've forgotten, this is only our second conversation, so you're the only one to blame for whatever assumptions you've made about me."

"You just don't seem like the type."

"Do you generalize all your customers?" I asked. "Or just the famous American ones?"

He ran a hand through his hair, and I tried to focus on being glad he was frustrated instead of being distracted by how good he looked. But with his hair on end like that, it was hard to ignore.

"I didn't mean to offend," he said, taking a step back. "Apologies."

If he was backing down, I supposed it wouldn't kill me to lower the guns, too. "You really don't believe in it?"

"Nah, not a bit, if I'm honest. At least not anymore."

"Then how'd you end up with the shop?"

"Dead uncle. How does anyone end up with a shop like this?"

His wry smile gave me permission to laugh, but that was the beginning and the end of my relief.

"But the website says you help people find books and things."

"I don't have to believe in witchcraft to read titles, Willow."

"But you don't believe in anything you're selling."

"That's business, isn't it?"

How could someone so cynical run a shop so charming? It must have all been his uncle's doing, and he just kept the lights on. Still, if he had any connections that might be useful to me, I wasn't ready to burn this bridge just yet.

"So are you going to help me or not?"

"I thought I was going to close up while you had a look around."

"I'd be out of your hair faster if you gave me a hand."

"Maybe I like you in my hair."

I took a step back as harsh wind whipped the windows, rattling the candles perched in the sills and breaking our eye contact. Eye contact that was charged in a way I felt all the way to my toes. Tingling, warm, unfamiliar.

"Suit yourself." I sighed, turning toward the stacks and trying to keep a level head. The cider swam in my veins, making it harder to ignore his presence. The fact he hadn't moved, was tracking me with his eyes as I roamed the shop.

It didn't take long to find Anthropomorphism tucked in between Zoomorphism and Chremamorphism, naturally, and I got to work exploring titles and tables of contents trying to find something about talking cats. Without the other customers, it should have been easier to focus, but being alone with Oliver was arguably worse than being approached by fans.

"That's popular," he said after a while, nodding to the book I was holding called *Alchemy of Anthropomorphism*. "Have to restock it quite a bit."

I turned it over in my hands, studying the back and the author's promise to teach basic anthro spells to bring any household pet to life. Seemed as good a try as any. One thing I could check off my list, at least.

"What else does your grandmother need?" he asked, propping a broom up against a wall and crossing his arms over his chest. "Don't forget, we had a deal."

"Three books, one question, I know," I said. "Except you already knew the answer to the first question. Doesn't that count for something?"

"If only," he said, and smiled. Crooked, lazy. Irresistible. "Come on, then. I'll give you that hand. Wesley can sweep when he gets in in the morning."

"I'm sure he loves having you as a boss."

"Wouldn't you?"

My deep breath wasn't enough to quell the electricity building in my chest, and when he leaned back and crossed his legs at the ankles, I fought to look away. I felt the chilling spell coming back. I watched in horror as frost began its slow creep across the windows behind him, its freezing fingers reaching toward the frame. *Shit.*

"I'll take that as a no," he said, whether at my silence or the look on my face, I couldn't tell.

Icicles began to drip from the brass curtain rods, leaving me scrambling to distract him before things got any worse and we had a full Elsa in the ice palace on our hands.

"All right, if you're going to give me a hand, let's do it, then." I motioned for him to follow me into the stacks, hoping the ice would disappear in the time it took me to pick out a few books and get the hell out of there.

"Right." He sighed. "Well, it looks like you've found how to make the cat talk, at least. Now what? We need to find something for your grandmother to be able to turn her back into a nurse?"

"Precisely."

"Very well. Follow me."

Instead of leading me to Reversals, Retractions, and Revocations, where I'd expected, he guided me toward his computer at the front desk.

"Don't bother googling it," I said. "I've already tried."

"I'm not googling it," he said, like I'd just told him not to bother flying to the moon. The audacity. "I'm searching our database."

CHAPTER 8
Oliver

This woman was a handful. What the hell would I be googling? Ways for an old woman who believes she's a witch to turn a cat she believes is her home nurse back into a person? I was sure that would yield loads of results.

She leaned over the counter while I applied filters to the search ("'spell reversal' + 'cat to human' + 'accidental shape-shifting'"), and I tried not to be distracted by her scent. Woodsy, slightly sweet, intoxicating. Vanilla. A cashmere jumper. Or her hair, falling in loose auburn curls over the till. Or the charming way she chewed on her thumbnail, brows furrowed as she watched me type.

"Who knew there was a whole database for books about magic?" she asked. "And that you could be so specific!"

"Everyone who owns an occult bookshop," I said, trying not to smile when she glowered. She wasn't very good at it, but that made it even more effective. "Right, let's see." Results began piling up, and I scrolled slowly, waiting for her to find something that stood out, because lord knows I was useless in that department.

"Wow." She exhaled. "This is a lot."

"Mm-hmm," I agreed. "And your grandmother didn't give you any more direction?"

She made a small sound, more to herself than to me, then shook her head. "No," she said. "This is it."

"This is a long way to come without really knowing what you're looking for."

"Don't I know it."

I kept scrolling, feeling strangely guilty for not being able to help her. Without anyone else in the shop, she didn't quite seem like the powerhouse I'd heard she was on-screen. She spoke softly and her eyes were searching in a way that told me this might have been about more than helping her granny reverse a spell.

"What about this one?" I asked, hovering my cursor over *Mr. York's Shape-Shifting Guidebook: 1896 Edition*. "I reckon this might be good for your grandmother."

She cocked her head to the side, assessing. "It's, uh, too old, I think. She practices more . . . modern magic."

Whatever the hell that meant.

I scrolled on, vowing not to make any more suggestions since I obviously had no idea what I was talking about.

"There," she said, grabbing my wrist to stop me from scrolling. Her hand was so small, it didn't wrap all the way around, and its warmth sent a chill up my arm. "Click on that one." She pointed to a title that read *Rewind: A Manual for Counter Magic*, and I opened the link in a new tab.

Rewind was apparently full of remedies for reversing accidental spells, with chapters sorted by time of day, season, emotion, sect of powers, geographical location, category of consequence—the list went on.

"There's no way I couldn't find the answer in there, right? It looks like it has everything."

"Your guess is as good as mine," I said, and shrugged.

"Where is it?"

I clicked around a few more times, feeling like I'd been doused with cold water when I came up empty. "How odd," I mumbled, more to myself than to Willow, trying a few more searches, all of which told me the book had been out of print for the last few years.

"But it has to be somewhere," she said. "Right? Otherwise it wouldn't have come up in the database?"

"Is that how the database works?"

"Oliver," she whined. The sound of my name in her mouth was intoxicating.

"Right, sorry. I'm sure it is somewhere. We just might have to do a bit of digging."

"I can do the digging," she said. "Just point me in the right direction."

"I'm afraid it might not be so easy. The database tracks the inventory of all occult bookshops in the city, so if it was as easy as sending you to another shop, it would say so here."

"So now what?"

When I turned to face her, she was closer than I'd realized. Her hopeful eyes had just the slightest tinge of desperation, but it was enough. Enough that suddenly I cared about this American celebrity who believed her grandmother was a witch. Enough that I found when I said "we," I didn't mean the royal kind. I was actively volunteering myself to find some ancient book of magic with a famous woman hiding from the paparazzi. A beautiful famous woman, no less, whose smoky voice and deep brown eyes had been haunting me since I first saw her in my shop. What could go wrong?

"Now we find the book," I said, as if it could possibly be that simple. "I have some contacts who might have some ideas, so I'll get in touch and see where it takes us."

She pulled her bottom lip between her teeth, and I felt that same freezing sensation I'd felt when she touched my wrist. Was there a window open?

"Are you sure this isn't something I could do on my own?" she asked. "I don't want to take too much of your time. Surely you're busy with the shop, and—"

"Do you want to help your gran or not?" She nodded. "And do you have any other ideas?" She shook her head. "Then we better get to work."

"I'm going to need you to repeat yourself," Minho said. "Slowly. Like you're explaining this to a primary student. Who barely speaks English."

"Should have paid attention the first time." I downed the rest of my pint in one gulp, relishing the buzz building in the backs of my eyelids. "Because I'm not going to explain myself again."

After Willow and I made a plan to be in touch once I heard from my mates at some other shops, I went directly to the pub to meet Minho and Lola. I needed a pint more than I needed to share this information with either of them, but it was bound to come out eventually, so I figured it was best to just rip off the plaster.

"He's become bloody best friends with Willow James, that's what he said." Lola was shouting so loud, I was certain they could hear us on the other side of the river.

"That's definitely *not* what I said."

"It's basically what you said," she argued. "You're planning to run around the city together looking for some old book for her witchy granny. What is that if not best friends?"

"My job."

"You own a bookshop. You don't have to help pretty American celebrities prance around the city to help dear old women, do you?"

"No one is prancing. And yes, I do. The website literally says I will help people find and procure old titles and shit."

"But this is Willow James, mate," Minho said. "She isn't just 'people.'"

"It's not like the website has a clause that says I can help everyone but celebrities, does it? Besides, she came in right as I was closing because she wanted to have a look around without anyone else in the shop, so I don't think she's keen on people knowing who she is or what she's doing here. Which means you two aren't going to go telling anyone about this, yeah?"

Two nods that said "obviously." Thank god we were at least on the same page about that.

"So you also have to be her bodyguard?"

"Are my words translating into some other language in your ears, Lo? Because you're hearing something completely different from what I'm saying, and I'd like to put an end to this miscommunication before someone overhears you and we're on the front page of some tabloid."

"Lighten up, will you? Aren't you even the least bit excited about this?"

"Excited about tearing this city apart to find some old book about magic that doesn't exist? Proper chuffed, if I'm honest."

The truth was, part of me was a bit chuffed. Not that I'd ever admit it to Lola and Minho. But I didn't mind the idea of spending more time with Willow. And perhaps I wasn't even ready to admit this to myself, but I didn't mind the idea of acting as her bodyguard, either. Her fake smile when she was spotted by those girls in the shop tightened a knot in my chest, and the pleading in her voice when she showed up at closing time tonight only pulled harder at the strings. I wasn't sure what it took for her to be here alone looking for something for her gran, but if I could protect her at all while she was doing it, well, then I'd have done my job.

Or maybe more than my job. But hadn't we already established that I didn't much care about semantics?

"All the good shit happens to you," Minho said. "And you don't even want it."

"Again, this is my job," I reminded them. "And you make like five times what I do, and Lo has a cooler job than either of us, so I wouldn't exactly say *all* the good shit happens to me."

"Can you admit it's at least a little exciting? Like, you don't go to these lengths for your other customers."

"My other customers haven't asked me to go to these lengths."

"But would you if they did?"

No. "Yes."

"I give up," Lola said, throwing her hands up, then dropping them in her lap. "When you're ready to be honest about your feelings on the whole matter, let us know."

"I'm sure you'll be here waiting."

"With bated breath."

"Another round?" Minho asked, already signaling the bartender. Thank god someone understood the assignment.

Though I couldn't quite blame Lola.

Usually, I would pride myself on being an intuitive person. It came with the territory of owning a bookshop, even if I didn't believe in what I was selling. I could still read people, make accurate assumptions about who they were and what they were looking for, find it before they even knew the answers themselves. *That* was the real magic of the bookshop.

But not Willow. For someone famous, someone seemingly so open and vulnerable, I couldn't read her past the first page. And I'd be damned if that wasn't the exact reason I'd keep coming back for more.

Besides, it really was my job.

Lola and Minho dropped the subject for the next round, sinking into our usual pub banter instead: football, Lola's newest video game designs, Minho's newest two-day relationship, Netflix's newest horror docuseries. Despite our endless group texts, we still always found something to chat about, and it had been that way since uni.

We'd lived across the hall from each other, Min and I as roommates and Lo with a girl we hadn't seen or heard from since first year, and it didn't take long for us to realize how much we had in common. We bonded over many late nights playing *Mario Kart*, eating frozen pizza, commiserating about women, and secretly caring way too much about our marks.

One Christmas, when Lola couldn't afford to fly home to her family in Spain and I wasn't celebrating because I'm Jewish, Minho invited us to spend the holiday at his parents' house in Hitchin, and we've been family ever since.

And as great as it was to have found this kind of friendship in one another, it meant nothing was off-limits and it was impossible to keep secrets. For better or worse, or whatever. So I shouldn't have been surprised when we came back around to Willow as we paid the tab.

"At least tell us your plan," Minho said. "When do you start the search?"

"Tomorrow," I confessed. "She's trying to spend as little time in the city as possible, I guess so that she can get back to her gran or her movies or whatever, and Wesley has been asking for more hours, so he can hold down the shop for the day." I typically hated leaving the shop during business hours, but even I had to admit, Wesley was getting good. And I wasn't exactly interested in working overtime to help Willow, so this would have to suffice.

"Where are you going?" Lola asked. "My boss is out of the office tomorrow, so I can sneak away to give you a hand."

"What help would I need from you?" I laughed. "Last I checked she wasn't designing a video game or listening to Gracie Abrams or making sourdough, so—"

"Rude," she said, swatting my arm.

"You just want to meet her."

"Obviously."

"If Lola gets to go, then I get to go," Minho said.

"This isn't a group activity. So unless either of you have become an expert in occult books and reversal spells for fake magic overnight, I don't want to hear it. She's supposed to be hiding from fans, remember?"

"We aren't *fans*, Oliver. We're your *friends*."

"At least promise if you do anything really exciting, we'll get to come along."

"I'm not sure what could possibly be exciting about looking for an old book, but sure. If suddenly this becomes a proper treasure hunt, I'll be sure to extend the invite."

CHAPTER 9
Willow

We'd agreed to meet on the South Bank in the morning, as the outdoor book market was coming to life. And once again, Vera and I wordlessly decided she'd stay in the hotel room. She didn't seem to love the Tube, and it was a nice day by London standards, so I figured she'd rather spend it lounging by the open window and watching the city than being stuck in the carrier on public transport. I hoped I was right.

I got a Vietnamese coffee from a street vendor and walked the length of the river while I waited for Oliver, contemplating any other way out of this mess. The book I'd brought home last night seemed to have what I needed to hopefully grant Vera the power to speak, but I was lacking the confidence necessary to cast a spell, and we all knew what happened when someone cast a spell without conviction. (See: literally any witchcraft movie where any spell backfires.) With my luck, I'd cast the spell and suddenly neither of us would be able to speak.

But since I couldn't leave her hanging, I'd have to find the confidence somewhere.

I stared at the river, watching it cut its centuries-old path through the city, murky and unforgiving and still somehow oddly peaceful, if I didn't think too hard about it. I tracked it under the London Eye and past Big Ben, watching it wend its way around landmarks it wasn't impressed or intimidated by. Landmarks that reminded me I was alone in the city, six thousand miles from home, solving a major problem with only the help of a man I'd met three days ago who didn't believe in magic.

I'd hoped the realization might give me the confidence I needed, might make me feel like an empowered woman on a mission, but instead it only made me feel more alone. And while I knew there was a solution to this feeling, it came at a price. One of endless mockery and *I told you so*s and the kind of teasing only family was capable of.

I was going to call my sister.

I hadn't done more than shoot my mom and my sister a quick text telling them I was headed to London for "work stuff," so calling Ivy would mean I'd have to tell the whole story, from the beginning. Fortunately, my mom was on some women's spiritual retreat in Banff all summer, so she was mostly unreachable. One fewer explanation of my stupidity. And one fewer burden on my family.

Even before I dialed, I was already trying to figure out how to spin it in a way that wouldn't make Ivy look like the Good Witch and me look like . . . well . . . even the Wicked Witch was way better at magic.

It was 10:00 a.m. in London, which meant it was 5:00 a.m. in New York, which meant Ivy was on her way to the gym before she put in another twelve-hour day doing whatever portfolio strategists did all day. Perfect. I'd catch her on the walk to her workout class, so we wouldn't have more than a few minutes to talk. That way, she couldn't ask questions. She couldn't be secretly annoyed or disappointed in me. She could just skip to the support part, and we could all get on with the day.

She answered on the second ring, and hearing her voice brought an unexpected lump to my throat.

"Morning, Wills."

"Hey."

"Everything okay? You sound weird."

"How do you know I sound weird? All I said was 'hey.'"

"Yeah, and it sounded weird." *Sisters.* Especially the witchy ones. They knew everything.

"I am weird," I moaned eventually. "I'm going to tell you what I'm really doing in London, but you can't freak out. I'm only calling for sisterly support, not unsolicited advice or reminders that I'm the black sheep of the family or anything, okay?"

"You're freaking me out. It's too early in the morning for me to be freaked out."

"But it isn't too early in the morning for you to go sweat your ass off in some fancy yoga studio?"

"Speaking of which, I'm almost there, so get to the point."

"Vera's a cat," I blurted. Silence. "Okay, now that that's out of the way—"

"Did you say a *cat*?"

"Yes, but I'll explain." I told the story as fast as I could under the guise of wanting her to get to her yoga class on time but really wanting to gloss over the part where I totally fucked up. Older sisters, however, are genetically predisposed to home in on precisely where you totally fucked up, so I don't even know why I bothered trying. Her DNA wasn't going to let me get away with it, so I didn't have much of a choice but to accept my fate.

"Wills, how did this even happen?" she asked, and I could practically see her rubbing the space between her brows like she could somehow massage my failures out of her frontal lobe.

"If I knew how it happened, I would have fixed it by now," I said. "That's the whole problem. Were you listening?"

"Truthfully, it was hard to listen to anything after 'Vera's a cat.'"

"Can you just say something supportive anyway? Pretend you listened and pretend I'm not the worst witch our family has ever seen and pretend you have something supportive to say."

"You are not the worst witch our family has ever seen," she said, more matter-of-fact than compassionate, but I had to take what I could get. "Aunt Clare is the worst witch our family has ever seen." Okay, I couldn't argue with that. To this day, none of us were sure Aunt Clare had *ever* conducted a spell correctly. And anytime we thought she did, we'd later find frog ears on her dog or vines growing from her showerhead or gibberish on the local news.

"And I don't have to pretend to support you," Ivy continued. "I always support you. I just wish you were more careful."

"It's not like I tried to make this happen," I said.

"I know, I know. I'm sorry." She always did this. When she sensed I was getting upset, she immediately backpedaled. That was also in her DNA, I supposed. It was what made her a good sister. She could get under my skin, but she hated to see me upset.

Growing up, and even now, it was like I had all the sensitivity for the both of us. She was practical, logical, sensible. And I was chaotic, emotional, creative. It was what made us good at our jobs. And what made her a better witch.

I didn't even mind that she was a better witch. I just minded that I was a *bad* witch. But true to form, Ivy snapped me out of my pity party before it really kicked off and ruined my day.

"Listen, Wills. You've got to dig deep here, okay? You do your best magic when you're in touch with yourself. And it sounds like you're outside, so that's already a good start. You have what it takes. You wouldn't have been able to cast the spell in the first place if you didn't. You just have to find it, which starts with believing it's in you. You aren't a bad witch, Willow. You're brilliant. The only thing you fail at is believing in yourself. So get your shit together, okay? Get Vera talking, then get your ass out and about in the city to find that book or whatever you need to turn her back into a person, then come home. And maybe choose a flight with a layover in New York. My class is about to start, so I have to go in. Call me later if you need anything. I love you."

Before I could even thank her and tell her I loved her back, the line was dead. But I got exactly what I came for. She might have sounded like she was all business, but her words carried more warmth than she even knew. Ivy had been my compass since we were kids, despite our differences, and I knew she was always right (even if I spent half our childhood telling her the exact opposite).

It was time for a Main Character Moment. The kind when the heroine stares out at a river with the wind in her hair and her face turned toward the sun, some vaguely familiar nineties song plays in the background, and the audience's eyes well up as she comes back to herself.

And it would have been cinematic, had Oliver not interrupted just as the soundtrack in my head was reaching its climax.

"Don't think too hard," he said, leaning on the railing beside me. "It's just a river."

I dug my elbow into his side, trying not to laugh when he did. "Some of us actually have something going on up here," I said, tapping my temple.

"Care to share with the class?"

"Isn't it obvious?" I gestured around, though the truth was, there was more going on in my head than I was willing to admit. I was thinking about Vera, sure, and my sister and how I was going to handle this mess, but I was also thinking about the undeniable flutter in my chest at the sight of Oliver. At the sound of his deep voice and his melodic accent and the size of his watch on his wrist and the easy way he leaned on the railing.

A crush was the *last* thing I needed right now. For a million reasons. I needed to focus on the task at hand and keep my magic under control and save Vera and *not* run the risk of having a single feeling for anyone whatsoever. That was a surefire way to make things worse, and I could not afford to make things worse. I could barely afford for things to be this bad.

"Nothing about what goes on in your head is obvious," he said. His tone was calm, collected, measured, but it didn't take away from the weight of his words. If anything, it only made them heavier. Was he just talking about what we were doing here, or was there more he wanted to know? And couldn't I say exactly the same about him?

"Well, in this case, I'm ready to find this book and reverse the spell and be done with the whole thing," I said, hoping that cleared things up.

"Isn't your gran reversing the spell?"

Had I seriously already almost slipped up? I'd been distracted by—what, his forearms? And forgotten the lie? Ivy was right. I needed to get my shit together. And fast.

"Yes, of course," I said. "I'm just getting her the resources. But she's impatient, so."

"Say no more." He stretched out his arm in the direction of the book market, but his face told me he had a plan.

"We aren't just browsing, are we?"

"Isn't it obvious?" He smiled, and I tried not to roll my eyes. Best not to bite the hand that feeds and all that.

"What's the plan?"

"I'm going to work my—" He cut himself off, bringing his knuckles to his teeth.

"Magic?" I asked, unleashing my best red carpet smile.

"It's an idiom," he grumbled. I let the small victory of getting under his skin propel me forward.

"Let's see it, then," I urged, and this time it was his turn to roll his eyes. I followed him in the direction of the market, secretly thrilled he had a plan. And even more thrilled I didn't have to spearhead said plan.

The market had only been open for fifteen minutes, but it was already teeming with families, older couples, young people with trendy tote bags and tortoiseshell glasses, and tourists with actual cameras around their necks. Thousands of books were piled on folding tables, crammed into milk crates, overflowing from vintage trunks and wicker baskets. It would have been so easy to get lost in the piles, spending all day digging through treasures under the bridge like some kind of literate magpie.

Except I didn't have all day, because Oliver was chatting to someone and waving me over like an impatient parent.

"Willow, this is Fergus, one of the most renowned purveyors of occult media in the city."

"Aye, in the world." He winked, shaking my hand. "You're a pretty little thing, aren't ya? Look like you could be in a film, there."

Thank god Oliver's snort demanded our attention, because I was frozen where I stood.

"Been telling her that," Oliver said, deadpan. "Maybe one of these days she'll listen and give it a go." I stepped on his foot and made no effort to be discreet about it.

"Ach, they never do, do they?" Fergus said.

"They, uh—" Oliver started, fumbling when he caught my eye. *Don't you dare agree with him.* "No matter," he said, recovering. "D'you have a minute? We've a few questions about an old book we're trying to find and I'm hoping you might have the foggiest where to begin."

"If you ask me, I'd say you've already begun," he said. "So you're well on your way. Good on you! What is it I can do for ya?"

I nodded along as Oliver explained our dilemma, and Fergus was shuffling through an old journal the size of my upper body before Oliver had finished the story.

"Haven't heard of anyone lookin' for a *Rewind* in yonks," he mused, licking his fingers as he turned the wrinkled pages. "Quite an unusual collection, that one." He hummed as he searched his diary, and we looked on, anxious and hopeful.

"But you've heard of it?" Oliver asked.

"'Course I've heard of it, boy. We just established I'm the top purveyor in the world of occult materials, did we not? Now if you'll just hush for long enough to let me find it . . ."

Oliver pressed his lips together, and I tried not to smile. Though watching someone else put him in his place was oddly satisfying.

"Ah, there it is," Fergus said, slamming his finger into the page.

"You have it?" I asked.

"'Course I don't have it! Old Bromley over there on the other side of the river has it, last I checked."

"'Course he does," Oliver muttered, casting his gaze toward the sky and blowing out a breath.

"Do you know who that is? Or where we have to go?" I asked.

"Indeed I do," he said. "Thanks, Fergus. I owe ya one."

"Don't get ahead of yerself now. I've no idea if he's still got it. He's just the last who had the collection, he is."

"Worth a try." Oliver smiled. "Take care."

As he guided me out of the book market and back in the direction of the Tube, I stumbled over my questions. "How do you all know so much? Does every occult bookshop owner know one another? You really know what he's talking about?"

"Slow down," he said. "It's a small industry, and we do get together for a convention once a year, so yes, most of us know one another. And in case you hadn't noticed, Fergus is about three hundred years old and has been in the industry for the same length of time, so he's a resource for the whole community. Somehow he never forgets a thing."

"And you still don't believe in magic?" I asked, earning myself a scathing side-eye in place of a verbal response. "Right."

"You have plans for the rest of the day, or you reckon we'll go back over the river to find this bloke and see how we get on?"

"My only plans from now until I help my grandmother are helping my grandmother, so I'm all yours. For the search, I mean."

"What else would you mean?" He raised an eyebrow, and I tried to conjure every spell in the book to stop myself from blushing. In vain. Hell, if there was a spell that could have stopped me from blushing, I'd have had a very different few years of middle school.

"You know what I mean," I mumbled, petulant. Why did he have to say everything out loud? And why did my only two remaining brain cells decide to take the day off every time he was around? "Where's his shop?"

"It's not so much of a shop," he said. "It's more of, er, a museum? Lots of odd volumes, antiques, that kind of stuff. And he gets cross if you touch anything you aren't going to buy, so keep your hands to yourself."

"Got it."

We slipped wordlessly into the Tube station, standing silent on the platform as we listened for the rumbling down the tracks. I pulled my hat a little lower on my head the longer we stood there, hoping no one looked in my direction, especially since I had nowhere to hide.

But, since the universe was a cruel mistress, right as I adjusted my sunglasses and ducked my head a little lower, someone caught me.

"Willow James? Bloody hell, is that you?"

People started looking, shuffling in my direction, craning their necks to see if the bystander was telling the truth. I should have been used to fans and paparazzi by now, but it never got any less unsettling for the crowd to close in and all sense of privacy to disappear in an instant. And in this case, hundreds of feet underground in the dim lighting, with the loud screech of the trains, it was almost unbearable.

I contemplated excusing myself and darting back up the stairs, but a warm hand on my back stopped me where I stood. Not a threatening hand. A comforting hand. Oliver's hand.

CHAPTER 10
Oliver

I wasn't sure what exactly came over me, but I was awash with a sudden sense of responsibility to protect her. Not that she couldn't take care of herself—she'd made it abundantly clear that she could—but in that moment, with the encroaching crowd and her eyes cast toward the ground, I didn't have a second to think before I acted.

With a firm hand on her back and an "Excuse us," "Sorry, no, you must have someone else," "Excuse us, please," over my shoulder, I ushered her around the corner and into a small cutout between the platforms. I tried to position my body so that it would block her from the fans without crowding her into the space, and her relief was palpable.

"You didn't have to do that," she said, taking off her sunglasses but not quite meeting my eyes.

"Do I seem like someone who does things they don't want to do?" At that, she raised her gaze and pinned me with those deep brown eyes. They held only the slightest trace of a challenge before they faded into something softer. Something that cut right through me.

"Thank you," she said. "I should do a better job of disguising myself, I suppose. Sorry you had to deal with that. Usually I can handle it better, just in the Underground, and with—"

"You don't have to explain yourself," I said. "I don't like crowds, either. I get it. It must be a lot to have people in your personal space like that."

"You don't like crowds?" she asked. "Even though you're, like, a head taller than everyone?"

"Even worse that way. Means I'm privy to everyone's business. And when I can see everyone, that means everyone can see me."

"I know how that feels. Not the height part, obviously." She gestured to her frame. "But the everyone-can-see-me part."

"Well, they can't see you now," I said, stretching my arms up to lean on either side of the cutout. "Why don't we wait here until that group gets on the train, then make a break for the next one?"

She nodded. "I like the sound of that."

✨

So that was exactly what we did. We waited in the cutout, Willow's breathing returned to normal, and the space between us disappeared one centimeter at a time. She smelled like rain and honey, and I couldn't take my eyes off the way her eyelashes fanned across her freckled cheeks. It was no wonder the camera loved her. The naked eye loved her, too. If she was America's sweetheart, maybe America wasn't so bad.

Just as I was contemplating pushing her hair off her shoulder, giving her a little more air, caving in to my temptation to touch her even just with the tips of my fingers, a train slammed on the brakes, sending a shower of sparks onto the platform.

The commotion was enough to snap us out of our trance, hurtling us back into reality at light speed.

"What the hell was that?" I asked, looking around the people on the platform and at the train, which hadn't appeared to sustain or cause any damage. Just a scare.

"Doesn't it do that sometimes?" she asked. Wisps of her hair floated up from her shoulders, surely a result of the electricity in the air, drifting across her face in a scene entirely too angelic for the grimy underbelly of the city.

"Not like that," I said. It appeared everyone was fine, and the sparks were definitely a sound distraction, so I nodded toward the train. "Ready? Now's our chance."

"Let's do it."

I grabbed her hand to make a break for the closing doors, ignoring the shock I felt at the contact. Again, electricity. Not at all a literal spark between us. Only she pulled hers away at the sensation, leaving me to take the hint.

We made it onto the train just as the doors slammed closed, and I was relieved when she stayed close, positioning herself between me and the doors the same way she'd been in the space between the platforms. Hidden, secure, protected. I liked her there. And judging by her return, she didn't seem to mind, either.

We got off the train at Camden Town, dodging the crowds outside the station until we could slip undetected onto a quiet side street. Fortunately, there were enough street vendors hocking knockoff designer bags and punks begging for a few quid for a photo that Willow's presence didn't demand any attention.

"You can exhale now," I said, looking around the tree-lined street to make sure no one noticed her. "Bromley's place is tucked away back here, so I doubt we'll be seen. Just a few minutes' walk up this way." I started up the street, exhaling as she fell into step beside me.

"That was crazy back there."

"Never been to Camden Town?"

"Can't say I have."

"The market is a good time, but the crowds make it nearly impossible to tolerate. Solid food, though. I'll take you back sometime if you fancy the best bao bun you've ever had."

My words shocked me as much as they seemed to shock her. What the hell was I doing, offering to take her to the market? I didn't even go through the trouble of taking women I was dating to the market. And here I was, technically on a work assignment, offering to take this woman for bao buns, even after she'd made it abundantly clear she was only here to get what she needed to help her gran and then go straight back to California?

In an even more surprising turn of events, however, she didn't run for the hills. "That sounds nice," she said. "I love bao buns. There's a place around the corner from my apartment that makes the most delicious vegetarian ones."

"Flat." I couldn't resist.

"Sorry?"

"Your flat. You're in England now, love."

"You know what they say." She smiled. "Can take the girl out of America and all that."

Why did I love the thought of taking the girl out of America?

"Just up here, then," I said, trying to bring myself back to the present before I said what I was really thinking.

"This one?" she said, pointing toward a townhome with smudged windows and a beat-up door.

"Mm-hmm," I confirmed. "I know it doesn't look like much on the outside, but trust me. It's a proper show inside. And remember, don't touch anything."

She made a show of shoving her hands into her pockets and arranging her features into something solemn. Or her version of solemn, anyway. Her eyes still sparkled and her full lips still curved up at the corners, but I appreciated the effort.

We climbed the rotting front steps, and I knocked before entering, so as not to alarm the old bugger. "Bromley," I announced, looking around the ground floor. "It's Oliver Hadley. Are you in?"

"Where else would I be?" he grumbled from the back room. "Come through, will you? I'm in my chair and I'd fancy staying in it if it's all the same to you."

"Come on," I said to Willow, trying not to smile at the startled look on her face "He's harmless. Trust me."

"Can I?"

"I'm on the other side of the bloody city on my day off looking for an old book for your gran," I said. "You tell me." When she said nothing, I took it as a concession. "This way, then."

We picked through the overflowing antiques and showcases that littered every square inch of his home: glass boxes displaying old dolls; large, yellowing books propped open down the middle; tasseled lamps and brass candlesticks and porcelain figurines.

"It really is like a museum," Willow whispered, closer behind me than I'd realized.

"Told you," I said as we reached the back room. "Bromley, nice to see you. Please, don't get up." I leaned down to shake his hand, noticing how much older he looked since the last time I'd seen him. "This is Willow. She's American, but I'm trying not to hold it against her."

He laughed, or rather exhaled a little harder than usual out of his nose, extending his hand to Willow. "What brings you in?"

I explained the situation with Willow's gran and our hunt for *Rewind: A Manual for Counter Magic*, mentioning that Fergus from the South Bank Book Market had sent us in his direction.

"How is that old bastard?"

"Old and a bastard," I said with a laugh. "But doing well. Sends his regards."

"No he doesn't."

"No." I smiled. "He doesn't."

"But because I like *you*, I'll give you both a hand, hm?"

"Thank you, sir," Willow said.

"Don't call me sir. What do I look like, an old man?" She pressed her lips together, whether fighting back a laugh or dying from embarrassment, I couldn't tell. "Fetch me that ledger there, would you?" He pointed to a book—not unlike Fergus's—buried under a stack of paperwork on a nearby writing desk.

I pulled it from the stack, careful not to disturb anything else on the desk. There was definitely a method to his madness, and I'd be damned if I was the one to disrupt it. Willow watched me, seemingly holding her breath, which I found impossibly endearing.

"Feel free to look around," I said to her as I handed over the ledger. "If you're interested in this kind of thing, there's some good stuff in here. Just—"

"Don't touch anything." She rolled her eyes. "I know."

She slipped back into the main room, and I returned my attention to Bromley as he flipped through the pages, muttering to himself and peering over the rims of his glasses. "There it is," he said eventually, jabbing the page with two fingers. If only he'd known how much he and Fergus were alike. Though if I pointed it out, I was certain I'd be forcibly removed from the shop, so I said nothing. "Looks like I sold it to an auctioneer a year ago. Over in Islington there."

Of course he did. And I was sure the auctioneer sold it to a client, and the client gave it to a friend, and the friend shipped it overseas to someone who buried it in the garden. He scribbled the name and address of the woman on a napkin and pressed it into my hand. "Should be able to find her there. So long as you get past security. Third floor, office with the green door hanging sideways from the hinges. Unless she's had the good sense to fix it, but I doubt that. Give *her* my regards, will you?"

He wiggled his eyebrows in a way that suggested he wanted me to give her more than his regards, and the thought made me nauseated. "Thanks, Bromley. Much appreciated." The moment I turned to leave, I heard a crash from near the doorway, and my nausea doubled.

"What the hell was that?" Bromley started to get up from his chair, galvanized by his irritation, and I had no choice but to jump in.

"I think I might have left the door open," I said. "Must have been a gust of wind. I'll take care of it. And I'll, er, purchase whatever that was. Do send an invoice to the shop, will you? We'll be getting out of your hair now. Willow? Let's be going."

I ducked into the front room to find Willow, white and still as a statue, standing over a pile of marble shards that might have once been a bust of Medusa. Hopefully it wasn't haunted.

"What the hell happened?" I whispered, grabbing her by the arm and pulling her toward the door. "What happened to not touching anything?"

"I didn't, I swear!"

"Then how did the bust end up in a million pieces on the floor?"

"It just fell!"

"Things don't just fall, do they?"

"In places like this they do," she argued, raising her voice as we made it out the front door and onto the street. The door slammed behind us, but not before we heard Bromley muttering a slew of obscenities and cursing those "damn Americans" as he picked up the pieces.

I didn't want to laugh. Really, I didn't. But she looked so horrified and adorable, I had no choice.

"This isn't funny," she moaned, letting her head roll back on her shoulders. "I swear it wasn't me."

"Must have been magic," I teased, laughing harder when she shoved me.

"You're the worst."

"If I was the worst, would I have this?" I waved the napkin in her face, pulling it back when she went to grab for it.

"What is that?"

"Our next stop."

The slow smile that spread across her face was worth every minute of chaos. And worth doing what I had to do to get us into the building.

I fired off a text to Minho as we got back on the Tube, saying a silent prayer he wouldn't ask too many questions.

> Need a favor. Think you can get us into the Islington North Creative Arts building?

His response came in as soon as we reached the next stop.

Minho: Who's we?

Me: Don't play dumb.

Minho: Yes to the building. But you know we can't do this without telling Lola.

Me: Is that really something I know?

Minho: Don't play dumb.

Me: Fine. But I swear to god, she better not make this a thing.

I closed out of the text thread and leaned my head back against the train window.

"Everything okay?" Willow asked. "We don't have to do this if you don't want to."

"No, no, it's fine. I just . . . I know this building. The one where the auctioneer is. My friend Minho is an architect and he did some work on the building a few years ago, and he still has a key fob, so he can get us in."

"That's great! Is it not? Why does your face look like that?"

"Because it means Minho is going to tell Lola, and Lola is, well, she's—"

"A girlfriend?"

"A fan."

"Ah." If I didn't know any better, I'd say the look on her face was something strangely like relief. Since when was she relieved about fans? "Well, we have to do what we have to do, right? As long as she isn't the crazy kind."

"As a person, she's insane. But as a fan, I'm sure she'll keep herself in check." *Because I'll threaten her within an inch of her life*, I refrained from adding aloud. I loved Lo, but if she added any stress to this situation, we were going to have a problem.

Though I had to admit, the thought of having my friends on board was oddly comforting, so long as they behaved. The harder it got to find this stupid book, the more relieved I was to be calling in the reserves. I hoped Islington would be the last stop, but judging by how the day had gone so far, I knew better than to get my hopes up.

@rachdeanareads822: has anyone heard from Willow James since she didn't show at the Solstice Party? #WhereIsWillowJames

@redspringmedia: Sources say she was spotted on the Tube in London this week. Reps have yet to comment. #WIWJ

@miamimanda_: when r we getting the willow james kit hayes movie??? r they filming yet???

CHAPTER 11

Willow

Willow, this is Minho and Lola. Minho and Lola, this is Willow." Oliver gestured impatiently for us to shake hands, hug, do whatever we had to do to get the pleasantries out of the way so that we could get on with the show.

"Pleasure," Minho said, shaking my hand with a firmness that did not match the goofy smile spreading across his face.

"I'm a hugger," Lola said, pulling me in before I could protest. Not that I would have. Something about her was so disarming, there was a chance I made the first move and hugged her myself. "Sorry, was that too much? People probably try to hug you all the time. I just didn't want to do anything out of the ordinary for me, because Oliver said to be normal, so—"

Oliver cleared his throat, and Lola clapped her hand over her mouth. "I'm sure you've realized by now I don't exactly have a 'normal,'" she said.

"No one does." I smiled. "It's nice to meet you both. And thank you for doing this. I'm sure you have much better things to do today, and I know this is a lot to ask."

"Nonsense," Minho said. "I've been meaning to get back into this building anyway, and Lo never has anything going on." Lola only shrugged. "Don't let Oliver here convince you this is a burden."

"No, no, he's actually been really helpful."

"Oliver Hadley has been helpful?" Lola asked. "Are you sure we're talking about the same guy? Bad attitude, general disdain for anything fun and whimsical, impossibly nice hair that women love even though he—"

"Thank you, Lola," Oliver cut in. "I'm standing right here. I think she knows which Oliver Hadley we're talking about. And is it so hard to believe I've been helpful? It's literally my job."

Obviously it was his job, but for some reason hearing him say it felt like just missing the train. I hadn't even been willing to admit it to myself, but this gut punch made it impossible to deny I'd been secretly hoping he'd been doing this because he wanted to, not because he felt an obligation.

But maybe the reality check was for the best.

"It's just that we don't actually think you like doing your job," Lola said.

"I like my job just fine."

"Yeah, we're all convinced," Minho said, and laughed, pulling a key fob out of his pocket and heading toward the door. "Are we ready, then?"

"You guys think I don't like my job?" Oliver asked, apparently unable to move on.

"It's not that," Lola said, softening her tone. "We know you like the *book* part. But we also know you don't like the magic part."

"It's not that I don't *like* the magic part," he clarified. "It's that I don't *believe* in the magic part."

"There's a difference?"

I was wondering the same myself, only I hadn't the courage to ask. Thank god for Lola.

"Do we have to talk about this now?" Minho asked. "I'd like to get in and out of here before anyone starts asking questions."

"Are we not allowed to be here?" I asked, suddenly worried I was about to get us all in trouble for trespassing.

"Technically we're allowed to be in here, but it isn't exactly encouraged. So I'd like to make this fast, if you don't mind."

"Which means you," Oliver said, turning to me and pulling the brim of my hat so low it almost covered my eyes, "need to stay hidden. Last thing we need is a scene." I slid my sunglasses onto my face and tucked my hair up into the back of the hat, and he nodded in approval.

"You two have gotten into quite the rhythm, haven't you?" Lola asked.

"Not the time, Lo," Oliver snapped. "Min, let's do it."

"Right." Minho scanned his fob, and we all breathed a sigh of relief when the sensor turned green and the lock clicked open. "Act like you know what you're doing."

"Third floor, green door," Lola repeated like a mantra, and we followed her with our heads down.

Fortunately, the first floor was bustling, which made it easy for us to blend in. Creatives of all ages shuffled around in Birkenstocks and trendy sneakers that were so ugly they were cool, wearing coveralls and chambray button-downs and acrylic glasses.

"What is this place?" I asked as we slipped unnoticed up the stone staircase that dominated the center of the room. It looked like if the Museum of Natural History had a baby with Mia Thermopolis's apartment in *The Princess Diaries*.

"Kind of a hybrid coworking space and artists' collective," Minho explained, nodding to someone we passed on our way up. "My company didn't do too much by way of the design, since we were trying to preserve the historic integrity of the building. Just reinforced the structure to bring it up to code."

"What did the building use to be?"

"Saw a couple different uses over the years. Churches, theater companies, art installations, auctions, that sort of thing. Been this collective for years now. Some locals rotate in and out and rent spaces, and others, like this"—he checked the paper in his hand—"Diane, I presume, have made themselves at home."

We rounded landings on the second and third floors, lined with faded portraits and ripped newsletters and cigarette butts in the windows. How a place could be at once so charming and vaguely gritty I wasn't sure, but something about it felt promising.

Diane's door was, indeed, painted green and hanging haphazardly from the hinges, granting us a peek inside. She sat in a ripped leather chair facing away from the door, her sleek gray bob a stark juxtaposition to the chaos around her. Stacks of books, dripping taper candles, dishes filled with vintage jewelry—the occult proprietors were definitely cut from the same cloth.

And they all reminded me of Granny Annie.

"Who's going in?" Minho whispered.

"Me," Oliver and I said at the same time.

"You've done enough," I assured him. "Let me handle this one."

"Let's do it together," he said, releasing the knot of anxiety at the base of my throat. "I met her at an auction last year and we got on. Well, we got on enough, anyway."

"That doesn't sound promising."

"What happened to trust?"

"You trust this wanker?" Lola whispered to Willow.

"Can't you two go wait outside?" Oliver asked, though it sounded like more of a demand. "Min, thank you for your help. And, Lo, thank you for your, er, moral support. Now let us get to it before we all get kicked out, will you?"

"Fine, fine," Lola said, raising her hands in surrender. "Let's go, Min. Let these two have their moment."

"No one is having a moment—"

"Oliver, stop taking the bait," Minho said, shaking his head as he followed Lola down the stairs in the direction of the front door.

"Ready?" I asked, trying to ignore how adamantly he'd insisted we weren't having a moment. Which we weren't. But why was he so desperate to convince them? And if he really was, why was he standing so close?

"Let's." He rapped twice on the door high over my head, careful not to knock it off the hinges entirely. "Diane Hughes?" he asked. "It's Oliver Hadley, from Coven and Codex? We met at the Occult Premier Oxford last year. Bromley sent me—well, my friend and me—and we're hoping you have some information about *Rewind: A Manual for Counter Magic*?"

The door swung open so quickly, I was pretty sure I gasped out loud. She stood with one hand on her hip and the other tapping her fingertips against deep purple lips, studying the two of us from behind wire-framed glasses.

"Arthur's nephew?" she asked. "Shop in Notting Hill?"

"The very one."

"And who is this?" She turned her gaze to me, and I swallowed hard.

"This is Willow," Oliver said. "An old friend from, er, childhood."

"Ah," she said, but it didn't seem like she believed him. I couldn't tell if it mattered. What I could tell, however, was that the pitch of her voice sounded exactly like my grandmother's, and I was suddenly overwhelmed by how much I missed her. How much I wished she was here to help me get out of this.

And how desperately sad I felt that she wasn't.

In the months since she'd passed, I'd returned to a sense of normalcy, and I was generally able to keep the tears at bay when I wasn't in the comfort of my apartment. My *flat*. But there were times I was bombarded with an unshakable longing. It wasn't grief, necessarily. She was an old woman who'd lived a beautiful life and she'd accepted it was her time to go, but that didn't stop me from missing her down to my bones.

And now was one of those times.

Tears pooled in the corners of my eyes in that kind of unstoppable way I hadn't felt more than a handful of times since I was a kid, and I knew there was no saving myself from the embarrassment of crying in front of near strangers who were going out of their way trying to help me.

"Are you all right?" Diane asked, squinting her eyes like getting a closer look would help her figure out what inappropriate emotion I might have been experiencing.

"Fine, fine," I said. "Thank you."

"Why d'you look like you're about to cry, then?" Oliver asked, his expression noticeably more concerned than Diane's.

"I'll just . . . If you'll excuse me . . . I'll just wait in the hall if that's all right," I mumbled before hustling out the door and into the hall, where I attempted a few deep, steadying breaths. With my back against the wall, I lowered myself to the ground, dropping my head onto my knees and breathing in the pattern I practiced with my therapist. Inhale for four, hold for four, exhale for four. Repeat. Repeat. Repeat.

"Willow?" Oliver asked after who knew how long. "Is everything all right?"

What was I supposed to say? He'd know I was lying if I said yes, but I couldn't go telling him my grandmother—the very woman for whom we were supposedly finding this book—was dead, could I?

"Just, um, a bit overwhelmed," I said. "Sorry."

"No need to apologize."

I waited to see if he would say anything else, but all he did was slide down the wall beside me into the same position on the floor. Wordless, but even more of a presence as a result.

"I just want to find the book, you know? To do the right thing, reverse the spell."

"You say that like you have something to prove."

"Are all Englishmen this perceptive? Or just the bookish kind?"

"Just the bookish kind." He smiled. "We're a rare breed. Speaking of which . . ." He pulled a slip of paper from his shirt pocket and waved it in front of me, smiling when I grabbed it from him.

"What's this?"

"Our next stop."

"You've got to be kidding me."

"That should be my line."

"Oliver, I can't let you do this. I'll take it from here," I said. I wasn't totally lying when I said I was overwhelmed. This was becoming a lot, grandmother or no grandmother.

"It's not only me you have to contend with now," he said. "You think Minho and Lola aren't going to jump at the chance to make another stop? Those two are bored to death. They're dying for something interesting to do."

"We can hear you," Lola called from the bottom of the stairs, making me laugh long enough for the tears to subside.

"Last stop," he said. "She's certain it's there." He got to his feet and held out his hand, warm and rough and twice the size of mine, helping me off the floor without a trace of judgment.

"Then what are we waiting for?"

CHAPTER 12
Oliver

Our final stop was the British Library. Though I'd never admit it, this probably should have been our first stop. In the occult bookselling community, we sometimes got so caught up in our own network, we forgot about the public network. The network that had seemingly innumerable resources available at all times.

And the British Library was home to more than 170 million items. A hell of a lot more than the occult bookselling community.

A short Tube ride let us out at King's Cross, where we were swept into commuter traffic.

"God, I forgot how bad commuting sucks," Lola complained as we joined the throngs funneling onto the escalators.

"You go to happy hour every other day," Minho said. "You're literally in these crowds the second your workday ends."

"You also go to happy hour every day," she argued.

"Which is why I'm not complaining."

I glanced over my shoulder to roll my eyes at their bickering, only to realize I'd been so hell-bent on getting out of the crowd that I'd stopped keeping Willow out of the public eye. While it might not have been technically as important as my other job, it was a job I'd assumed nonetheless, and I was failing at it. And I hated failing at a job.

The second we stepped off the escalator, I hooked a finger through her belt loop and pulled her to my side. "Stay close," I said. "The crowds are a good place to hide. Keep your eyes low. I've got you."

If I wasn't mistaken, I could have sworn I felt her exhale.

I guided her through the crush of people with a hand on her hip and Min and Lola close behind, taking my own deep breath when we finally spilled out of the station and onto the street.

It was a balmy night, the heavy kind that wrapped its arms around the city at the end of the summer and made it impossible to go inside.

With the spectacle of St. Pancras behind us and the British Library ahead, I could imagine what the city looked like to a tourist. Grand, historic, full of promise. So long as you didn't look too closely at the rubbish in the streets or the panhandlers surrounding the station entrance or the vague blanket of smog that hung in the air.

"Could it really be as easy as the British Library?" Willow asked as we approached the entrance. "Why didn't we start here?"

"Because Oliver's a wanker, that's why," Minho said, clapping me on the back.

"Mmm," I confirmed. "He's right. I dragged us all over the city just for fun when I've known it's been right here all along. Because of my love of witchcraft and all. Just wanted to see a few more stops along the way."

"All right, all right, we get it," Lola said, shoving me through the door.

No matter how many times I came to the British Library, I never got used to its grandeur. The floor-to-ceiling stacks, the glass, the iron, the private rooms and hidden studies and thousands upon thousands of years of stories, tucked neatly against each other for any curious mind to get their hands on. Ancient Greeks housed in the same stacks as modern literary fiction and the Cold War and cookbooks and music history and every encyclopedia humanity could get its hands on.

It was this kind of variety, this kind of bottomless well of knowledge, that made me want to work in a bookshop in the first place. The very idea that I could spend my days in a place people came to to learn, to be entertained, to escape, to discover themselves. Bookshops saved me more times than I could count over the past thirty-two years of my life, and I'd always thought it would be a privilege to own one that could save someone else. That could bring someone back to themselves—or far away from themselves—or that could bring someone comfort or answers or questions or a sense of belonging.

What I didn't dream of was the occult.

But I didn't dream of my granduncle dying before his time, either, so. Life was nothing if not full of surprises.

"Right, then." Minho clapped his hands, bringing me back to the present. "Where do we begin?"

I rubbed my jaw, trying to remember Diane's instructions. "We need to find Basil Whitlock, at the second-floor research and reference desk. He's supposed to be able to grant us a day pass so we can access the occult collection, and it's apparently in there."

"I can't believe it's as easy as the bloody British Library," Lola said.

"Don't jinx it," Willow said. "Nothing about this has been easy."

"Superstitious?" Lola asked.

"She's witchy," I said, waving my hand. "Or her gran is witchy. So she's witchy by association."

"She's standing right here," Willow said, gesturing to her body. A body I had no business admiring in the British Library. A body with soft curves that were somehow still no match for her face, if I was honest. The more time I spent with her, the more I noticed every freckle, the deep set of her dimples, the smooth lines of her jaw, the changing shades of her brown eyes.

And the more ridiculous I felt for feeling anything for this woman, this American celebrity, who was likely to leave London on the first flight out the second she had her hands on this book. This woman who believed in witchcraft.

"Let's get to it, then," Minho said. "There are a couple pints calling our names when we're done here."

"Min, it's been a long day. I'm sure Willow wants to—"

"A pint sounds great, actually," she said. "Hopefully we have something to celebrate."

"That's the spirit!"

"One thing at a time," I said. "Let's find the second-floor research and reference desk and go from there."

We poked around the library for longer than I'd have liked before we stumbled on the occult section, hidden down a winding corridor. An older gentleman, one I hoped was Basil Whitlock, sat at a nearby desk thumbing through a stack of crumpled papers. The kind that looked like the ones you used to make with a wet tea bag for a school project.

"Excuse us, sir," I said, approaching him like one might approach a deaf dog. He seemed easily startled, and I needed him on our good side. "Are you Mr. Whitlock?"

"Who's asking?" He lowered the stack of papers, skeptical.

"I'm Oliver Hadley, sir. Of Coven and Codex in Notting Hill. Diane Hughes sent us."

"Diane!" he shouted, entirely too loud for a library. "Why didn't you say so?"

"Didn't you *just* say so?" Lola whispered, and I stepped on her foot.

"What is it you're looking for?"

"*Rewind: A Manual for Counter Magic*," I said, holding my breath while I waited for his response and sensing the others doing the same.

"Aye, a *Rewind* volume," he mused. "Let me see here, now," he mumbled to himself, banging his keyboard one key at a time. "Would you look at that!"

"You have it?" Willow asked, stepping up to my side.

"Indeed I do, my dear. Right this way now."

We followed him like moths to a flame, hot on his (very slow) heels as he wove through the stacks, clicking his tongue and humming a quiet tune. He ran his knobby knuckles over the spines, repeating the call number until he found exactly what we'd all been looking for.

"Here we are," he said, pulling it gently from the shelf and presenting it like the grand prize it was. "Now, you can't check it out, as I'm sure you know, but you can look at it as long as you'd like. And since you're friends of Diane's," he whispered, leaning in, "I'll look away if you take a photo."

He returned to his desk as we thanked him profusely, assuring him we'd be out of his way long before closing time.

"I can't believe we found it," Willow said, turning it over in her hands. "Well, I shouldn't say *we* found it. *I* didn't do much of anything. *You* guys found it."

"Don't be silly," Minho said. "Lola didn't do anything, either."

"Does moral support count for nothing?" she argued.

"Not exactly an emotionally taxing journey, this," I said, ignoring Lola's middle finger when she flipped it in my face.

"Thank you," Willow said. "Seriously. I know this might be Oliver's job, but this kind of treatment, especially on a day off, was above and beyond. From all three of you. I'll find a way to thank you properly."

"Tickets to a premiere wouldn't hurt," Lola said, and I was impossibly relieved when Willow laughed.

"I'm sure I can make that happen." She might have been smiling, but the worry wasn't gone from her eyes. It manifested in a glassy sheen and two identical, impossibly cute wrinkles between her brows.

"Well, go on," Lola said. "Open it."

"You can't possibly be interested in this part," Willow said. "You've all done more than enough. Please go back to your real lives before I feel even guiltier for taking so much of your time."

"Are celebrities usually this humble?" Lola asked. "This feels very far from what I've read of Americans in general, let alone—"

"Must you always say exactly what you're thinking?" I asked. "Seriously, is there anything stopping you from spewing your every thought directly into the universe?"

"Yeah, you," she said, "complaining all the time."

"Well, apparently I'm not doing it enough, since you're still—"

"Children, please," Minho said, taking his turn as peacekeeper. "Willow, we've come this far—"

"You've been to two stops—"

"—to not see this through. Do please open the book and let us know if it has what it needs for your gran."

"I couldn't bother you with all that. You don't even believe in witchcraft, and—"

"*Oliver* doesn't believe in witchcraft," Lola said. "Open the book, love. In case you've not noticed, we're very clingy. And now we're invested in your business, so we need to see how it plays out."

"It might take a while . . ."

"We've nowhere to be except the pub," Min said.

Willow looked at me with expectant eyes, undoubtedly awaiting my approval. It wasn't about me, so it didn't matter whether I believed in witchcraft. What mattered was that she got the answers she came here looking for, and that I did my job and helped a customer procure an old volume. Then she could be headed off to LA or New York or Toronto or wherever her next film would take her, and I'd head back to Coven & Codex like this never happened. A simple fact, a preferable solution, really, that shouldn't have made my stomach turn.

"Go on," I said, savoring the flicker in her eyes when she finally opened the book.

"Remind me again what kind of spell we're looking for?" Lola asked.

"One to reverse a spell completed on the solstice," Willow said without looking up from the page. "Which sounds ridiculous, I know, but still. And this book has some old reversal spells, especially some that have to do with shape-shifting and the seasons . . ." She let her sentence trail off as she frantically flipped through the pages, their crinkling the only sound in the room. For all we knew, it could have been the only sound in all of England.

After a while, she stopped flipping pages. Stopped mumbling. Stopped breathing, as far as I could tell. "Did you find it?" I asked, trying not to sound as eager as I felt.

"I found it, all right."

"Why aren't we excited?" Lola asked. "We should be excited, right?"

Willow turned the book around, and the three of us fell into a trance as we stared back at a page filled with a list of six tasks, all of which were required to complete the spell. Willow's hard swallow was audible in the silence.

"Holy shit," I whispered. "This was only the beginning?"

"This was only the beginning."

CHAPTER 13

Willow

This was only the beginning. How could I have been so stupid to think it'd be as easy as finding the book? I didn't want to think Lola had jinxed it, but she might have jinxed it. Six tasks? To complete one spell?

When I was younger, even simple spells often had requirements for completion. Small offerings, easy lessons to learn, that sort of thing. Ivy and I didn't mind; it kept us occupied, and we were excited to have experiences other kids weren't having. But as we got older and learned more advanced magic, we no longer had to cover the prerequisites.

But even in those early days, I'd never seen something this involved. The tasks were so daunting, I could hardly process them one at a time, and instead I just stared at the open book like it was on fire. Just held it in my hands, wide-eyed, slack-jawed, speechless.

Time slowed, and I finally read the list.

I. Forage for *Clinopodium menthifolium*, grown locally. Prepare and consume locally in accordance with your preferences.

II. Conduct an Orientation spell with the Wharram Percy Pendulum. Use its direction as a guide.

III. Complete the Ritualistic Restoration Cleansing in a pond, lake, or slow-moving river to prepare the body for the Reversal.

IV. Participate in a Full Moon Ceremony. Stay awake until the following sundown for maximum effect.

V. Commune with those who have passed on. They know more than any of us who remain in our mortal forms on Earth.

VI. Convince a skeptic of the existence of magic. Use the experience to fortify your powers to effectively produce the Reversal.

"I'm sorry," Lola said, "but does your gran have to do all of these things?"

All I could do was nod.

"Ritualistic cleansing?"

Nod.

"Chat to the dead?"

Nod.

"Saints alive," Oliver said, exhaling. "'Convince a skeptic'? How the hell is she meant to do that?"

"She's got the time," Minho said.

"What d'you mean?"

"Look, there," he said, pointing a long finger at the fine print at the bottom of the page.

> If the initial spell is cast on the summer solstice, the reversal must be cast on the winter solstice. If the initial spell is cast on the winter solstice, the reversal must be cast on the summer solstice. Regardless of seasonality, Reversal spell and all prerequisite tasks must be completed in the city in which the caster finds this text.

I couldn't believe what I was seeing. The *winter* solstice? It was June, for god's sake. That meant I couldn't turn Vera back into a person until *December*? And I had to be in *London* to do it? My head was spinning. And my palms were sweating and my throat was dry and my lungs were tight and my eyes were burning and I no longer knew which way was up.

It made sense, given the solstice was the catalyst for the spell in the first place—which I'd feared even at the time—but that didn't make it any less shocking.

"Maybe you should sit down," Lola said, resting her fingertips at my elbow and trying to guide me to the floor. Instead, I slammed the book shut and walked slowly, calmly out of the room. With the book still in my hands. And with the three of them at my back, whisper-shouting about how I couldn't take the book out of the stacks. Their voices broke over me like waves and I couldn't stop my feet from carrying me out the door.

"God damn it," I heard Oliver mutter from somewhere behind me as he jogged to my side. "Willow, come on," he said. "Can't you just take a photo for your gran? You don't have to steal the whole book, do you?"

"I do," I said, without adding any other information. Mostly because I couldn't quite explain why a photo wouldn't suffice. I knew I needed to be holding the book in my hands while I worked out how to conduct the spell, but I had no plans to reveal *I* would actually be the one doing the conducting, so I didn't have much else to say.

Neither of us spoke for a moment until he dropped his head back and exhaled toward the ceiling. "Fine," he said. "At least let me help. Here." He held out his hand, and I gave him the book, watching with unabashed appreciation as he tucked it into his inside jacket pocket. "Cover me."

"I thought you were covering me?"

Without another word he pulled me tight to his side, right up against where the book was bulging from his pocket. We shuffled arm in arm like that out of the section, past Basil at the desk, then out of the library and back in the direction of the Tube, much to the horror of Minho and Lola.

"Didn't that bloke say he was going to look away?" Minho asked, out of breath from trying to keep up.

"If we took a photo," Oliver said. "Not if we took the whole bloody book."

"Stealing from the British Library has to be some kind of indictable offense around here."

"I hope we never find out," I said. "I didn't mean to make you guys accessories to a crime. I just . . . I needed to get out of there."

Lola held up her hands. "We've all been accessories to far worse crimes."

"Speak for yourself," Oliver said.

"Please, go to the pub," I urged them. "Enjoy the rest of your night."

"You aren't coming with us?"

"This has become a bit more involved than I'd thought," I said, "and I need to get this book to my grandmother." *And I need to get back to Vera, who is probably shredding the wallpaper in the hotel by now, even though this is all for her own good.*

I should have been used to the lie by now, but talking about Granny Annie as if she were alive felt like swallowing glass, so I needed to get out of there before things got any worse.

"Tomorrow, then," Lola insisted, squeezing my arm, then following Min in the direction of the pub.

And while I wanted to resist, to untangle them from this mess, I had to admit it felt good to be invited to something as low-key as the pub. By someone who seemed genuinely interested in this journey.

In LA, everyone's version of magic was green-juice cleanses and holistic healing and homeopathic remedies in place of modern medicine. People didn't believe in the occult, but they worshipped at the altars of celebrities and plastic surgeons and anyone with a good tan and straight teeth and a daily Pilates routine.

Here, with the exception of Oliver, far more people seemed to believe magic was possible. Judging by the size of the section in the British Library, people had been believing in the occult for thousands of years. And if this many people believed these spells worked, then maybe I could, too.

"Are you sure you're okay?" Oliver asked, holding me at arm's length and lowering his head to make eye contact. "You ran out of there like the whole lot was on fire."

I sighed, resisting the urge to bury my face in my hands. Though I suspected if I wasn't looking at him, then it was possible the sparking in my chest would stop, and I definitely wouldn't complain about that. "I was so overwhelmed by finally finding the book, and then the list, and all I have to do to reverse the spell, and I just—"

"All *you* have to do? I thought it was all your gran had to do?"

Shit. "Oh, it is! It's just . . . I have to get the book back to her and then help her with the tasks, and you know how it goes, and that's a lot of work, so—"

"Is all of this actually for your gran?" He dropped his arms and took a step back, like I'd burned him. Though the sparking was so common by now that I probably had.

"What?" I asked, though I'd heard him perfectly fine; I just needed to buy myself time. Only my plan backfired, because hearing him repeat the question a second time stung more than the first.

"Is this actually for your gran? Or is it for you?"

"Can't it be one and the same?" I asked in a last-ditch attempt to save face.

"Willow." He exhaled, running his hands through his hair and looking away just long enough for me to see the firm, unhappy set of his jaw. "All of this can't really be for *you*, can it?"

"Why couldn't it be?" I didn't want to confess, but I wasn't about to let him stand there and make me feel bad about witchcraft, either. Just because he didn't believe in it didn't mean it didn't exist. We all had things we didn't believe in, but it wasn't up to us to decide what was real for someone else, and I wasn't about to let him try.

"You seem . . . I don't know. Smarter than that."

I scoffed so loud, a pigeon flew from its spot at our feet. How had this taken such a turn? Sure, I hadn't wanted to tell Oliver the truth, but that was because I knew he didn't believe in magic and didn't want to have to explain myself, not because I thought he was going to turn around and be a dick about it. "So you think witchcraft is stupid?" I asked. "You run an occult bookshop, and not only do you not believe in your products, but you think the people who do aren't smart?"

"I'm not saying I think you're stupid," he said, raising his hands and immediately dropping them again. "I'm just saying I didn't think you'd buy into all this nonsense."

"Nonsense? This is how you make a living, Oliver, in case you'd forgotten. And just because it doesn't make sense to you doesn't mean it's nonsense. Maybe *you* aren't as smart as you think you are if you can't understand that."

I hadn't meant to come to blows outside King's Cross Station, but I couldn't just let him talk down on such a fundamental piece of my identity. I could deal with his cynicism, but I couldn't deal with his condescension.

But at the same time, as soon as the words left my mouth, I realized they sounded a whole lot like *I know you are but what am I?*, which brought me right back to my childhood days of my malfunctioning powers and trying to explain away every weird thing that happened to me so that the neighborhood kids would stop looking at me like I was growing a second head. I wanted to be proud of this part of my identity, not burdened by it. And I'd be damned if he made me feel that way.

Even if up until this moment he'd been a gentleman. A charming—if edgy—intelligent, considerate gentleman. One who was passionate about books and secretly loved helping people even if he pretended he didn't. And one who was so impossibly handsome, every time he looked at me with those green-gray eyes, my bones turned to liquid.

It didn't matter much anymore. Not that it ever should have mattered in the first place.

"It's hardly just a belief system so much as it's science," he said. "The universe has laws and rules and things, you know? I'm not saying I don't believe in it because I'm trying to be an arsehole. I'm saying I don't believe in it because it would be impossible."

There were so many questions I wanted to ask. I wanted to know how he could possibly think that when we hardly knew the first thing about the capabilities of the universe. How he could even remotely assume everything that ever happened abided by those "laws" and "rules."

Instead, I said, "Right."

"That's all?"

"I'm not going to argue with you here outside the Tube station. We hardly know each other. And I don't need you to believe in any of it. All I needed was your help finding the book, for which I'm grateful, by the way, but now we can go our separate ways."

"And you're going to complete the list on your own?"

"It's not like you're going to help me, is it?" Silence. "That's what I thought. Have a great rest of the night, Oliver."

Before he could say another word, rude or otherwise, I disappeared down the stairs and into the throngs of the Underground. Just me and the stolen book and the impossible list and a lump in my throat and six months laid out ahead of me before I could even give this thing a shot.

I couldn't remember all the circles of hell, but this had to be one of them.

@JewelsBlogs: Is Willow James studying in London? Read more about star-studded MFAs and how Hollywood is overtaking academia at the link in bio!

@IDreamOfDragons: no way is she in grad school. I bet she's filming something new. #WhereIsWillowJames

CHAPTER 14

Oliver

When you own an occult bookshop in a popular neighborhood of a major tourist city, there are few things left to surprise you. Really, you start to think you've seen it all.

And yet . . . I was shocked.

Which didn't make proper sense, given how little I knew about this woman, but something wasn't clicking in my brain. *This* woman thought she was a witch? This celebrity, famous for dramas and thrillers and films Lo and Minho informed me were serious, no-nonsense affairs. Though I supposed it was acting, after all. She was merely playing a role.

The same way she'd been with me, running the story about her gran. How stupid was I that I didn't see what was really going on? Maybe this was why she was nominated for an Oscar or whatever Lola said.

My head was spinning, and before I knew it, I was headed in the direction of the pub. I would have to confess the whole thing to Min and Lo at some point, so, much like telling them about the search in the first place, I figured I'd get it over with.

They'd dropped a pin in our group text when they left, so it was easy to find them at Mack's, just up the street from the station.

"That was fast," Lola said when I slid onto a stool beside them.

"Yeah, well, we had nothing left to say to each other, so." I drank half her pint in one gulp, ignoring her raised eyebrows and her open mouth. "I'll get the next round," I said.

"Are you going to fill us in?" she asked. "Or are we going to have to guess why you look like smoke is about to come out of your ears?"

"Nothing to fill you in on," I said, finishing her beer.

"Might as well just tell us whatever it is now, mate," Min said. "You know you're going to have to eventually. Let's have at it, then."

"She lied," I exhaled. "And she thinks she's a witch. Are we ready to move on now? Have another pint and go back to living our lives like this never happened?"

"She what?" Min asked.

"And she *what*?" Lola added.

"Please don't make me repeat myself," I said.

"We're going to need a little more information," Minho said. "She lied about what? And what do you mean she's a witch?"

"She *thinks* she's a witch," I corrected him. "She can't be an actual witch because witches aren't real."

"But what about her gran?" Lola asked.

"There is no gran," I said. "Or maybe there is . . . I don't know. But Willow was looking for the book for herself the whole time."

"Which means—" Min started.

"Which means she has to do the tasks," Lola said, a note of excitement creeping into her voice. "Which also means she's going to be in London for at least six more months, doesn't it?" That piece I had yet to acknowledge, even to myself. I'd mentally prepared for her to leave after today, and I had no idea what to do now that she was staying. Surely I'd run into her. And surely I didn't want to. Or at least I shouldn't have wanted to.

"Oliver, you have to keep helping her."

"Are you mad? Absolutely not."

"Are *you* mad? Meeting Willow James in the first place was the opportunity of a lifetime. And now you get to help her do a whole lot of witchy tasks to turn someone back into a person? Come on."

"You come on. Are you even listening to yourself right now?" I argued. "None of this is real, Lo. And even if it was, it doesn't take away from the fact that she lied."

"Oh, boo-hoo. She told you she was helping her gran and she wasn't. Hardly a lie, is it? Min, help me out here."

He raised his palms and his eyebrows: a universal signal for *Leave me out of this.*

"I'm pretty sure every nontruth counts as a lie, doesn't it?" I said. "What else is she hiding, you know?"

"We'll never find out if we don't help her."

"When did this become a *we* situation?"

"When you made it perfectly clear you weren't capable of doing this on your own," she said. "And we haven't even cracked the surface of the real issues here, so you need all the help you can get."

"What are you talking about? What real issues? And can we at least have another beer before this conversation? I'm not exactly keen on the direction it's going and I'd love a pint or twenty to make it through to the end, if you don't mind."

"It's my turn," Min said, jumping up from the table, and headed toward the bar, undoubtedly thrilled to get away. I envied him.

"The fact that you feel you have to protect her," Lola said, counting off "issues" on her fingers. "And the fact that you fancy her."

"You've officially lost the plot."

"God, Oliver, for someone who's so upset about lying, would it kill you to be honest for a second?"

"It might, yes," I said, but she didn't laugh. "I don't fancy her. And I don't feel the need to protect her from anything. She's fine on her own. I was just doing my job."

"And a hell of a job you were doing," she said, gratefully accepting a pint as Min returned. "It's not a crime to fancy her, you know. Everyone else does." For some reason, hearing that felt like jumping into a freezing lake. Of course everyone fancied her. She was a celebrity, for Christ's sake. And a beautiful one. A kind, down-to-earth one. Or so I thought.

"We definitely do." Min shrugged.

"*Now* you decide you want to contribute?" I said.

"I'm just saying, mate. Not the end of the world if you fancy her."

"Can we stop talking about if I fancy her?" *Because obviously I fancy her.*

"We can talk about why you seem to feel obligated to protect her, instead," Lola suggested. "Is that better?"

"Hardly."

"Why? Because it's also true?"

"You lot are bloody irritating, d'you know that?"

"That's why you're friends with us." Lola smiled, a hand placed delicately under her chin.

"I can assure you, it isn't."

"No, it isn't," Min agreed. "You're friends with us because we're always here for you, without judgment." He cut his eyes to Lola, and she mouthed something incomprehensible, then dropped her gaze to her beer. "Which means it's okay if you fancy her. More than the general population, I mean. And it's okay if you want to protect her from the paparazzi or the fans or whatever. I don't blame you. And that doesn't mean she can't take care of herself. It just means you want to do what you can to help. Nothing wrong with any of that."

"What he said," Lola said with a sigh.

I wanted to be comforted by what Min had said—and I was, in a sense—but it didn't *feel* like there was nothing wrong. I wasn't usually charmed, which meant I wasn't usually disappointed, which meant I had no idea where to put myself now that I was experiencing both. It had only been a day. Three, maybe, if you counted from when she first came into the shop.

And I should have counted from when she first came into the shop, because I hadn't stopped thinking about her since. I didn't *want* to care. But that didn't mean I didn't.

"I can't possibly help her," I said eventually, resigned to the truth. "I don't believe in anything she's doing, and I think I hurt her feelings when I tried to explain that before." It really wasn't my finest moment, come to think of it. "If I tried to help, I'm sure I'd only hurt her more. And I'm not even sure where I'd begin. I doubt she even wants my help at this point, anyway." I was spiraling, and I needed to stop. I wasn't someone who spiraled, and I wasn't keen on starting now.

"One thing at a time," Lola said. "Do you *want* to help her? Yes or no."

"I mean—"

"Yes," she said, "or no."

"Yes." There was so much more to it than just that one word, but it appeared I wasn't going to have the chance to explain that.

"Right." Lola nodded. "So on to the next. What happened when you tried to talk to her about it before?"

"I said some shite about science—which is true, by the way—and

I might have implied she was stupid. Or at least she thought I was calling her stupid."

Lola dropped her head into her hands, and Min bit his lip trying not to laugh. "You're hopeless," he said.

"He is not," Lola said. "And we're going to help him. And then we're all going to help Willow."

I wasn't going to touch that just yet, but I did *not* plan for this to be a group activity.

"So it sounds like the first thing you need to do is apologize," Lola said.

"I don't even know how to get a hold of her."

"She's staying at the Charter."

"How the hell do you know that?"

"Saw the key card in her wallet when she went for her Oyster card."

"You're a creep, Lo." She only shrugged. "Still, it's not like I can just show up to the hotel and ask for Willow James. *Hi, yes, would you mind terribly giving out the room information for a high-profile guest? Just want to apologize for being a wanker and then I'll be on my way.*"

"Ye of so little faith." Lola tutted. "You let me worry about how we're meant to get in touch with her. You worry about what you're going to say when you see her."

"I'm capable of a proper apology, you know."

"I'm not the one who needs convincing."

"Thank god."

"Then what?" Min asked.

"Then we offer our help on the quest," Lola said.

"Must you always talk like we're in a video game?"

"Must you always try to change the topic?"

"How's this for staying on topic," I said. "It isn't *our* help on the quest. If she's willing to accept any help at all, it'll be from me. Seeing as I work in the occult industry, after all."

Lola laughed, but not because anything was funny. "If you think we're letting her try to complete that list with only the help of someone who doesn't believe in magic, you're even more delusional than I thought."

"I don't have to believe in magic to make sure she does what she needs to do without being hounded by fans," I said.

"But you do need someone to believe in magic to keep morale up when times get tough," Lola argued. "She needs support, not just a bodyguard and a couple connections."

"You don't know what she needs."

"Neither do you."

"Only one way to find out," Min said, clapping his hands.

"We can't really be doing this," I said. "This whole thing is absurd."

"You can't change your mind now," Lola said. "You're just scared."

"What could I possibly be scared of?"

"I don't know," Lo said. "You fancy her, she's going to go back to America eventually, she 'lied,' which is problematic to you even though it wasn't really a big one and it was kind of her prerogative anyway, and maybe you're afraid you're not actually going to be able to help her, which would be quite the hit to your ego—"

"We get it," I said.

"You asked."

"And I regret it."

"Before we leave, I do feel like we have to address the elephant in the room," Min said. "Or the cat, rather."

"Please don't," I groaned. "I can assure you, whatever cat there is has always been a cat and will always be a cat."

"In your world, maybe," Lola said.

"There's only one world."

"Try telling that to the cat."

"You guys are about to get yourselves banned from the quest."

"Does that mean we're officially allowed to be part of the quest?"

"Doesn't seem like I could have said no if I wanted to, does it?" Even though I really, really wanted to.

"We're going to be helpful, you know," Lola said. "Min has just as many connections as you do around the city and I know everything there is to know about the hero's journey. And I believe in magic. And Min doesn't care enough one way or another. So we'll be great for moral support. We're trying to help you both, Oliver. We aren't just fans of Willow or meant to be a thorn in your side."

The softness in her voice made me feel bad for giving her such a hard time, even though she had been doing the same to me. But she was right. They were trying to help, and it seemed Willow and I both needed all the help we could get.

"I know." I sighed, scrubbing my hands over my jaw. "Thank you."

"Don't thank us yet," Minho said. "We've got quite a bit to do first. Starting with a trip to the Charter."

We clinked our glasses together and gulped down the rest of our pints, for liquid courage or because we were suddenly racing against the clock, I wasn't sure.

All I was sure of was that I was on my way to a hotel to attempt to track down a celebrity to apologize and to propose we help her on her quest to complete a list of tasks to perform a spell to turn a cat back into a person. There weren't enough pints in the world.

CHAPTER 15
Willow

It was nearly eleven thirty when I heard a knock on my door.

I'd gotten so used to staying in hotels alone over the many years of traveling for work that I'd more or less stopped freaking out every time I heard a sound, but a knock on the door was unusual. A knock on the door close to midnight in a hotel where no one even knew I was staying was even weirder.

I glanced over at Vera to confirm she'd heard it, too, and her little head was peeking up from the foot of the bed, her wide eyes darting back and forth from me to the door. So it wasn't just me.

"What the hell was that?" I whispered to her, and she blinked back like my guess was as good as hers.

By the time I got back to the hotel and realized I was no longer in the right headspace to conduct the spell to get Vera to be able to speak, we'd decided we'd have to wait until morning. Or at least I'd decided, but she'd seemed to agree. Ivy had given me the confidence I needed, but I was so tired from the day, I had a feeling that if I did manage to get Vera to speak, it would be in another language or she'd only be able to communicate in early nineties song lyrics or something equally tragic.

When I tried to explain this to her, she seemed to understand. Or at least I hoped she did. Everything I was doing was for her own good, and until I got the spell to work, I just had to hope she knew that.

So she still couldn't say anything, but her eyes told me all I needed to know: the knock was real.

I slid off the bed and crept toward the door, straining on my tiptoes to see through the peephole. All I could see was the chest of a man in a hotel uniform. I was about to ask who it was when I heard whispering on the other side.

"This is insane."

"Just trust me."

"We're going to scare her to death. Why didn't anyone think of that sooner?"

"It's going to be fine as soon as she realizes it's us."

"Unless she calls the police first and we're all handcuffed before she can even open the door."

"Don't be ridiculous."

"Do you want a chance to apologize or not? Focus on what's really important here."

I swung the door open in the middle of their argument, all four of us equally shocked to see each other. Me because they were dressed like hotel staff, and them because I opened the door.

"Willow, hi," Lola said, smiling wider than I'd even known was possible. People in my industry would have killed for teeth that straight.

"Hi." I resisted the urge to look down at my pajamas, suddenly painfully aware I was standing in the doorway in nothing but boxer shorts and an old UCLA T-shirt. Bare feet, hair tied into a low braid, bleary eyes. Definitely not my best look. And definitely not a way I'd ever allow anyone else to see me, either.

But I couldn't deny my curiosity.

"How did you guys find me?"

"Please don't be mad," Lola said. "But I saw the key card in your wallet, and then everything after that was like a bad spy movie. Uniforms hanging in the service entrance, key fob in the pocket, easy access to the computer, a few clicks, and—"

"Does anyone else know I'm here?"

"No." Oliver stepped forward, shaking his head. "And it's going to stay that way. I just owe you an apology, and we didn't know how else to get in touch with you. It's not like we can just find your email or, I don't know, DM you on Instagram."

"No." I laughed a little. "I suppose it isn't."

"Are you mad?"

"Not mad," I said. "Confused, maybe. And a little impressed? And a little concerned, you know, with security and all that." If it was this easy for them, would it be that easy for someone else?

"That's part of why we're here," Lola said, gesturing to Oliver to continue. I furrowed my eyebrows, hoping he was going to make sense of the late-night visit. He cleared his throat and glared down at Lola, and she nodded like she'd just remembered the plan.

"We're going to, er, be down the hall." She grabbed Minho by the arm and dragged him in the direction of the elevators, disappearing around a corner.

"Hi," Oliver said, and exhaled, clearly gearing up for something. "I'm sorry it's late. And I'm sorry we barged in like this."

"This is the British version of 'barging,' I assume."

A smile, small and tentative.

"And mostly I'm sorry for the way I acted earlier."

When we'd parted ways and I got the Tube, I'd convinced myself I didn't need an apology. That I'd never see him again, if I was lucky, and it didn't matter what he thought, anyway. I knew what was real, and I didn't need to convince anyone otherwise.

Except I did.

Item number six. Right there at the bottom of the page. *Convince a skeptic.*

Though if I could do anything to help it, he wouldn't be the one I tried to convince.

"Go on," I said, eager to hear what else he had to say, if only to unclench my jaw. He said some shitty things earlier, and I wasn't about to let him get away with a simple *I'm sorry.* Not that it seemed like he planned to, what with all the deep breaths and the squared shoulders and the practiced cadence of his speech.

"I was a wanker. I shouldn't have said I thought you were smarter than someone who believed in magic, and I shouldn't have been so pushy about my beliefs. It isn't nonsense. And I'm sorry I said it was."

Well done. "Thank you." I sighed. I didn't have it in me to hold a grudge. Especially against a man I hardly knew. I had enough to keep me busy.

"And I do hope you can forgive me, because I—we—would like to help." This last part came out a bit like he was announcing he wanted a root canal, but the words held meaning all the same.

"The three of you?" I asked. "Want to help me . . ."

"With the quest," he said, smiling a little when I laughed at the word. "Lo's been calling it that and it just kind of stuck."

"But you don't even believe in any of this. Why would you want to help me?" It made sense for Lola and Minho to want to help, but Oliver?

"Well, those two are interested in the list itself," he explained. "The tasks, the items, the whole lot."

"And you?" I asked, holding my breath.

"I'm interested in you," he said. The words floated between us like snowflakes: beautiful and sparkling and gone before I knew it. "Your safety, I mean. I'd like to come along to make sure you aren't swarmed in the Tube station or anything like that." The callback to our moment in the cutout made my face warm. As did his four simple words: *I'm interested in you.*

In fact, my face was *really* warm. Warmer than was appropriate for a comment that was quickly modified to be something entirely platonic.

"Are you all right?" he asked. "You've gone quite . . . rosy."

I tried to laugh, to seem like I had control of the situation, but as he brought the back of his hand to my forehead and I pulled away, my hair started to float up from my shoulders, and I knew it was hopeless.

"Fine," I said, closing the door a little. He didn't budge. "Just a bit warm in here. You know how it is, no AC here in England." I tried to shrug, but it was manic. More of a twitch, really. An unfortunate muscle spasm.

"Are you sure? Your hair, it's—"

Smoking. My split ends were *smoking*.

"Heat damage," I yelped. "Anyway, thank you for the apology and for the offer to help. Let's talk tomorrow? I'll come by the shop? It's late, so I should just, you know, good night, Oliver."

I closed the door before he could respond and dashed into the bathroom, dunking my head in the sink and turning the faucet on full blast.

Fire? My hair was catching on *fire*? Because a man touched the back of his hand to my forehead to make sure I was all right?

I wanted to accept their help, but I needed my magic to work now more than ever. I couldn't afford for it to go haywire because Oliver touched my forehead with the back of his hand, for god's sake.

If I was going to accept their help, I needed a plan.

And no one was better at a plan than Vera. Which was why, first thing in the morning, I was getting her to talk.

✧

Sip of wine on the edge,
Pruning like you would a hedge.
All that's left is an
Upright walk.
Big deep breath
And now you talk.

The spell was simple enough in nature: formulaic, like the ones we practiced as children. Only I really had to muster the conviction not to mess this up. The words were basic but the magic was advanced, and I couldn't afford any more mistakes.

"All right, Vera," I muttered, studying the spell once again. Wine on the edge because alcohol and nerves made everyone talk too much; pruning and upright walking because the more animals acted like people, the more likely they were to speak. It made sense. I believed in it. And I believed in myself. Or at least I believed Ivy believed in me, which was even better. "Here we go."

I used nail scissors from the complimentary vanity kit in the bathroom to trim the hair around her eyes and on her tail, brushing her gently and smoothing every stray whisker into place. She was as beautiful as a cat as she was as a person, even before I started the grooming, but I hoped this would do the trick.

Then, with my feet hanging off the edge of the bed (it was the best I could do in the hotel room), I poured us both a healthy swig of minibar wine, held Vera by her front paws with her back feet planted next to mine, and recited the spell.

I said the words loud and clear and with a slight rhythm, the way Granny Annie had taught me, believing every one of them. I envisioned Vera speaking, put all my energy into doing something for her, all my energy into that moment, the moment she opened her mouth and—

"Thank god," she said.

My eyes sprang open, and I collapsed onto my knees on the floor. "What? Was that you? What did you say?"

"I said *thank god*. I was getting so sick of listening to you ramble to yourself and not being able to say anything back to you. And if you didn't get your shit together and find some conviction to get this done, I was prepared to start shredding the curtains." She stretched out her paws and admired her nails. "Quite the manicure, don't you think?"

"You can talk," I cried, pulling her into my chest and resisting the urge to sob. "Oh my god. You can talk."

"But I can't hug, and you're crushing me," she said.

"Sorry." I laughed, holding her out in front of me. "I'm so relieved."

"Put me down, you psycho," she said. "Well done, Willow. I knew you had it in you. Thank you for this."

"Please don't thank me ever again," I said with a shudder. "I haven't exactly done anything good. Just made the horrible situation I put us in slightly less horrible."

"At this point, we've got to take what we can get. Especially since it's going to be another six months before I'm a person again."

"You've been able to understand me this whole time?" She nodded. "Oh god, Vera. I'm so sorry. I had no idea I'd have to wait for another solstice to do the spell again. I wish there was another way out of this. I'm going to keep looking. I can't leave you like this until December."

"Willow, I'm just glad you've found *any* way out of this," she said. "What's important is you do what you need to do between now and then so you can reverse the spell when the time comes. We have plenty of time to prepare, and we need to make sure we use it to our advantage. Do things right."

"But, Vera—"

"I'll be okay until then," she said. "I'm getting used to being off the grid, spending all my time in a luxury hotel in a beautiful city with nothing to do. That's what all celebrity managers dream of, isn't it?"

"You're being such a good sport about this," I said.

"I'm always a good sport."

"You've never been a good sport."

It felt good to laugh together.

"I know you didn't do this on purpose, Willow. I just need you to be ready to get me out of this when the time comes, okay?"

"I will be," I said. "I promise."

That promise was either going to hold me accountable or eat me alive, and there was only one way to find out which.

"But in order for me to do that, we need a plan."

"Beyond the obvious?"

"Beyond the obvious," I confirmed. "I need Oliver to, uh, keep his distance. Or maybe I need to keep my distance. Either way—"

"I saw the whole thing," she said. "Burning hair and all." I collapsed onto the mattress, properly mortified. "This is what we're going to do."

"Talk to me," I muttered with my face pressed into the sheets.

"We're going to make it seem like you and Kit are seeing each other. Nothing serious, still early days. Just enough to make Oliver think you're involved with someone else, so he doesn't go doing anything else sexy like . . . checking your forehead for a fever."

"What if you just killed me instead?" I asked, face still shoved into two-thousand-thread-count Egyptian cotton.

"Have you forgotten I'm a cat?" Vera said. "Besides, this is going to be a piece of cake. No killing necessary. Right before the summer solstice party I saw a fan edit of the two of you on Instagram. Photoshopped together, you know the deal. Let's find it again, set it as your phone wallpaper, *et voilà*. That's all you need to do."

I might not have liked it, but it was a plan, and I was desperate. Besides, when had Vera failed me before? There was a reason she was one of the most coveted managers in the industry, and it wasn't lost on me how lucky I was. I needed to trust her.

Even if I hated the idea of Oliver thinking I was with someone else. Though for all I knew, *he* could be with someone else. What mattered was that I was removing any temptation, which would hopefully reduce the threat of errant magic, and we would be on our way to reversing this spell without causing any other damage in the process.

Easy enough.

CHAPTER 16

Oliver

Coven & Codex was so peaceful in the mornings, it was easy to remember why I agreed to keep it running after Uncle Arthur passed away.

The shop might not have housed the kind of books I loved, but I was surrounded by books nonetheless, and I would have been a selfish bastard to complain about that. And first thing in the morning, with the pale light streaming through the windows, the silence, the warmth of the fireplace, and the day stretching lazily ahead of me, I couldn't think of anywhere I'd rather be.

Mondays were the slowest days—the "Hours" sign on the front door read *Mondays: Maybe*—but I often kept the shop open while I inventoried, caught up on paperwork, and did the other boring administrative tasks that came with the territory of being a shop owner.

It was easy to fulfill special requests, reorganize, clean, and update seasonal displays when I was mostly alone in the shop, and for that reason, I didn't hate Mondays. A slow start to the week, just me and the shop and a to-do list with things I was actually able to check off by the end of the day.

This morning, I was rearranging the windows to include a new series by a local author, surrounding the stacks of books with flickering electric tea lights and crystals of varying colors and sizes. I hadn't the foggiest what any of her books were about, but if I wanted good business, the shop had to look the part.

The series was called Cosmic Collision, and each cover featured a constellation. The author, Agatha Hemlock, was doing a reading here next week, and I'd hoped the display would attract some guests. Her lecture was meant to cover something about unlocking your inner Urania, whatever that meant. Where did these people get this from? Maybe I'd have Wesley cover the floor that night . . .

I was organizing a selection of crystals in a way that would hopefully catch the light, when I heard a faint tap at the front door. It wasn't uncommon for tourists to peek in before or after business hours, so at first, I ignored it, hoping they'd read the sign and come back if I decided to open the shop later.

Only when I heard it again, more insistent this time, coupled with a faint call of my name, I realized exactly who it was.

After she'd slammed the door on me last night, I wasn't sure I'd ever see her again. Not to mention whatever was happening to her face . . . and her hair? I grew up with a sister, I'd heard all about heat damage, but I'd never seen it actually . . . smoking. Maybe we'd just interrupted her in the middle of styling it. Or, more likely, I was just tired and seeing things. That must have been all it was.

I left the stones scattered in the windowsill as I climbed out of the display and raced to the front door before she gave up and left. The morning was wet, and she was huddled against the door under the awning, signature hat pulled low and trench coat wrapped tight around her waist. Raindrops sat on her shoulders and her hair, and the way they shimmered under the light of the doorway made her look like a painting. I could have stood there, on the other side of the translucent glass, watching London paint her a million times over. The only thing more tempting than an art study was opening the door and letting her in.

"Willow," I said, my voice scratchy. This was the first word I'd said all morning. I cleared my throat and started again. "Come in, get out of the rain." I opened the door wider and gestured for her to step inside, relieved at her grateful smile.

"Sorry I'm here so early," she said. "I hope it's okay. I was just trying to avoid the crowds, and I figured it was my turn to apologize for yesterday. For being so abrupt last night. I just needed . . . I was tired, and embarrassed, and overwhelmed. And I'm sorry."

See? I knew that was all it was. "Apology accepted," I said, nodding firmly for emphasis. "Thank you."

"And I wanted to take you up on your offer," she said. "If it still stands. For help on the quest."

It didn't seem like it was easy for her to say these words, and I wondered if she was someone who had a hard time accepting help. There must have been certain help that came with the territory of being an actor, of course, like managers and security and hair and makeup teams, but those were paid employees. We were strangers. And we knew nothing about her and nothing about this fake magic, and it seemed none of us knew where to begin, so I couldn't blame her for struggling to get the words out.

"And if you three changed your minds, that's okay," she continued. "I understand it's a big ask, and will require a lot of time and energy, and since you don't even believe in any of this in the first place—"

"We haven't changed our minds," I said. "And I don't have to believe in it to help you stay safe and check items off the list. We're in, Willow."

"Thank god," she said, and exhaled, like she'd been holding her breath since I left last night. "I was starting to wonder how I was going to do any of this on my own."

"I'm sure you'd have been just fine," I said. "But now you've not to worry."

Even as I said the words, I had no idea whether they were true. Didn't we all have to worry? This whole thing was barmy. I had no idea how she thought we were going to fix a problem that couldn't have existed in the first place, and Lola and Min were definitely going to get too invested, and I was more than likely to put my foot directly back into my mouth every time we talked about "magic," which was likely to be most of the time. What the hell were we thinking?

But when she thanked me, when I caught the warmth in her eyes and the pleading written across the lines in her forehead, I remembered exactly what we were thinking. And I feared Lo and Min weren't the only ones who risked getting attached.

As soon as I remembered this whole thing was about her thinking she was a witch, however, I snapped back into myself. Whenever I needed to keep my distance, I just had to remember I didn't believe in what appeared to be quite a large piece of her life, and for that reason, among millions of others, we'd never work. Not that I wanted us to work. But sometimes my imagination ran away with me. I was a bookseller. It happened to all of us.

"So, I guess whenever you're ready to get started . . ." she was saying when I refocused. "Though I suppose we're not in a rush, since I'm stuck here until December." *Stuck.* I hadn't expected such a simple word to hurt, but there was an undeniable twinge in my chest. This wasn't a holiday for her. She wanted to get out of here as quickly as possible: another reminder to keep my imagination in check.

"Right, yeah, of course," I said. "Maybe we'll, er, meet Minho and Lola at the pub this weekend and figure out a plan?"

"Perfect," she said. "Thank you."

"This is going to be a long journey, Willow," I said. "You don't have to thank me every time we make plans. Especially if we're only meeting at the pub."

"That's going to take some getting used to."

"You're not one of those overly polite Americans, are you?"

"Isn't that supposed to be the Brits?"

"Ah, come on. You know the type. *Yes, ma'am. Pardon me, ma'am.*"

Her laugh cut through the stillness of the morning, and I felt it all the way down to my toes. "*That's* your impression of an American accent?"

"What's wrong with my accent?"

"Other than everything?"

"Like you could do a better British one." I rolled my eyes.

"I'm an actor. I can do a perfect one," she said, in what was indeed the most perfect British accent I'd heard from an American in all my life.

"Fair play to ya," I said, raising my palms.

"So no, I'm not one of those overly polite Americans." Her smile alone was enough to take the chill out of the morning. "But I am terrible at accepting help, especially if I feel like it's a burden to someone else. So it would go against everything in me to not thank you every five minutes."

So I was right. "Even if you know it'll drive us crazy?"

"Even if I know it'll drive you crazy."

The longer we stood in the entrance to the shop, with the city coming alive just behind her head, framing her like a halo, the more certain I was she was going to drive me crazy in more ways than one. Hell, maybe I was already crazy for agreeing to any of this. If so, she was sure to make me lose my mind completely.

And I was walking directly into the fire.

CHAPTER 17

Willow

"You're stressing me out," Vera said, watching me pace our hotel room to kill time before I was supposed to meet Oliver, Minho, and Lola at the park. "Can't you just stretch or watch ASMR videos or put on another coat of mascara or whatever you normally do? Your energy is all out of whack and it's making me itchy."

"I figured out how to make you talk and this is what I get in return?"

"You also turned me into a cat, in case you'd forgotten, so I'm not exactly sure making it so I can speak is a major accomplishment."

She had a point.

Over the past few days, we'd learned a few things: cats required way more sleep than humans, baths were suddenly a freezing nightmare, and I was the only one who could understand Vera when she spoke. Well, me and Siri, apparently. I guessed since robots didn't have to believe in magic, there was nothing stopping Siri from comprehending.

The bellman, on the other hand . . . not so much.

We'd been avoiding him since a vicious meowing incident a few days ago.

Otherwise, Vera didn't much mind hanging out in the hotel. And in a few days, we were going to relocate to a short-term apartment on a ground floor with a garden, so Vera could enjoy the next six months as much as possible while I got us sorted out.

As far as our jobs went, Vera was supposedly on a silent retreat, and we'd concocted a story about me also needing an unexpected break to relax and recharge before I took on new projects, said a few more Hollywood buzzwords about wellness, then put up a vague out-of-office message and hoped for the best.

"Imagine how my energy is making me feel." I sighed, finally sitting down next to her on the windowsill. "I know I shouldn't be nervous. It's just a few people at a park. And not even a popular park, so hopefully no one will recognize me."

"Right, so . . ." she said, seemingly waiting for me to identify a problem. "Is this about Oliver?"

"Of course it isn't about Oliver." I had a sinking feeling it was very much about Oliver. "It's just . . . I've never gotten help from strangers with my magic before. And it's only a matter of time before they find out I'm terrible at it. If they even believe I can do it at all. And that's assuming they don't change their minds before then, which they probably will, so maybe I actually have nothing to worry about."

"Spiraling doesn't look good on you."

"So what do you suggest, hmm?"

"I suggest you take a deep breath and remind yourself who you are."

"Secret, shitty witch who turned her manager into a cat? American actor incapable of doing a romance because she can't get her magic under control?"

"Strong, thoughtful woman, capable of anything," she said, staring straight into me with her marble-green eyes. "Maybe one who's doing a little too much whining right now, but a powerful one nonetheless. And if you ever forget that, we're both doomed. So time to buck up and put your game face on, Willow James. You're not the only one in this mess, and I'm counting on you."

"No pressure," I said, and laughed. "Thank you, Vera." She knew exactly what she was doing. If I couldn't gather courage for myself, I could at least do it for her. And part of what made her such a great manager was that she always knew exactly what I needed to hear, and that hadn't changed just because she was a cat.

And as much as I didn't want to admit it, Oliver might have also had a point. I couldn't spend the next six months thanking them incessantly for something they volunteered to do and frankly, with the exception of Oliver himself, seemed excited about. I would drown in the feeling of being a burden, and there would be no way I could muster the strength to turn Vera back.

I needed to remember that my success (or lack thereof) didn't define me, and I could be a good witch even if it was hard. And that I could be someone who accepted help from willing strangers whom I would trust not to judge me for the lack-thereof part.

I squared my shoulders, swiped on another layer of lip gloss, settled Vera in her spot in the window with a room-service branzino and a *Sex and the City* marathon, and slipped out the door into the cool London night.

We'd agreed to meet at a quiet park near the Notting Hill Gate Tube station, hoping anyone who might recognize me would be farther into the hustle and bustle of the city and not hanging out in some unknown local spot without so much as a picnic table.

It was a perfect plan for more reasons than one. Back home,

Vera was constantly whisking me to parties and galas and openings and birthdays and events whose purpose I couldn't even remember. This kind of social calendar came with the territory, and Vera busted her ass to get us in front of all the right people wearing all the right things and I couldn't complain about any of it, nor did I want to, most of the time. I was living the life younger me would have killed for.

But on the quiet walk by myself through the city, past the Victorian homes with their pillars and their checkered entryways, past the old couples and young families out for the night in this charming part of the city, without cameras or couture gowns or champagne that cost more than my rent, I felt like myself again.

Like the me before the films and the fame and the spell that changed everything.

If only for a second, I was the sensitive, curious Willow of my youth, wide-eyed and entirely unaware of what would happen next. That kind of blissful ignorance that only feels good when you're too young to know how blissfully ignorant you are.

The feeling didn't last long, but it was enough that when I arrived at the park, I was cracked open with vulnerability. The kind that makes you emotional at even the slightest act of kindness from a stranger, never mind the waving hands and the open can already in front of a spot on a picnic blanket where I was meant to sit.

"You made it," Oliver said, scooting over on the blanket and stretching out his long legs as I approached. "Figured you'd be a pale ale kind of girl. Hope I wasn't wrong."

"You a mind reader?"

"No such thing." He smiled, and I rolled my eyes.

"Glad you're here," Lola said, reaching over Oliver's lap and touching my knee.

"You sure this park isn't a pain? I'm not sure where you usually go, but it is kind of quiet here . . ." I looked around, clocking no more than a few young couples and a group of kids who didn't look a day older than thirteen sharing a cigarette.

"We love it here," Minho said. "We're regulars."

"You are not."

"I'm serious. Found this spot when Lola was trying to hide from an ex years ago and loved it so much we kept coming back. It's never too empty that it's creepy, but it's never crowded, either. Even on the rare two days of the year when the weather's nice. Perfect spot to have a bev and watch the sky."

"Did the ex find you?"

"Like hell she did," Lola said. "She thought she was too good for parks in Zone 2."

"Didn't she live in like, Ealing?" Oliver asked.

"She was the worst," Lola said, waving her hand.

"Which explains why you dated her for, how long was it? Two years? Three? Min, do you remember?"

"Why have you chosen violence today, hmm? Are you off your meds?"

"Piss off," Oliver said with a laugh.

"Willow gets it," Lola said. "You've had shitty exes, haven't you? I'd say we all have, but these two only have like, one and a half exes combined, so."

"Actually, I haven't," I said, trying not to have a visceral reaction when all three sets of eyes snapped up at me. "I'm, uh, not great at dating, so whatever I'm involved in usually fizzles out before it can become a real breakup, anyway. Most of my 'exes' are from high school, and I don't think those count."

Lola nearly choked on her beer, which I supposed I should have expected. "What about the tabloids? All the rumors?"

"Just rumors," I said. I knew what she was talking about. As much as I tried not to read online gossip, it was unavoidable. Vera usually filtered it for me and only told me what I needed to know, but that didn't mean I still hadn't heard my fair share of headlines: *Willow James Spotted on Steamy Date in LA* or *Willow James Seen with Lover at LAX* or *Who's on Willow James's Arm at Brunch?*

The "steamy date" was with Ivy, my "lover" at LAX was my driver, and the man on my arm at brunch was a childhood friend asking for industry advice. Hardly anything worth writing home about.

It was just easier this way. I kept telling myself it wouldn't be forever, that I'd get a hold of my magic and it would stop interfering with my love life, but that day had yet to come. All I could do was hope it would be soon. Well, not *too* soon, because I had other things on my plate, but soon enough. I wasn't getting any younger.

"What about now?" Lola asked. "I take it you aren't seeing anyone?"

"This isn't an interview, Lo," Minho said.

"I'm making small talk." Lola shrugged. "We're friends now. This is what friends do."

Friends. Not strangers. And friends helped each other.

I'd been so busy relishing the word and the idea that I wasn't just a celebrity to them or a charity case that I'd forgotten I was supposed to answer.

And that my answer was supposed to be a lie.

"I'm, uh, it's early days," I said, grabbing my phone from the picnic blanket and sliding it into my back pocket. Suddenly nervous about the grand reveal of Kit's face, I decided I'd leave them with only half the lie for now. Maybe it would do the job. "But I doubt it'll become anything, so—"

"That's so exciting." Lola grabbed my arm again, suppressing a squeal. "Early days is the best part of a relationship. Honestly, I wouldn't mind if it never got past early days."

"That's about when people realize you're insane, so that checks out," Oliver said, dragging his fingertips through the grass. He didn't look up at Lola, or at me. Just traced a steady pattern in the earth and followed it with his gaze. I wondered if I was hallucinating the firm set of his jaw.

"Better than you, Mr. One Ex It Took Me Years to Get Over," she said. "When was the last time you even went on a date?"

Hold on. Oliver Hadley was hung up on an ex? And he was obviously grumpy, but he really didn't date? A man this handsome wasn't out charming the entire population of Notting Hill?

"First of all, you're the one who keeps bringing her up. Everyone else has moved on. And last I checked, we were here to make a plan for Willow's problem," he said, "not pick apart my romantic history."

"Picking apart the whole thing would only take us a minute, anyway," Minho said.

"Doing yours would take half the time, so should we start there?"

"They don't get out much," Lola stage-whispered to me.

"We get out plenty," Oliver snapped. "We just aren't concerned with going on a date with all of bloody London."

"Guilty." Lola smiled.

Their banter was soothing. The less I had to talk, the less I was bound to reveal, and at this rate, they already knew more about me than nearly anyone else in my life. They didn't need my sordid dating history to add to the file.

And if ending this conversation meant Oliver could release his shoulders from his ears, then I was even more in favor. Whatever had washed over him in the last few minutes wasn't a good look, and I wasn't exactly keen on trying to unpack it. Mostly because I knew where my train of thought would lead, and I needed to get off before that train left the station.

"Oliver's right, though," Min said. "We *are* here to discuss Willow's problem, and I'm buzzing to get started."

"Do you have the list?" Lola asked.

I'd copied it onto a sheet of hotel stationery so that I didn't have to lug the book around, and I held my breath as I unfolded it and slid it across the blanket to Lola. It was real now, in a way it hadn't been when we were in the library, which made it even more frightening. As if completing the tasks and reversing the spell weren't daunting enough, now I had an audience.

An audience who was hopeful and generous and invested and who would be disappointed if I failed. An audience who was holding me accountable, who would watch me struggle, whose time would have been wasted if I couldn't pull this off. And I thought Vera was putting me under pressure.

"What the hell is *Clinopodium menthifolium*?" Lola asked, eyes glued to the paper.

"Wood calamint," I said. I'd had to look that one up last night. Hell, I'd had to look up half the list last night.

"My grandmother used to make tea with calamint," Minho said. "Used to complain it was harder to find in the UK than it was in Korea. Which was fine by me, because I never liked it."

"Love that," I said, "given I have to find it, grown locally, and consume it."

Minho shuddered. "We'll help you with the search, but you're on your own with the consumption. I haven't seen my grandmother in years, and I've no interest in reliving the calamint tea of my childhood."

"Lucky for you, you're not the one who has to cast the spell," Lola said, slapping him on the back. "So you're all set there." He rolled his eyes, and I envied him. I wished I wasn't the one who had to cast the spell.

"It says here it flourishes in late August on the Isle of Wight," Oliver said, scrolling through an article on his phone.

"Late August?" That was nearly two months away. So much for getting a jump on things.

"That a problem?" he asked. "In case you've forgotten, you're stuck here until December, so it's not like we're in a rush, are we?"

"Would have been nice to get started," I said, and sighed. "But you're right. What the hell are we going to do until then?"

"What everyone does in London in the summer," Minho said. "Enjoy the city."

CHAPTER 18

Oliver

The summer passed by much the same as it always did. Long, slow days in the shop, endless pints outside pubs with other patrons spilling into the streets. Longing for a holiday but refusing to close Coven & Codex and miss out on the business when tourists were infiltrating Notting Hill looking to spend their money.

Only this summer, we had the addition of Willow.

After our first meeting at the park, she kept to herself for a few weeks. Moved into a flat nearby, said she was settling into the city, arranging to have some of her stuff sent from LA, adjusting to the idea of living in London for a whole lot longer than she'd anticipated. We gave her space, getting on with our routines like we didn't even know she was here.

Only we did know she was here. *I* knew she was here. And I couldn't stop thinking about her being here. I no longer read on the Tube, but instead kept my head on a swivel looking for even the slightest trace of her auburn hair. Every short, curvy woman waiting to cross every street bore a passing resemblance, until I got a closer look and was reminded no one could even hold a candle.

"Why don't you just invite her out already?" Lo asked one night as we wandered down the Regent's Canal in Little Venice, eating ice cream and kicking rocks off the path.

"What?"

"Willow," she said. "I know you're thinking about her. You've been checking your phone incessantly for the past few weeks, and you never check your phone. Why don't you invite her out with us?"

Having perceptive friends was starting to feel like more of a curse than a blessing.

"Am I being that obvious?"

"Only to me," she said. "And to Min."

"You've talked about it? Should I just jump into the river right now?"

"Since when are you one for drama?" she asked. "We haven't *talked about it* talked about it. We've just noticed it seems like you're distracted, that's all. And since she's the only thing in your life that's changed in quite a while, it adds up."

"Not sure it matters, though, does it? What with the guy she's seeing and all that shite about 'early days.'"

"That's just something people say after they've been on, like, one date," she said.

"Is one date enough for the bloke to be her phone background?"

Lola stopped in her tracks, but I kept walking.

"She's got a bloke set as her phone background?"

I nodded. "Saw it that night in the park. Before she slipped it into her pocket. You don't reckon she has a brother or anything, do you?"

"I wish I could say yes, but I think only a sister. What did he look like?"

"I only got a glimpse. Shouldn't have even been looking in the first place," I confessed. "Tall, much taller than Willow—"

"Everyone's taller than Willow."

"Light brown hair, kind of messy. On purpose. Like he's trying too hard to look younger than he is."

"Holy shit," she said, grabbing my arm. Again, I kept walking. "Was it Kit Hayes?"

"I don't know what Kit Hayes looks like."

"God, Oliver, at least pretend you've seen a rom-com."

"Why would I pretend I've seen a rom-com?"

"Focus," she said. Little did she know, now that we were on the topic of Willow's dating life, it was impossible for me to think about anything else. Even though I knew I should have been thinking about literally *everything* else. "Did he have kind eyes?"

"Did he what?"

"Don't be difficult."

"Of the two of us in this conversation, I wouldn't say I'm the one being difficult."

"I heard a rumor she and Kit were supposed to do a film together. I bet it was him. In which case, this is worse than I thought."

"Grand," I said, kicking a rock harder than necessary into the river. "Care to fill me in?"

"One of those guys who looks like a golden boy but is actually a dick," she said. "You know the type."

"Everyone in Hollywood seems to be the type," I said, hating what the thought of someone being a dick to Willow was doing to my body. My irritation was visceral, rising in my chest like hot lava. Or maybe it was acid reflux. Likely one and the same, if I was honest. "What do we even know about him, anyway?" I was desperately hoping whatever preconceived notions Lola had were only hearsay, headlines from shit tabloids or gossip from her coworkers.

"We know he was rude to a server at a restaurant in Mayfair last year," she said. "And that he supposedly fired his valet in front of an entire red carpet."

"How do we *know* those things?"

"Same way we know anything about celebrities," she said. "TikTok? I don't know. The point is, he's a wanker. And if even you aren't going to be with her, we still don't want *him* with her."

"Slow down," I said, finally stopping mid-stride. "First of all, it isn't up to us who she dates. She's a grown woman with agency and all the trappings of the twenty-first century—"

"Bugger off—"

"—and second of all, we don't *actually* know anything about this bloke. Maybe he isn't as bad as everyone says." I was trying to convince myself more than Lola, but fortunately, she didn't notice. "And third—"

"There's a third?"

"We hardly know Willow that well, either. Maybe they have a history."

"They don't."

"Lola."

"Are you done?"

"No," I said. "Last but most certainly not least, I don't want to be with her. We need to get that idea off the table before we start this whole thing in earnest, because I cannot have you watching my every move and wiggling your eyebrows for the next five months. And the whole point of me going along with this thing, aside from my connections in the city, is to make Willow comfortable. What good would I be if I was chatting her up? Especially while she's seeing someone? Get it out of your head, Lo. I mean it."

"You first."

I grabbed her shoulders and shook her in the direction of the river, letting go only when she screamed.

"You bastard." She laughed, smacking me on the arm. "Why d'you have to take everything so seriously?"

"I don't," I said. "This is just something that happens to be serious."

"Everything is serious with you."

"That's not true." Was it? Did I take things too seriously? I mean, I was no comedian, that was for sure, but wasn't that part of my charm? The whole grumpy British bookshop owner, quiet, reserved, contemplative. It was an archetype. People loved an archetype.

"Unfortunately it is," Lola said. "But that's quite all right. Now's the perfect time to try out a little spontaneity. Take out your phone."

"Absolutely not."

"D'you want to be a killjoy your whole life, or d'you want to have some fun?"

"We *were* having fun," I said. "Before all this. When we were just walking and talking and eating ice cream. That was fun, wasn't it?"

"That is a Thursday," she said. "We do this all the time. Let's get you out of your comfort zone."

"You've been doing that since uni. Can't I have five minutes to just enjoy my comfort zone?"

"Not when you're racing against the clock. She's going to be gone before you know it. Or properly dating that tosser, and then we're really going to be screwed."

"You know, if you didn't make everything such a 'we' situation, you wouldn't have to be stressed about all of this."

"I'm a masochist," she said with a shrug. "What can I say? Your phone, please." She held out her hand, wiggling her fingers. We both knew I had no choice but to hand it over, so it was better I didn't fight it. I slapped it into her hand, and she rolled her eyes, using my face to unlock it before she opened WhatsApp.

"The fact that you even have bloody Willow James's number is mental," she said. "D'you know how many people would kill for that?"

"I don't, and I'm not interested in finding out. Please don't make it a big deal."

"You're not giving me enough credit. I haven't even asked for it yet. Haven't forced you to make a group chat or anything, either. The Lola of Two Years Ago would have already driven the poor woman straight back to Los Angeles. I'm making progress."

Thinking about the Lola of Two Years Ago made me smile. She was right. She was only slightly insane now, compared to fully unhinged like she was when we were younger. And I *wasn't* giving her enough credit.

"You're right," I said, holding my hands up in surrender. "Do your worst."

"Careful what you wish for, Hadley."

✧

Three hours later we were sat at a pub on the water, packed into a snug and waiting for the arrival of one Willow James. As much as I took the piss out of Lola, she did know what she was doing. As soon as she convinced Willow this was another unknown pub and we could hide out in the back, promised her we wouldn't talk quest if she didn't want to, we just wanted to check in on how she was adjusting to the city and buy her a pint, she was sold.

Pints on me, though, she'd said. Lola had happily obliged.

"Do you think she's offering to buy a round because she's rich and she feels sorry for us?" Lola asked when we slid into the booth.

"I think she's offering to buy us a round because she's a decent human being," Min said. "And you have your own two-bedroom flat in the center of Notting Hill, Lo. You aren't exactly struggling."

"Fair play," she said.

Before any of us could say anything else idiotic, I caught sight of Willow slipping through the front door, careful not to let it slam behind her. Her hair was in one long braid over her shoulder, a few wispy strands in front obscuring her face. It was the first time I'd seen her without a hat since she first came into the shop, and I was paralyzed.

Even with the wisps of hair obscuring her eyes, there was a certain clarity to her expression that had been shadowed by her hat this whole time. Out from under the brim, she was practically glowing. Her auburn waves and her peachy complexion were nearly the same color, giving her a kind of otherworldly appearance that made it easy to understand why she was the star of every red carpet, or whatever Lola said.

Unfortunately, I wasn't the only one who'd noticed. As she made her way to our table at the back of the pub, nearly every set of eyes turned to follow her path. Either she didn't notice or was really good at pretending she didn't notice, because she just kept walking, but I noticed, and I couldn't cope with the way people were gawking at her.

I was out of the booth before I could think better of it, cutting a path through the pub to meet her halfway.

"Gemma, great to see you," I announced loudly as I wrapped an arm around her shoulders and steered her in the direction of our snug. "I'm so glad you're back from South Africa."

"What are you doing?" she whispered, trying not to laugh.

"Dispelling suspicions," I said. "People were starting to notice you. Now they just think you're a doppelganger."

"A doppelganger who's meeting an insane person for a pint," she said, letting the laugh loose and reclaiming everyone's attention.

"Sorry we didn't all go to acting school," I said. "I mean"—I raised my voice again, if only to make her laugh—"sorry we didn't all join the Peace Corps after uni."

"Jesus, Oliver. You didn't tell me Gemma was Mother Teresa. I'm not sure I look the part." She looked down at her jeans and trainers, but I couldn't follow her gaze. I was too busy staring at her face, her flushed cheeks and her clear eyes, thinking she might actually be a saint after all.

"You look grand," I said, snapping myself out of my trance and reminding us both what we were doing here. "The others are just in the back there."

"Gemma, welcome back," Minho said as we approached the snug.

"You heard all that?" I asked.

"Oh, we did indeed," he said, turning back to Willow. "Do please tell us about the Peace Corps."

"It was wonderful. South Africa is beautiful this time of year."

"All right, all right, enough," I said. "I did this for your own good, you know."

"And I appreciate it," she said, softening her tone. The honey in her voice matched the rest of her so perfectly, for a second I wasn't sure she was real. *God, mate, get it together.*

"How have you been?" Lola asked. "Adjusting to the city okay?"

"More or less," she said. "Moved into the new flat almost three weeks ago, and most of what I needed from LA arrived last weekend, so I'm settling in."

"Have you seen much of Notting Hill?"

She chewed her lip, and I forced myself to look away. "It's, uh, I've just been, well, no." She forced a laugh. "I keep telling myself I'm going to explore the city, but then I chicken out when the time comes. Which I know is stupid. But this is the first time my life has been quiet in so long, and I don't want to do anything to disrupt the peace, you know?" We didn't really know, since we weren't international celebrities, but the three of us did enjoy quiet lives, more or less, so we could imagine. *I* could definitely imagine. "Sorry, that was a massive overshare and kind of a downer right out of the gate. Enough about me. What have you guys been up to? Having a more fun summer than I am, I hope?"

"A whole lot of this," Min said, gesturing around the pub. "Weather's been shite, obviously, so we've just been kicking around."

"We're bored to death, he means," Lola said. "We're glad you came out with us tonight. We're sick of staring at each other. We needed someone new to stare at."

"What Lola means is it's good to see you," I said, shooting a sideways glance at Lo, who only shrugged.

"You guys, too. It's good to get out of the flat. I probably should have done this sooner."

"No bother." Lola smiled. "What's important is you're doing it now, and we're happy to have you here."

Thank god. Something normal. Willow's bright smile reached her eyes this time, and I relaxed for what might have been the first time since she got to London. It was good to have her out with us before we started the quest. To get to know each other without all the witchy shit.

To just be four friends in a pub in London in the summer, before we started the quest and all hell broke loose.

@Coastal_Lisa: Just watched French 75 for the first time. Willow James is iconic. Is she filming anything new?

@Mich316: No one knows where she is. I think I read she's in Scotland working on a rom-com? #WIWJ

@WritePretty: Subscribe to my blog for updates as I track her down. Exclusive updates from insider sources pending.

CHAPTER 19

Willow

Meeting everyone at the pub had seemed like a great idea at the time. Getting out of the flat, letting myself think about something other than the spell for five minutes, remembering that the three of them were good people and their willingness to help was earnest.

This morning, however, made me regret every decision I'd ever made leading up until now. The throbbing headache behind my eyes made it hard to even hold them open long enough to rummage through my bag for a rogue Advil, and when I did find one, I swallowed it without water, wincing as it slid down my dry throat like a marble.

When was the last time I drank that much? Did I even drink that much, or was I just terrible at drinking? Maybe it was the beer. I wasn't sure I'd ever had that much beer.

Trying to figure it out was making my headache worse, so I collapsed back onto the mattress and stopped asking myself questions I didn't need the answers to.

At parties and bars in LA, packed with everyone who was anyone in the industry and more cameras and smartphones than people, I kept it to two cocktails and then club soda for the rest of the night. I couldn't risk making any kind of a scene, slurring a word, stumbling, even. I had to be the picture of professionalism. Especially because I was also battling the magic, which made me embarrass myself more times than I was willing to count. Adding alcohol to the mix was a recipe for disaster.

But in London, far from my real life, I'd apparently forgotten myself.

I sat up to find Vera staring at me from the foot of the bed, her blinking so aggressive I was surprised I couldn't hear it, like a cartoon. *Blink blink.*

"If you have something to say, please say it," I said. "My stomach can't handle anticipation this morning."

"Just checking you're alive," she said. "Those few pints caught up with you, didn't they?"

"It had to have been more than a few."

"When you got home last night, you told me it was four."

"I was lying."

"You never lie to me."

I flopped back onto the mattress. "That's all it was?"

"That's all it was."

"That's embarrassing."

"Indeed it is."

"Vera!"

"Kidding, doll. I take it you aren't feeling so hot?"

"I'm feeling like I had four pints last night is how I'm feeling," I groaned. "Did anyone see me? Am I all over the tabloids? Where's my phone?"

"Relax," she said. "I had Siri read me the headlines and every email in my inbox. You were properly undercover in your weird pub or wherever you were. But you won't always be this lucky, Willow. You need to be careful."

"I know, I know," I said. She was right. I couldn't get too comfortable. "That's what I have Oliver for," I said. "He's supposed to be making sure no one notices me."

"Oh, is that what he's doing?"

"Come on."

"I'm just saying." She didn't sound teasing. She sounded disapproving, and it made my arm hair stand on end.

"I probably should text them, though," I said. "Apologize for having a few too many."

When I finally found my phone, I saw it was them who'd sent the first texts. In a group chat, apparently.

Minho: Anyone else in dire need of a full English?

Lola: just the toast. give me all the toast.

Minho: You need the protein. We've got a big day ahead of us.

Oliver: @Willow, get ready for your first full English.

Normally, I hated a group chat. Always got nervous about what to say, got overwhelmed by the notifications, could never keep up, and hated having unread texts. They were always with people

I barely knew, didn't remember meeting, or was fairly certain I'd never met in the first place. But this one felt . . . normal. Or at the very least how I assumed normal would feel, given I wasn't sure I'd ever actually experienced it.

But so far, it seemed no one was trying to pitch me something, introduce me to someone, ask me questions I didn't want to answer, or convince me to do anything other than simply go to brunch. And in this state, I could definitely handle brunch.

This is something I have to get ready for? I asked.

Lola: she lives.

Me: You weren't doubting me, were you?

Minho: We started to, but Oliver put us straight.

My stomach turned one way at the thought of them thinking I might have been down for the count, then turned immediately back the other way at the thought of Oliver standing up for me. The flip-flop made me nauseated. But maybe not in a bad way.

Me: Chivalry isn't dead, after all. How does one get ready for their first full English?

Minho: Meditation.

Oliver: Empty stomach. Vague hangover.

Lola: stretchy pants

Me: Done, done, and done.
Jury's out on meditation.

Oliver: Clever girl. Meet at
Crown Court in an hour?

Minho: Grand.

Lola: already know i'll be late

Me: See you there.

I closed my phone and stared at Vera, both of us wondering what the hell was going on.

"I'm going for a full English," I said, but made no move to get up. "And I'm supposed to wear stretchy pants."

"Do you even know what's in a full English?"

"I suppose I'm about to find out."

"Didn't we *just* talk about being careful when you're out and about?" she said.

"You think I want to be seen?"

"Of course not." She sighed.

"I need them for the quest. I'm not just running around the city making friends." Even if it felt like I was. Drinks, then brunch the next day? Neither of which I needed a glam team for? Never mind a glam team—I didn't even think we needed a reservation. When was the last time I just walked into a restaurant and asked for a table?

"It's my job to look out for you, Willow," Vera said. "And if I can't do it outside this hotel room, I have to make sure you're looking out for yourself." She nudged my sunglasses in my direction, and I took the hint.

"Thank you," I said. With this headache, honestly, the sunglasses would be working overtime. "Do you need anything?"

"You know what I need," she said. "You safe, and me back in my human body. Until then, I'm fine here."

Since we moved into the flat, things had gotten much easier for Vera. I meal prepped and made sure all food was accessible to her when I wasn't home, all the technology in the flat could be accessed by voice controls, and there was even a doggy door that led into the garden. When she said she was fine, I knew she meant it.

Armed with my stretchiest pair of pants (a gauzy cotton wide-leg situation), my largest pair of sunglasses, and a tote full of antacids, I said a silent prayer and headed for brunch. The restaurant wasn't far from my flat, so I took my time breathing in the fresh air and wandering through the streets.

It was damp, as London always is, but in a way that filled my lungs and made me feel inexplicably clean. The neighborhood was quiet, save for a few dogs and a few small children, and I savored the walk, focusing only on putting one foot in front of the other, watching the rows of homes go by, clearing my head of every thought that didn't have to do with a slow, lazy morning.

By the time I arrived at the restaurant, my hangover subsided enough for the hunger to set in, and I was eager to dive into a full English—whatever that meant. I kept my sunglasses on as I looked around, relieved when I quickly spotted Lola at a table in the back.

"Good morning, sunshine," she said as I slid into the booth across from her. "Are the sunglasses part of the disguise, or are you too hungover for overhead lighting?"

"Both?" I laughed, wincing only slightly as I pushed them onto my head.

"Those pale ales will get ya," she said. "You don't do a lot of drinking in the Hollywood party circuit? I thought those parties were all about booze."

"Trust me, they are. I'm just more of a two-cocktails-only kind of girl."

"You're a four-pints kind of girl now," she said.

"I hope I wasn't embarrassing? Please say I wasn't embarrassing."

"Hardly. Unless you count being impossibly charming and picking up two rounds even when it wasn't your turn embarrassing, which we definitely do not."

Relief washed over me like warm water. "It's the least I can do."

"Nonsense." She waved her hand. "You don't owe us a thing."

"I have a feeling once this quest starts, you might change your minds."

"Well, we're about to find out." She smiled, waving Oliver and Minho over to our table. "Because we start today."

✧

THEY WERE RIGHT about the full English. In order to enjoy a massive plate of eggs, bacon, sausages, baked beans, grilled tomatoes, mushrooms, toast, and who even knew what else, one definitely needed a pair of pants three sizes too big and a hangover to match. I could practically feel the food soaking up the booze and restoring my will to live.

Which I needed desperately, because when we got down to business, the nerves came back full force.

"Now that we're stuffed to the brim and grease is oozing from our pores, are we ready for a road trip?" Minho asked, signaling the server for the bill.

"Not when you say it like that," Lola groaned. She was clutching her stomach and leaning against the back of the booth, rolling her head side to side.

"Grow up, Lo," Oliver said. "Get the gluten-free toast or stop complaining."

"That crumbly shite? Never."

I dug in my bag for the digestive enzyme I used for award shows, handing one over and instructing her to take it with a full glass of water.

"Saint Willow," she said, and sighed. "We're keeping you around forever."

It was no secret I'd be going back to LA as soon as we finished the quest and reversed the spell, but the reminder that I wouldn't actually be here forever, going out for pints and brunch and being treated like the girl next door, stung more than I'd expected it to. For a fleeting, agonizing second, I allowed myself to wonder if it could always be like this.

"What's the plan, then?" I asked, eager to change the subject before I went too far down that rabbit hole.

"We're headed down to the Isle of Wight," Oliver said, clapping his big hands together. "A little earlier than we'd planned, but it's now or never. Minho will drive, and if we leave now, we should be there around half one. There's a farm in town that does a proper market of hundreds of locally grown herbs, so we're certain to find your calamint there."

It sounded almost too good to be true. All we had to do was drive there and buy the herb? In my circumstances, however, I wasn't exactly prepared to jinx it, so I kept my mouth shut. Maybe I'd actually be in for a streak of good luck. Maybe it really could be this easy.

"At the very least, let me pay for gas," I said.

"It's called petrol, and we'll see," Oliver said.

"This is fun for us, too," Lola said. "I've been dying to get down there this time of year. You already know I want to have a lie on the beach."

"And Min and I want to try their seafood," Oliver said. "So we'll make a proper day of it."

"You really don't have to—"

"Willow, respectfully, are you going to do this every time we make plans?" Lola said, and I snapped my mouth shut. "We're locked in. That's all there is to it. You aren't forcing us to do anything. We're excited. Now, are we ready to go?"

I was grateful she hadn't given me much of a chance to respond, because I wasn't sure what more there was to say other than "Thank you."

"That better be the last thank-you I hear out of your mouth today," she said, looping her arm through mine as she got out of the booth. "Min, take us to the isle."

Oliver sat in the front to help navigate while Lola and I lounged in the back with the windows down and fresh air flowing through the car. I unraveled my hair from its bun, letting it whip this way and that, trying not to care about the knot it would be in later. It felt too good to just let it be.

It was easy to let my guard down for a few hours in the car, where no one would notice me and I didn't have to do anything other than sit there and watch England pass by out the window. But with my guard down, there was room for Oliver to slip in, which was arguably even more dangerous than being seen.

From my spot in the back seat, I had the perfect view of his profile: strong, angled jaw, curl of dark hair behind his ear, the kind of long eyelashes and sharp cheekbones my makeup artist would kill for. I studied the veins on the back of his hand as he scrolled through his phone, curating the perfect road trip playlist and keeping Minho on track with directions. He had a certain kind of grace I wasn't sure even existed in America, and I wondered if I'd find myself looking for it when I got home.

Which I already knew I shouldn't be.

My wondering was abruptly interrupted, however, by flashing dashboard lights and wipers on high speed. Both of which I knew were not a malfunction of the car.

"What's going on?" Oliver asked, clicking around aimlessly while Minho tried to get the wipers to turn off.

"I've no idea," he said. "Should I pull over?"

Get it together, Willow. Stop staring at his damn wrists and focus on something else before the car dies completely and we're left stranded on the side of the highway.

"I'm sure it's fine," I said, immediately regretting it when Oliver and Lola both looked at me like I'd said *I'm sure it's Beyoncé* instead. "I mean, it's just wipers and lights, and look, they're already slowing down."

Lola looked back at the dashboard, but Oliver kept his eyes trained on me, one brow raised. I wished it was the other way around. All I could do was shrug, but he seemed satisfied as the wipers came to a slow stop and the lights stayed on.

"See? Totally fine," I said, trying to keep my voice from wobbling.

"Min, I swear, if this car breaks down, I'll scream at the top of my lungs," Lola said.

"It's not going to break down, you cow. That was just a blip."

A blip. Exactly. And if I could help it, there wouldn't be another blip. We would be blip-free. Which meant I had to concentrate on anything other than how good Oliver looked with his elbow resting on the window frame and his hand in his hair.

We pulled up to the ferry port just before things could get any worse. Or rather, just in time for things to get worse.

No one told me we were taking a ferry, which meant I didn't tell anyone I got horribly seasick. Without Dramamine in my system, I was doomed.

"Nice day for a ferry ride," Minho said, pulling onto the platform. "Will be good to get out and stretch our legs a bit."

We'd only just driven onto the boat, which was still sitting in the port, and I already felt my stomach churning. The full English that had saved me this morning was now my worst enemy. I wound my hair back into a bun to get it off my neck, willing the ferry to move for some airflow and for the ride to be one step closer to over.

"You okay?" Lola asked, craning her neck to catch my eye.

"Fine, fine," I said. There was no way I was going to add seasickness to my list of ways I was inconveniencing them. "I'm just going to get out to, uh, get some air." I had no idea if being on the top deck was going to make this better or worse, but either way, I couldn't be around them.

"I'll come," she said, unbuckling her seat belt.

"No, no. I'm fine, really. You stay. I'll be right back."

I practically ran from the car, hoping she wouldn't follow, taking gulping breaths of salty air as I made my way to the top. The ferry finally pulled away from the harbor, and I leaned my forehead on my arms, which were folded on the railing, continuing to breathe slowly and deeply, hoping to keep the nausea at bay.

"Keep your eyes on the horizon," came a voice from over my shoulder. I couldn't look up, but I knew it was Oliver. "I'm serious. It helps." I lifted my head slowly, dragging my eyes to the spot where the sea met the sky. "Good girl."

The last thing I needed was to hear those words out of his mouth at this moment. The butterflies in my stomach warred with the nausea, and the sensation was overwhelming. I swallowed hard, trying to tamp it down. *Good girl.* In that accent? Did he even know the effect that had on people? What a reckless, irresponsible man.

"Fancy a ginger ale? Might help. Happy to go down to the bar for ya."

"This is mortifying enough," I mumbled. "I'll be fine. But thank you."

"Nothing mortifying about a bit of seasickness. Happens to the best of us."

"How'd you know?"

"Other than the way you legged it out of the car?" He laughed. "Your face had gone white as a ghost. None of the usual flush to your cheeks."

He noticed the usual flush on my cheeks? And thought to bring it up now, while my head was hanging over the side of the damn boat? Maybe I'd be better off if I jumped. Just right into the sea and sank to the bottom. I couldn't be embarrassed at the bottom of the sea.

"Come with me," he said suddenly, grabbing me by the elbow.

"What? Where?" I was terrified to leave the edge of the ferry but didn't seem to have much of a choice.

"Just trust me."

I didn't say anything else, mostly because I couldn't for fear I'd throw up, but instead stumbled behind him as he pulled me by the arm to a secluded corner of the lower deck, with a half-wall instead of a railing, lined with a few wooden stools.

"Helps to be closer to the water," he said. "Even if it seems like it would do the opposite. And if you alternate between sitting and standing, your body will feel the movement of the boat a little less. And the wall is better than the rails. Feels more like you're on solid ground and less like you're out to sea, doesn't it?"

"How do you know all this?" I asked, sliding onto a stool and trying to breathe.

"My granduncle used to love the ferry, so we'd take rides all the time when I was a kid. I used to get quite seasick, and this always helped."

I kept my eyes on the horizon, willing my stomach to settle and trying to distract myself. I wondered about his granduncle. He talked about him in the past tense, with a sort of nostalgia I knew all too well, and I couldn't help but figure we had something tragic in common.

"I'll be back in a minute," he said. "Hang tight."

Seeing as I couldn't move a muscle without feeling like my stomach was turning itself inside out, I didn't have much of a choice.

He returned a few minutes later with a ginger ale and a damp towel. "Take slow, small sips," he said, handing me the soda. I obeyed, my hand shaking as I brought the can to my lips. As I drank, he pushed my baby hairs off the back of my neck with a gentle sweep of his fingers, then held the cool towel against my skin. The sensation bordered on erotic.

"How does that feel?"

All I could do was nod.

The pressure of his hand on the back of my neck, the cool towel, the intimacy of his care, it was almost too much. When I finally tore my eyes from the horizon to risk a glance at him, I was surprised to find he was already looking at me.

"You're okay," he said. "Keep looking straight. We'll be there before you know it."

I did exactly as he said, and he was right.

CHAPTER 20
Oliver

The vulnerability of Willow's seasickness left me shaken in ways I wasn't willing to admit. The way she relaxed back into me when we made it to the lower deck, trusting my advice and letting me take care of her, filled me with a sense of pride I hadn't felt in a long time.

I didn't want to *want to* take care of her like this. I hadn't planned to feel a swell in my chest every time she looked to me for support, every time she let me take the lead. She was seeing someone, she believed she was a witch, and she was going back to California in a few short months, and none of that made it okay for me to feel this way. I needed to get this crush under control.

But then I remembered Lola saying that the guy Willow was seeing was a real dick, and I was back at square one: wanting to protect her, look out for her, even though I knew she didn't need either. It didn't stop me from wanting to be the one she could lean on.

Which, I knew, was insane.

I tried to snap myself out of it as we arrived at the Isle of Wight, focusing instead on my surroundings and our plans for the day and the welcome break from the heat of the city.

"Tell me we're here," Willow said from the back seat with her eyes pressed shut. "Are we here?"

"Indeed we are," I said, likely as relieved as she was that she'd made it in one piece. It was touch-and-go there for a second, but fortunately she pulled through.

"Thank god," she said. "Sorry for the drama."

"Oh, please. That was nothing compared to the drama Lo's capable of," I said.

"He's right. I'm more dramatic by nine o'clock in the morning than you've been this whole time you were fighting for your life," Lola replied.

"See what I mean?" I said.

"I can't even make fun. I really did feel like I was fighting for my life there for a second. I owe it to you for saving me," Willow said, reaching up to the front seat to touch my shoulder. A fleeting, gentle touch I was certain I'd be feeling for the rest of the day.

"That's what I'm here for," I said, resisting the urge to turn around and check to see if the color was back in her face. Instead, I kept my gaze locked firmly out the window, watching the coastline turn into rolling hills as we crept closer to the farm.

I'd been to the Isle of Wight a handful of times as a child, but I hadn't been back since, and this drive alone was making me wonder what took me so long. As the cliffsides and wide beaches turned into sprawling green, stone cottages, and high streets that looked like they hadn't aged a day in hundreds of years, I was reminded how silly it was to spend so much time cooped up in London when this was only a few hours' drive away.

It wasn't that I didn't love Notting Hill. It was a beautiful place and I was well aware how fortunate I was to call it home, but that didn't mean I didn't notice the gritty underbelly of the city, the increasing flocks of tourists, the sometimes never-ending monotonous drone of the workweek. The isle seemed like a place where hardly anyone even worked, but instead spent their days browsing the markets, wandering the coastline, and tending their gardens. And as far as I was concerned, there were far worse ways to live.

"Can you imagine living here?" Willow said, taking the words right out of my mouth.

"Beautiful, isn't it?" Min said.

"You've all been here before?"

"Every person who lives in England came here as a kid," Lola said. "It's a popular holiday spot."

"Puts our holiday spots to shame," Willow said. "There's so much character here."

"Arguably too much, sometimes," Min said with a laugh. "Wait until we get to the market. Everyone's as old as the buildings themselves, and they're all a bit mad."

"In the fun way," Lola added. "You've nothing to worry about. We'll find that calamint in no time."

I hoped she was right. I could see the tension return to Willow's shoulders even as she marveled at the countryside, undoubtedly nervous we wouldn't find what we came for. And as much as I wanted to be the comfort she needed, I, too, was vaguely nervous we wouldn't find what we were looking for.

While I didn't believe in any of this, it was obviously causing her a great deal of stress, and I wanted to be able to mitigate that. Even if there was a perfectly logical explanation for why she seemed to believe a person was now a cat, she wasn't interested in logic, and it wasn't exactly my position to try to convince her otherwise. My job was to help my customers find what they were looking for, and that was exactly what I was doing. Whatever happened after that, well, that wasn't my business anymore.

The farm stretched out before us in varying shades of green, dotted with pitched white tents, wooden farm stands, and a stone barn standing proudly at its center. It was worlds away from London, and while I was mildly anxious about leaving the shop to Wesley for a full day, I couldn't deny how good it felt to take a breath in the countryside.

"Right, well, this is it," Min said as he put the car in park. "Are we ready?"

"No time like the present," Lola said.

We climbed out of the car, and I gave in to the temptation to really look at Willow. Full bottom lip between her teeth, eyes wide. "You all right?" I asked.

"Cautiously optimistic."

"Me too," I said, surprised I actually meant it. "But I have a good feeling. Come on." We both relaxed as she fell into step beside me, and the four of us made our way into the market.

It was more crowded than I'd anticipated, but that made it easier for Willow to blend in. Not that this was really the crowd that would notice her, anyway. It was mostly locals and the elderly, so I had a feeling she'd be pretty safe. Still, I'd keep my head on a swivel so she wouldn't have to.

"Where do we even begin?" she asked, looking around like a deer in headlights.

"Looks like herbs are over there," I said, nodding toward a row of stalls lining the left side of the market. "Let's just start at the first one and make our way through?"

"Works for me," she said.

So that was what we did. We wandered from stall to stall, browsing their offerings and inspecting every bed for signs of wood calamint. When we came up empty after the fifth stall and Willow's shoulders started to sag, I had to take matters into my own hands.

"Excuse me, sir," I said to a man running what looked to be the largest of the stalls. "D'you know where we can find wood calamint?"

"Aye, it's wood calamint yer after, is it?" He scratched his jaw. "You've come to the right place, but you've come at the wrong time, I'm afraid. We've had so much rain this year it's been a bit of a faff to grow the bloody thing, and I reckon most of us have sold it by now."

"Ah, come on, mate," I said. "Someone's got to have it here, no?" There was no way we came all the way over here for nothing.

"You could try that bloke down the end there," he said, pointing toward a stall on the outskirts of the market. "He's got some rare shite. Might have a bit of calamint in there yet."

"Thank you," Willow said, shaking his hand with both of hers. His scowl instantly dissolved into a gentle smile, the wrinkles between his eyes softened, and he bowed his head.

"A pleasure, dear. Tell him Ewan sent ya if he gives you a hard time. And if he doesn't have what yer looking for, do come back and I'll sort you right out."

As we shuffled away from his booth and in the direction of his mate, Lola bumped Willow with her hip. "Maybe you should be in charge," she said. "You're way more charming than Oliver."

"I'm standing right here."

"Well aware," Lola said.

Willow laughed. "It isn't a contest," she said. "I just want to get the job done."

"I know you aren't exactly keen on showing your face around

the city, but it isn't a bad idea out here. People like your face. Obviously," I said.

Willow tutted. "Don't be silly. It has nothing to do with my face. He was a nice guy."

"Maybe he just didn't like *your* face," Min said, nodding at me. I was relieved for a change in subject, even if it was at my expense. I knew Willow didn't like to get her way because she was famous, and it seemed she liked getting her way because she was beautiful even less. I made a mental note to tell Lola later not to push it.

"Then he has terrible taste," I said. "Let's see what this other bloke has to say."

Had Ewan not directed us to this stall, I wasn't sure we would have even known it was part of the market. It didn't have the same pomp and circumstance of the others: no signage, no tent, no A-frame out front. Just a boy who looked no older than fifteen sitting behind a wooden table stacked with bundles of herbs.

"Are we sure this is our guy?" Minho asked, tilting his head to the side as he studied him.

"Only one way to find out," Willow said, approaching the stand. "Hi." She smiled, but he hardly looked up from his book. "We're looking for wood calamint? Ewan sent us over, said you might still have some."

"Doubt it, but can look for ya," he said, though he still hadn't moved.

"Only if it isn't too much trouble." This woman knew what she was doing, and it was working. When he finally lifted his gaze to her, he dropped his book in his lap and pushed his sloppy hair out of his eyes.

"Bloody hell," he said, his voice gruffer than I'd expected for a kid his age. "Are you Willow James?"

Willow opened and closed her mouth but said nothing. I could tell she hadn't expected this. Perhaps we should have, given he was a good forty years younger than everyone else here, but being on the isle felt like going back in time, and it was almost hard to believe this kid had even seen a film, let alone one Willow was in.

"She gets that all the time," I said. "Don't you, Gem?"

"I do," she said. "But I'm afraid I'm just a doppelganger."

"I could have sworn you were her," he said, eyes narrowed in disbelief.

"If only. Mind if we—"

"Can we take a photo anyway to send to my mates? I bet they'd fall for it."

Even his mates knew who she was? Jesus. "Listen, we're just here for the herbs," I said, stepping between Willow and the kid.

"Aye, all right," he said, raising his hands and shrinking back behind his table. I wasn't often intimidating and rarely used my height to my advantage, but I didn't like the way he was looking at her and knew she was too polite (or maybe too heavily media trained) to deny him the photo, especially when he had something we needed, so I figured I'd be the bad guy on her behalf. "The calamint then, is it?"

"Please," she said, her wide smile offsetting my frown.

"Now tell me," he said as he pushed herbs around with his gloved hands, "d'you plan on growing it or eating it?"

"Uh, steeping it in a tea?" she said.

"Right, then it'll need to be soaked in cold water overnight first," he said, pulling a thick bunch from a pot. "To remove the toxins and that."

"Toxins?"

"Just yer standard," he said. "We don't use pesticides or anything, but we do treat some of our herbs there with chemicals to prolong their lifetime and protect them from insects and that. Just a good overnight soak'll do the trick."

An overnight soak.

Undoubtedly, all four of us were on exactly the same page. The instructions in the spell said to "prepare and consume locally." Meaning Willow couldn't take them back to London. Meaning we either had to drive back and forth or—

"We're going to have to spend the night," she said, turning to face the three of us. I didn't think it was possible for her eyes to get any wider, but she was full of surprises. "Unless we drive back and forth, but—"

"All in favor of spending the night?" Minho asked, raising his hand. This was not in the cards. I had shit to do at the shop, none of us had anything packed, and I feared we would be hard-pressed to find a hotel in the area. But when Lola's hand shot up, followed by Willow's, albeit much slower, I realized I was outnumbered.

"That's three to one," Lola said. "Get on board, Hadley."

"I'll find us a hotel." I sighed. It wasn't that I didn't want to help Willow. It was just that I wasn't exactly the spontaneous type, and this definitely wasn't part of the plan. Besides, the last thing I needed was to be spending the night in the same place as Willow James.

CHAPTER 21

Willow

"This is it?" I asked, squinting my eyes to read the faded sign hanging haphazardly above the doorway. *Sonny's Inn. Vacancies.*

With one eye closed and my head tilted to the side, I supposed it did have a sort of old English charm. Whitewashed, pebble-dash exterior, dark shingled roof, a pale blue door with chipping paint and a curtained window. In its prime, it was probably beautiful. Though its prime was likely generations before even our great-greats would have stayed here, but that wasn't the point. The point was everyone had agreed to stay on my behalf, and Oliver had been kind enough to make the arrangements. I wasn't about to forget that just because the bed-and-breakfast looked like it might crumble to the ground as soon as we stepped through the door.

"The Isle of Wight is apparently more popular than we thought," Oliver said. "This was the only spot I could find in town with rooms available. If it's not okay, I can keep looking for something further inland, or try calling some places that didn't have availability online. Just, er, let me know."

"It's great," I assured him. "Thank you for doing this."

"Don't thank me yet. We've not been inside."

"He's right. Might be a proper shithole."

"Thanks for the confidence, Min," Oliver said. "You can sleep in the car if you'd like."

"And miss out on this cultural experience? I think not."

"Inside, the lot of you," Oliver said, nudging everyone toward the entrance. We followed his orders, packing ourselves like sardines into the minuscule lobby between the door and the check-in desk. With Oliver pressed up against my back, I could no longer ignore the reality of the situation: We were spending a night in the same bed-and-breakfast. Sleeping just down the hall from each other, painfully aware the other was a mere few feet away.

Or at least it was painful for one of us.

I didn't want to be thinking about him in his room alone. Picturing what he might look like underneath his clothes, with his hair a mess, his shoulders relaxed, and his eyes tired. I didn't want to wonder what he sounded like late at night, or in the morning, or in the moments in between. But I'm only human, and some (most) things were out of my control.

"Name?" the receptionist asked, just peering over the top of her ancient desktop.

"Hadley," Oliver said over my shoulder. "Should be a reservation for four."

"Ah, yes," she said, clicking around, "in the Hampshire Suite."

"It's a suite?" Oliver asked.

"Do believe I mentioned it over the phone," she said, seemingly uninterested in discussing it further. "One bunkie and a queen bed, there. Should be more than enough room for you lot. Let me just get the key for you."

I snuck a glance at the three of them while she looked behind her for a key hanging on the wall. I was hoping for validation, but I found Min and Lola as unfazed as the receptionist. Oliver, on the other hand, looked equally spooked.

Is this okay? he mouthed.

Fine, I mouthed back. What else was I supposed to say? *Thanks for arranging all of this on my behalf, but I actually can't share a room with you because the whole thing might burst into flames? I'm trying hard not to be attracted to you, but spending the night in the same room is going to ruin all my progress? The way you're mouthing words to me right now and forcing me to focus on your lips is making it impossible for me to answer?*

It was going to be a long night.

"Well, should we go see our digs?" Minho asked, shaking the old brass key in the air.

✨

Our digs were, well, what we expected after the receptionist dropped the bomb, I supposed. Bunk beds pushed up against one wall, a queen bed pushed up against the other, about a foot of space between the two. Aside from a small bathroom tucked into one corner and a writing desk in the other, there wasn't much else. No distractions, nowhere to hide. Just the four of us crammed into the world's tiniest room for an unexpected overnight.

"This is . . . cozy," Lo said. "Oliver, you're sure—"

"I'm sure."

"Well, then," she said, and clapped. "Should we go find dinner while the mint soaks?"

"I thought we'd all just stay in here, actually. Plenty of space. Maybe get a bit of room service, check out the hotel bar . . ." Minho said, unable to suppress a smile.

"We get it," Oliver snapped. "Would you rather have driven back to the city tonight, then? Come back first thing in the morning just to drink the tea?"

"Touché," Min said, pushing past Oliver and out the door before he could see Min roll his eyes.

"Tough crowd," I whispered.

"You're telling me," he said. "Willow, honestly, if you aren't okay with this, please speak now. We all practically lived together like this in uni, and we're used to shitty houseshares, but we were strangers to you not too long ago, and I'm sure you're used to much nicer accommodations . . ."

"Oliver," I said, reaching out to touch his arm. Letting my hand linger. Watching his eyes flick from my hand back to my face, softening. "It's fine. Honestly. Perfect, even. The thought of having to do that ferry ride any more than necessary is light-years worse than having to share a room."

"You say that now. Wait until you hear how loud Lola snores."

"I heard that," she called from the hallway. "Are you two coming, or should we leave you alone in the honeymoon suite?"

"Bugger off," Oliver said. I watched the tips of his ears turn the same pink as his cheeks—my only indication that maybe I wasn't alone in feeling . . . whatever this was. "Why don't you make yourself useful and find us a place for dinner, yeah? We'll get the mint soaking and meet you in the lobby. Maybe that charming receptionist has some ideas."

With an aggressive salute with her middle finger, Lola disappeared down the hallway toward the lobby with Min in tow, leaving me and Oliver alone in the room. He cleared his throat loud enough for me to get the message: *Let's do what we have to do and get out of here.*

"I'll just, uh, get the mint soaking, then," I said, fumbling in my tote for the bundle. As I unwrapped it, he filled a small glass with cold water from the sink and set it on the desk, reaching his hand out for me to pass him the herbs.

"Thanks," I said. "Listen, I—"

"I just want to—"

We both laughed, gesturing for the other to go ahead. "You first," he said, leaning back on the desk and gripping the edge with his hands. His long fingers curled around the wood, and I felt a tug deep in my stomach.

"I really appreciate all you've done for me today, and I'm sorry we're all stuck in here because of me."

"Rubbish," he said, shaking his head. "We all chose to do this, remember? Besides, we could all use a break from the city, anyway. Really, it's no bother."

How one man could at once be so grumpy and so relaxed, I wasn't sure. It made me want to know what else lurked beneath the surface, but I knew better than to try to find out. My powers didn't include prophecy, but that didn't mean I couldn't see exactly how that story ended.

"What were you going to say?" I asked, holding my breath while I waited for the answer.

He crossed his arms over his chest, uncrossed them again, white knuckles on the edge of the desk. Let go, ran his hands through his hair, dropped them at his sides.

"Spit it out, Oliver," I said.

"I know you're seeing that bloke," he said, "and I don't want any of this to be weird because of that."

"I . . . What?" He didn't have to explain what he meant by "any of this." I knew he wasn't just talking about the small room. He was talking about the energy between us. What I didn't know was what "bloke" he was talking about.

"I saw your phone screen," he said. "I didn't mean to pry, honestly. It just lit up on the picnic blanket in the park that night and I caught a glimpse. Lola mentioned he was another industry bloke, and I just— I don't want you to think— And I'm sorry if any of this was invasive, which now that I hear it out loud, it definitely was—"

"No, it's fine." I sighed, realizing I should have been relieved the phone wallpaper did its job, but instead I felt the opposite. Frustrated. Disappointed. "Like I said, it's early days, so. Hardly worth the mention, really." If Vera was here, she would have killed me. Our plan worked exactly as we'd hoped, and instead of letting it be, I was poking holes left and right.

This should have been what I wanted. If Oliver thought I was seeing someone, it might relieve some of the tension, and there would be less of a risk of my magic going haywire. But I was never good at doing what I *should* be doing, so I dipped another toe into the fire.

"Are you seeing someone?" I asked. "I'd hate to think I was monopolizing all this time when there was someone—"

"There isn't," he said. Not short, not curt, just matter-of-fact.

"Well then." It was all I could think to say that wouldn't further incriminate me. That wouldn't add to the lingering look and the shrinking distance between us.

"We should meet the others," he said, but it came out hoarse and shallow. Like he was only saying it because he had to and not because he meant it. After another second of excruciating eye contact, I pulled myself away and headed toward the lobby.

Dinner was in a pub that looked almost identical to the bed-and-breakfast: quaint, rustic, older than America itself. We ordered from the small menu—pub grub, they called it—and pulled greasy fish and chips apart with our fingers, sipped light beers, and chatted mindlessly if only to kill time before we were forced to head back to our one-room abode.

It was nice. Familiar, even. Almost like they weren't near strangers who were about to have the intensely intimate experience of seeing me sleep.

Though I supposed at this point, they were hardly strangers anymore, were they? And they definitely weren't going to be after tonight. I couldn't believe I was making what might have been some of the only true, normal friends I'd made in my adult life, and I was going to leave them as soon as I completed the spell.

Although they'd go right back to living their lives, probably thrilled this whole mess was over. I doubted they'd give it a second thought. Not that I needed to worry about any of this now, but I couldn't help it.

"Ground control to Willow," Lola said, snapping me back to reality. "You in there?"

"Yes, sorry. Just thinking about this stupid mint, that's all," I said. "Hoping none of this is a waste."

"Will we know anything after tomorrow?" she asked. "Will you feel any different after you drink the tea? Or will you not know if any of this worked until you try the spell?"

"I won't know anything until I try the spell, I'm afraid," I said, trying to ignore the way I saw Oliver tense up every time we talked about magic. "But if I do everything I'm supposed to do, I don't see why it wouldn't work. I'm trying to remain optimistic." *Because if*

I let the self-doubt creep in, then I don't stand a chance of doing the spell at all.

"I think that's the right idea," Lola said, and smiled. "I'm sure it'll be grand."

Easy for her to say. But still, I was glad someone was saying it. I needed a vote of confidence to offset the irritation in Oliver's locked jaw. With his lips pressed together and his eyes looking everywhere but in my direction, it was easy to remember why I needed to keep my distance.

Late that night, however, under the cover of darkness, in the room with only his whispers and the deep breathing of Lo and Minho between us, it was nearly impossible.

"How'd you know I was awake?" I asked after I heard him whisper my name from the bottom bunk. Lola and I were sharing the queen bed, and with her on the inside, Oliver and I were spitting distance from each other. A sliver of moonlight painted a clean stripe down the side of his face, illuminating only one glassy eye and the corner of his lips.

"Shot in the dark."

"It was a good shot."

"Usually is."

I smiled, but I wasn't sure he could see it. "Why are *you* awake?"

"Not a great sleeper even in the best conditions. Quite hard to relax with you right across from me there, tossing and turning and sighing dramatically every other minute."

"I wasn't—"

"I'm kidding." He reached out and rested a warm hand on the side of my head, and I was no longer certain I had a body. Every nerve ending I had was condensed to the space of his touch, firing on all cylinders and lighting me up from the inside out. "About the drama," he clarified, dropping his hand and letting it linger over the edge of the bed, tracing patterns on the wooden floor. "I'm not kidding about it being hard to sleep with you right there."

"I offered to try to get us another room somewhere," I said, walking the fine line between whispering and breathless.

"I said it was hard, Willow. I didn't say I didn't like it."

Every ounce of air that was left in my chest escaped in a rush. It must have been audible, because I could hear his smile in the dark. "I'm sorry. I know I shouldn't be saying things like that."

"Doesn't mean I don't like it." *What the hell was I doing? And why couldn't I stop myself?*

"I trust you'll tell me if you change your mind," he said.

"Does that mean you plan to continue?"

"It's going to be a long five months, you know." He stopped tracing patterns in the wood and tucked his hand under his head, propping it up and looking straight at me. Searching. For what, it was hard to say, but I felt scrutinized, even if I couldn't see more than a fraction of his face. And for once, I didn't mind. "So we might as well be honest with each other."

Of all the things he could have said, it had to be *that*? When I was in the middle of a lie about my fake boyfriend so that he wouldn't hit on me, while I was also simultaneously encouraging him to still hit on me? No wonder I was shit at being a witch. I could barely handle being a human.

"Tell me something, then," I said, hoping to turn the attention onto him before I confessed and ruined the moment.

"What'd you like to know?"

The list was endless. *Who you are outside of the shop. Why you don't believe in magic. What usually keeps you up at night. What your kisses taste like and how you sound in bed.*

What you think about when you're alone.

"Tell me about your granduncle," I said instead, trying to stay in safe territory.

"Ah, Uncle Arthur," he said, rolling onto his back and folding his hands behind his head. "He was quite the man. The kind of man everyone wishes to have looking out for them. Especially if you have a shit dad and no one else to rely on. Uncle Arthur died a couple years back. Dementia and that."

"I'm so sorry," I whispered. "I bet you miss him."

"You've no idea," he said with a sigh.

"I think I do." He rolled back over to look at me. "The grandmother I pretended we were finding the spell for? She died a few months ago."

"God, Willow, I'm sorry. I had no idea. I wouldn't have given you such a hard time about the lie if I—"

"I know," I said. And I did. "I didn't say that so you'd feel bad. I said it so you'd know we have more in common than you think."

He laughed softly, and I wanted to wrap the sound around me like a blanket. "I didn't think we had anything in common, if I'm honest."

"Pleasantly surprised?" I asked. "Or terribly disappointed?"

"Bit of both, to be fair."

"Can't argue with that."

"You tell me something."

"I just did."

"Doesn't count."

"Why not?"

"It was in response to my thing."

"That doesn't mean it wasn't something."

"Hey, wankers, some of us are trying to sleep," Lola said at full volume, making both of us jump.

"Saved by the bell," Oliver said. "Don't think I won't hold you to this."

"Fine by me," I said. "Plenty of time to think of a suitable lie."

"What am I to do with you?"

"Go to sleep," Lola said. "That's what you're to do."

We both laughed, and Lola pulled the covers up over her head.

"Good night, Willow."

"Good night, Oliver."

"And good night, Lola," we said at the same time, before rolling over and finally nodding off to sleep.

CHAPTER 22
Oliver

I'm telling you, the faster you drink it, the easier it is," Minho said, handing Willow the cup of calamint tea. "Just shoot it. Down the hatch."

Willow's eyes darted to Lola and me, and all we could do was nod encouragingly. "Quicker you get this done, the quicker we get back to the city and on to the next task," I said. That was what she wanted, right? Better to keep our eyes on the prize.

Especially after last night, where for a blip in time, it felt like our eyes were everywhere *but* the prize. Or maybe on a different prize altogether. Best not to dwell on either.

"Count me down," she said.

"Three, two—" She tossed her head back and swallowed the entire cup of tea in one impressive gulp. All this, the past twenty-four hours, the travel, the bed-and-breakfast, just for one single gulp of tea. I hoped it was worth it.

"Good girl," I said. "How'd it taste?"

"Delicious."

"Really?"

"Absolutely not."

"Grandma Dae would be proud," Min said, trying not to laugh when Willow hiccupped.

"So, that's it?" Lola asked.

"That's it." Willow shrugged. "Sorry it was kind of anticlimactic. I guess it won't be in the long run, but right now . . . that's it." I hated the hint of apology that laced her tone.

"No bother," I said. "We aren't here for excitement. We're here for the list, and now we can check that off. Well done, you." Her smile eclipsed her apology, and I felt something in my chest loosen.

"Are we ready to head back, then?" Min asked.

Willow dropped her head back and blew out a hard breath. "Someone just knock me out for the ferry ride. I beg."

"The drama," I teased, and she snapped her head in my direction.

"At least now I know who to throw up on."

"Looks like whatever moment you two were having in the middle of the night didn't translate to the morning, did it?" Lola said.

"What moment? What'd I miss?" Min asked.

"Just these two chatting each other up in the middle of the night and keeping me awake," Lola said.

"No one was chatting anyone up," I said, shooting her a look. "Get your shit. We have a ferry to catch."

"None of us have any shit, remember?"

"Any votes to throw Lola overboard?"

"If I go down, I'm taking you down with me," she said.

"Good. Then we won't have to listen to your bickering. Car's leaving in five. Be in it or I'm leaving the lot of you here." Min was out the door before we could argue, which was for the best. Lola was quick to follow, leaving Willow and me at the back of the pack, alone, once again. By design, I was starting to presume.

As far as Lola's went, there were far worse schemes.

"Promise if anyone's going overboard, it's me," Willow said. "I don't know if I can handle that again."

"Stick with me and you'll be just fine."

I led her out of the bed-and-breakfast with a hand on her lower back, relishing the way she relaxed into my touch. Every time I tried to remind myself she was seeing someone, I remembered Lo saying he was a dick, and I remembered Willow brushing it off every chance she got, minimizing it, sweeping it under the rug, whispering to me in the middle of the night, and I found it harder and harder to keep my distance.

The ferry ride back was much like the ferry ride there, only this time we at least knew what to expect. Willow and I made a beeline for our spot, and this time she did the breathing techniques with less panic, letting me gather her long hair and hold it off the nape of her neck. She didn't wince at the intimacy of the moment. Didn't shy away from my touch. Let me run my fingers from her scalp to her ends to soothe her, let me hold her hair wrapped around my fist so she could get some air, without so much as bothering to open her eyes.

Her vulnerability with me was the highest compliment.

For someone like Willow, someone always in the public eye, someone hiding out here from anyone who might recognize her, desperate not to be seen, to let her guard down, letting me take care of her even for the short ferry ride felt like nothing short of a miracle.

When we got back to the city and made plans to find the Wharram Percy Pendulum in a few weeks when the four of us next shared a free weekend day, I found myself disappointed I wouldn't see her in between. Strangely satisfied by the quest and already wishing there was more of it. Even if it was meaningless. That didn't mean everything that was happening along the way was, too.

But it wasn't like I could ask to see her before we looked for the pendulum. I could flirt with her, sure, but I couldn't go asking her out. Especially when Min was out of town for two weeks for a work thing and Lo had a wedding next weekend and I couldn't even make it a group thing. So we parted ways at Notting Hill Gate, and I started the countdown to the bloody Wharram Percy Pendulum search.

✧

As EXPECTED, SIX weeks without Willow felt like three years. I was distracted in the shop, giving shit recommendations and losing track of inventory, and I couldn't seem to get my head back on straight. Nor was I trying terribly hard, which was equally concerning.

But when the day came that we planned to meet and the bells above the door announced her arrival to the shop, everything slotted into place.

"Hi," she said, a slow smile spreading across her face. Was she equally happy to see me?

"Hi." I leaned my forearms on the counter, desperate to be closer to her. "You look well. How've you been?"

"Fine, thanks." Another perfect smile. "Eager to get the show on the road today. I've just been cooped up in the flat for the past few weeks."

"You're always welcome to hang out here, you know." This was news to me, too, even as the words tumbled out of my mouth.

Might as well double down. "There's quite a nice lounge space in the back, perfect for reading or whatever. Out of view of the customers. And you can always come in when we're closed to . . . browse."

Had Lola or Min been here to hear me offer this, they would have wound me up for weeks. They knew I wasn't keen on any more social interaction than was necessary, and I hardly even let them in the lounge. And opening and closing times, with my headphones and my cleaning routines and the silence in the shop, were sacred. Until now.

"That would be really nice," she said, sounding equally surprised. "But I couldn't possibly impose."

"Hardly an imposition when there's an invitation, yeah?"

"You make a good point there, Hadley."

"So I've been told."

She leaned on the counter across from me, and had Lola and Min not walked in exactly then, there was no telling what might have come out of my mouth next.

"Are we ready to get this party started?" Lola asked, throwing her arms in the air and doing a weird little shimmy.

"If you call looking for an old pendulum a party, then I guess," I said.

"Everything's a party if you have the right attitude."

"I'm not sure I have the right attitude."

"We know," she said. "Willow does, though. Right, Willow?"

"I guess so?" She laughed, and even Lola seemed charmed.

"I'll take it," Lo said. "What's the plan?"

"So, the pendulum was originally found in Wharram Percy, obviously," I said, "but thankfully it's in the city now, so we don't have to make another trip into the countryside. At least not today. I made a few calls last week and it seems to be in the East London Museum Obscura, so I reckon we go have a look?"

"Can you, er, cast a spell if it's in a museum?" Min asked.

"So long as it's hanging freely, should be fine," Willow said. "And so long as nobody's looking."

"You can't cast a spell if anyone's looking?" Lola asked.

"Definitely not," Willow said. "It's, uh, it's an old family thing. Can't prove the existence of magic with magic, either. My grandmother didn't want me to have to prove myself to anyone when I was a kid, so she made it nearly impossible to do magic if someone was watching, especially if I was trying to make a point, or if anyone was looking for evidence, et cetera, et cetera. Blessing then, but a curse now." All three of us stared at her, slack-jawed to varying degrees.

"So how are you supposed to do the last item on the list?" Lola asked. "How can you convince anyone magic exists when you can't actually show them magic exists?"

"Your guess is as good as mine." Willow sighed. "Trying to just take it one thing at a time."

"Well, then. Let's go find that pendulum," I said.

✧

THE MUSEUM WAS on the opposite side of the city, and we sat with our shoulders and thighs pressed together for the entire length of the Tube ride. Even as people filtered out, we didn't move.

Not until a group of women stared at Willow for a second too long, and she turned in to me to keep her face hidden. Before I could think better of it, I twirled a lock of her hair, letting my hand linger in front of her face for long enough that the women put down their phones and looked away.

I knew I was pushing it. Knew I probably could have just stood in front of her or pulled her hat a little lower. But I was losing my grip on whatever it was that kept me in check all these years, and every time she leaned into my touch, I lost it even more.

"That was close," she whispered when the women got off the train.

"I told you I got you."

Lola scoffed on the other side of me, and I pretended not to notice.

She stayed close when we got to our stop and wove through the crowds and out onto the street, closer still as we wandered in the direction of the museum.

London's east side was more crowded than the west. Grittier. Younger and edgier and more likely to know Willow. She had a sun hat with a wide brim on today, despite the dense clouds hanging in the sky. Ridiculous as she looked, it was a sound disguise. We just had to get in and out of the museum and back to Notting Hill before anyone looked too close.

"How have I never been here before?" Min asked, staring up at the building in awe. "I've read about it, but I've never thought to come see it in person. *This* is what I've been missing?"

The museum was an architectural wonder, I'd give him that. Like something out of a storybook, it was hard to believe the building could hold itself up. All sloping rooftops and rogue turrets and random bursts of modern styles that had to have been later additions. It was like Strega Nona had moved in with Bill Gates.

Bizarre.

"What the hell is this place?" Lola asked. "Who built this?"

"Omari Mbatha," Minho said, reverent. "Something about the juxtaposition is supposed to mirror the oddities inside. I read an article about it years ago."

"Hopefully one of those oddities is the pendulum," Willow said.

"Only one way to find out."

The inside was even more obscure than the outside. All sorts of witchy shit around every corner, crystals and mirrors and books and cloaks and floor-to-ceiling plaques and stained glass. A winding staircase dominated one side of the room, a glass elevator on the other.

"Where do we reckon the pendulum is?" I asked, looking around without moving my feet. I got a weird feeling in there. And the quicker we found the pendulum, the quicker we could get out.

"Upstairs, definitely," Willow said.

"How do you know?"

"Just do." She shrugged. "Gut feeling."

That made me feel even weirder. Was she *that* intuitive? And if she was right, what else did she know based on a *gut feeling*?

We climbed the staircase in a single-file line, running our hands along the ornate banister and looking over the edge at the museum below. I couldn't tell if the dull electric current I felt in my fingertips was because of this strange museum or because I was only a step behind Willow and could just smell a faint trace of her shampoo, but either way, I was ready to leave before I got zapped.

"Told ya," Willow said as soon as we got to the top of the stairs, bounding around a corner and into a room with none other than a pendulum hanging in a glass box nearly as tall as Willow herself.

"This is it?" Minho asked, walking a slow circle around the box.

"It is," she said. "I've been reading up on it all week. Sometime in the sixteenth century, when Wharram Percy was largely deserted, the pendulum was found in the ruins of an old family estate. In pristine condition. Untouched by whatever natural or unnatural forces turned the estate to ruins in the first place. It was apparently in a box like this, just swinging there. When the travelers who found it asked for a guide and it swung violently to the east, they followed, which eventually led to a new settlement that flourished for centuries after. They'd been looking for a safe place to land, and, well, the pendulum led them to their village, I guess."

We looked at her in a collective trance for longer than was necessary, at least on my end. I'd never been one for a history lesson on witchcraft before, despite my profession, but the cadence of her voice made me wish the story didn't have an ending. I could have listened to her talk about this stupid pendulum for the rest of my life and never complained.

"Wow," Min said eventually. "And is that what we're meant to do today? Ask it for directions?"

"In a sense," Willow said. "It hasn't swung like that for just anyone since—hence the need for the Orientation spell. But if it works, it should point in the direction of the next task."

"The cleansing?" Lola asked.

"Yes," she said. "Should tell us which direction the current should flow. Or where the sun should be at the time of the ritual."

"Go on, then," I said, hating the buzzing in my chest and the conflict I felt hearing Willow talk about witchcraft like it was factual. "You're going to be grand," I added, so she didn't think I was rushing her because I was a dick.

"Hope so," she said, and exhaled. "Well, if you guys will just . . ."

"Right, right, sorry. You're meant to be alone," Lola remembered, ushering the two of us out of the room. "What if someone else comes up?"

"I'll make sure they don't," I said. "We all will. Willow, we'll be at the top of the stairs whenever you're . . . done?"

"Thanks," she said, still staring at the pendulum as we left the room. Whatever the hell she was planning on doing, I really hoped it worked.

I. Forage for *Clinopodium menthifolium*, grown locally. Prepare and consume locally in accordance with your preferences. ✔

II. Conduct an Orientation spell with the Wharram Percy Pendulum. Use its direction as a guide.

III. Complete the Ritualistic Restoration Cleansing in a pond, lake, or slow-moving river to prepare the body for the Reversal.

IV. Participate in a Full Moon Ceremony. Stay awake until the following sundown for maximum effect.

V. Commune with those who have passed on. They know more than any of us who remain in our mortal forms on Earth.

VI. Convince a skeptic of the existence of magic. Use the experience to fortify your powers to effectively produce the Reversal.

CHAPTER 23

Willow

Part of executing a successful spell was staying focused, which was becoming increasingly more challenging with Oliver in the vicinity. Especially on the other side of a glass wall, where I could just make out the outline of his broad shoulders and the wave of his hair as he pushed it behind his ears.

The truth was, I hadn't focused on much of anything since that night on the isle. Every glimpse I got of Oliver's personality that went beneath the surface pulled me like a magnet, further and further from the point of the quest.

I was drifting away from the shore with every stolen moment, and I was rapidly losing sight of my life raft. Pretty soon, I'd be flailing in the middle of the ocean with nothing to save me but his strong hands and his green-gray eyes and the sound of his voice in—

Stop it, Willow. I shook out my shoulders and turned my attention back to the pendulum, trying desperately to get myself back on track. I'd lost the past few weeks to daydreams of Oliver—I couldn't lose this, too.

The pendulum hung proudly in its glass box, still as a statue, reflecting the dim light around the room like sunbeams. The Orientation spell was one I knew by heart, as my grandmother taught it to me and Ivy when we were finally old enough to go out and about in the city on our own.

Only, back then, we used to use Granny Annie's old locket or tattered flags on hot dog carts instead of centuries-old pendulums behind museum glass. Still, the phrase was familiar on my tongue. All I had to do was channel all my energy into making the pendulum move. Make the pendulum and the universe believe I meant what I said, believe I had the conviction necessary to cast a spell. Was confident in my craft. Focused. Intentional.

Swing, swing,
Lead the way.
Point to where
I'm not astray.
North, south,
East, or west,
Show me a sign
And I'll do the rest.

The pendulum drifted only slightly, like there'd been little more than a gentle breeze. I mumbled the words again, with my eyes closed, envisioning the pendulum swinging hard in whatever direction I was meant to go. I knew this spell. This was an easy spell. There was no reason for this not to work.

Unless . . . there was.

When I opened my eyes, the pendulum was in the far corner of the box. Only, as Oliver moved on the other side of the glass, pacing the floor with his head down, the pendulum moved with him.

Followed him. Swung slowly back and forth as he walked, tracing his path.

Come on, I mumbled, willing it to work with me. *Show me the sign.*

All at once Oliver stopped . . . and the pendulum stopped. *You've got to be kidding me.*

I whispered the spell again, trying for even more conviction. Eyes closed, seeing the pendulum pointing the way, showing me the direction of the river, leading me one step closer to transforming Vera back into a person. Said it two more times for good measure. Begged, even.

When I opened my eyes again, it was pointing straight ahead. Northwest. Nearly horizontal. Right at the center of Oliver's back.

In college, I took a psychology course and learned about confirmation bias. Learned what it means to look for information that supports existing beliefs. And I couldn't stop wondering if that was what was happening here. Was the pendulum actually pointing to Oliver, or did I want the pendulum to be pointing to Oliver? Surely it could have been swinging back and forth in the direction of a flowing river, couldn't it?

Only, the thought alone rang the gong of disappointment so hard, it rattled through my skull. Something in this building must have altered my brain chemistry, because there was no way I was *actually* hoping the universe was giving me a sign that Oliver Hadley was the way to go.

It didn't matter that he was gorgeous, and thoughtful, and protective, and that just being near him made me feel like anything could happen, magic or otherwise. What mattered was that we were from entirely different worlds and his didn't include magic beyond his day job, and that about said it all.

Though I couldn't even lie to myself and pretend that I hadn't watched the pendulum trace his path with a dangerous bubble of hope in my chest. But reality came crashing in as soon as Lola turned around, and the pendulum dropped right back to its resting position.

She tapped on the glass, then made a *wrap it up* motion with her index finger. It looked like Minho and Oliver were talking to someone, undoubtedly stalling, so I had to get out of there. Last I saw, the pendulum was pointing northwest, so that would be our guide.

Overthinking would be the kiss of death, and we had to keep moving. I didn't have time to wonder whether the universe wanted me to step further into the orbit of an incompatible man. No matter how gorgeous, how contemplative and brooding. No matter what my name sounded like in his accent; no matter how he looked at me through his dark lashes like we were the only two people in any room.

No matter how much I wanted to.

"Did you get what you needed?" Lola asked as soon as I rounded the corner. "The lads are causing a bit of a scene trying to stall and I think we need to leg it out of here before things get any worse."

"We're going northwest," I confirmed. "But right now, we're just going anywhere but here. That guy doesn't look happy, and I don't trust Oliver with someone looking at him like that."

"Bloody hell," Lola said, looking back at the guy and Oliver, now chest to chest like two idiots in this quirky museum. "Let's make a break for it." She grabbed my arm and pulled me in the direction of Oliver and Min, calling, "Excuse me, sorry, excuse me, sorry," to the people we brushed by in our hurry to get out.

"Time to go," she said, intercepting the men at the top of the stairs and ushering them toward the door.

"Not with the mouth on this bloke," Oliver was saying, shaking his arm free from Lola's grip.

"Ol, come on," she said. "All you were meant to do was stall. No one asked for a fight."

"That was before he started running his mouth about Willow," he said, and I froze where I stood. "Telling his mates he thought he saw her, talking shite to me and Min trying to get by. Saying she needed a real man, like."

"He said that?" Lola asked. "Ew. Why did he think you two even knew her?" Thank god for Lola, because she was asking all the questions that were stuck in my throat.

"I guess he thought we were her security," he said. His voice was rough, scraped. Something I shouldn't have found impossibly sexy, especially in that moment. "We just told him someone was busy in that room and he could go in in a minute, and things just, they escalated."

"Since when do you have confrontations with strange blokes in public places?" she asked.

He looked at me with such intensity, I was certain there would be a shadow on the floor when I stepped away. The shape of my body, seared into the carpet.

"Since I've had something to give a shit about," he said eventually, dropping his voice to something low and sultry. Like he wasn't talking to Lola at all.

"Well, if you don't mind, can you give a shit outside before we cause any more of a scene?" she said, looking back and forth between us but fortunately sparing us the commentary.

Oliver raised his hands above his head, letting Lola shove him out the door. *I* was the thing Oliver gave a shit about? Why hadn't he given a shit about anything before? And why *me*? It was no secret we'd be terrible for each other in the long run. And the short run, quite frankly.

Not that that changed how I was beginning to feel about him at all. But surely he had a better grasp on his emotional state than I did, didn't he? I didn't really have him pegged as the type to follow his heart instead of his head.

So many conflicting thoughts pinballed through my head, it made my teeth ache. I was losing track of which way was up, caught on the edge of a landslide riddled with caution signs screaming *MUTUAL DESTRUCTION* and *TURN BACK*.

But out on the sidewalk, watching Oliver's breathing return to normal as he looked me over, clocked that I was okay, I couldn't help but take another step toward the edge.

"Thank you for that," I said, touching my fingertips to his forearm. Letting them linger. "When you said you'd protect me from the fans, I didn't quite expect you'd go toe-to-toe with them. I'm sure that's not at all in your job description."

"Willow, we are so beyond my job description."

The heat that spread through my body at the sound of those words was another warning sign, and I tried to listen. Tried to put some space between us. If I kept this up, there were going to be consequences.

And right now, those consequences were coming in the form of squawking birds.

"What the hell?" Lola asked, turning her face toward the sky only to quickly lower it into her elbow. "Where did all these birds come from?"

It wasn't quite Alfred Hitchcock, but it sure as hell wasn't normal. A whole flock circled lower and lower, fluttering through the trees lining the sidewalk and screaming like it was end of days.

"Jesus," Minho said, trying to look up and flinching away.

"Come on." Oliver grabbed my hand, pulling me in the direction of the Tube stop. "Min, Lola, let's go."

I shouldn't have loved the feeling of my hand in his. Shouldn't have loved the bossiness in his tone as he made the move to get us out of there. Especially since it only seemed to make the birds squawk louder. Fly lower.

By the time we ducked into the Tube station, they finally swooped back up into the sky, and we doubled over to take deep, heaving breaths.

"What the fuck was that?" Oliver asked, leaning over with his hands on his knees and breathing slowly. I watched his back expand with every breath, caught a glimpse of a gold chain just beneath his collar.

"Maybe you pissed off more than just those blokes in the museum," Lola said, fanning herself with the bottom of her shirt.

"Bothered the whole animal kingdom there, did you?" Min laughed. "God, that was weird. Has anyone ever seen that happen before?"

"Not outside of a horror movie." Lola shuddered.

"Are you okay?" Oliver asked, returning to his full height and taking a step closer to me.

"Fine," I said. The last thing I needed was to cause any more drama today, which meant the last thing I needed was Oliver this close. Even if it did feel good to have him check on me. To be the one he gave a shit about. "Ready to call it a day on step two."

"Yeah?" he asked. "You've got whatever it is you need?"

I nodded. "We're headed northwest for the ritualistic cleansing, and that's about all we need to know."

"Grand. Sounds like the Heath to me, doesn't it, lads?"

Lola and Minho nodded, like the Heath was obvious. I didn't know what that meant, and judging by how today had gone, I wasn't sure I was ready to find out.

When I finally got back to my flat, I found Vera listening to an audiobook on the porch. She was stretched on a chaise even though it was starting to get cold, and her eyes were closed but her ears were up, telling me she was awake.

I flopped on the chaise next to her, closing my own eyes and matching my breathing to hers. The book was some kind of mystery, and the small-town detective was about to approach the victim's father in a bar.

"Do you want to talk about it?" Vera asked.

"Not now," I said. "We're about to get to the good part."

"Hey, Siri, pause this chapter," she said, and I groaned. "Let's hear it."

"I let loose a swarm of birds today."

"You what?"

"We were in the museum so I could do the spell with the pendulum, which seemed to just be tracking Oliver, so I don't even know if that worked, then he was supposed to be standing guard with Minho and they got into some confrontation with these guys who recognized me, then Oliver said he has something to give a shit about now, and that something is me, I guess, then I tried to thank him and he confessed this was all way beyond his job description, and I got overwhelmed by the subtext and tried to put some distance between us, and then the birds happened." I sighed.

"That is . . . a lot to unpack." She sat up, and I did the same. "Did the spell work?"

"I think so. Or I hope so, anyway."

"Did the guys talk to you?"

"No, Oliver and Min held down the fort. They recognized me, but I think Oliver fed them the same lie we've been feeding everyone else, so it was probably fine. Either way, they didn't get pictures or anything, so I doubt anyone would believe them even if they said something."

"So I can cross PR nightmare off the list of things we have to handle today?"

I nodded.

"Excellent. Next order of business."

"Don't say Oliver."

"Oliver."

"Please, can we skip right to the birds? I'd love to talk about the birds."

"In this new form, I'd hate to talk about the birds," she said, glancing down at her body. Couldn't blame her for that. "Doesn't he think you're with Kit?"

"He thinks . . . well . . . he thinks it's early days. Not important, really."

"Willow," she scolded. "You were supposed to make him think you guys were together."

"I know, I know. I just . . . I like the way he looks at me," I confessed. "And we were alone in that inn and I got carried away and I just didn't want him to stop flirting with me." Leave it to Vera to get me to say things out loud I'd yet to say to myself. "Is that so bad?"

"It is when you release a swarm of birds!" she cried. "What's next? Locusts? The slaying of the firstborn?"

"Maybe *you* want a career in the dramatic arts," I said. "Someone get this woman an Oscar."

"I'm serious, Willow. We don't know what's next, and the more of a scene you create, the more you run the risk of being noticed. Everyone at home thinks we're on some post-awards-season retreat, remember? Spas, unplugging, the whole nine. Not running around Notting Hill with some handsome local and endangering the entire population."

"Okay, that's an exaggeration," I said. "Four people is not exactly the entire population. And we aren't *running around*, either. Lest you've forgotten, we're trying to find everything I need to get us out of this mess."

"And where exactly does developing feelings for each other slot into those plans, hmm? Did the spell say *Fall in love with the handsome local*?"

"Who's in love?" I asked. "Is that what you think this is? I blush one time talking about a man and now I'm in love?"

"Oh, don't be so literal." She waved a paw. "You know what I mean. This just wasn't part of the plan, that's all."

"And it isn't going to get in the way of the plan, either. Trust me. I have the whole thing under control."

"For an actor, my dear, you are a terrible liar."

"That's because I'm telling the truth."

"You don't think I know you well enough by now to know when you have things under control and when you don't?"

I groaned, flopping back onto the chaise. If I wanted this treatment, I would have called Ivy.

"If you're really into him, Willow, then perhaps we need to be having a different conversation altogether."

"It doesn't matter either way." I sighed. "My focus needs to be getting my magic under control. And we both know focusing on Oliver would do the opposite. And we're going back to LA at the end of this, so."

"Why do you sound disappointed?" she asked. "We *are* going back to LA, aren't we?"

"Of course we are," I said. Though I had to admit, I wasn't as excited about the idea as I was when we first arrived. It was my home, of course, and it was where my career was, but did I feel like myself there the way I was starting to here?

"You know, maybe I should meet him," Vera said, thankfully moving on from that topic. Though I wasn't sure this one was much better. "Get out of the flat, do some sightseeing . . . What do you think?"

I could already tell there was no getting out of this. It wasn't like anyone but me could hear her speak, so it wouldn't be the end of the world to bring her along. Especially to the Heath, which I'd learned by now was a park with a few ponds and acres upon acres of grassy fields. It would be cruel to say no. Even if the real reason she wanted to come was to spy on Oliver on my behalf.

"Fine," I said, throwing up my hands. "But don't be too critical, okay?"

"Am I ever?"

"Almost every time you meet someone, yes."

"For your own good," she said, putting her paw over my hand. "This way we can figure out what's really going on here. Because at the end of the day, if you're going to lie to yourself, Willow, the least you could do is tell the truth to me."

The problem was, I didn't *know* the truth. Was this a harmless flirtation? Or was my infatuation with Oliver on the brink of turning into something more legitimate? Did it even matter?

But I couldn't stop spending every day apart from him wondering what he was doing, wondering if he was thinking of me. Couldn't stop dreaming about what it would really be like to be his to protect, to take care of, to share things with. I couldn't help but wonder what it would be like to shed my identity as Willow James, Celebrity, and just be plain old Willow.

Either way, it was beginning to feel like I had to add "seeking the truth" to my list of things to do before I left London. With only a few months left to go, I had to get a move on. I had a feeling this step was going to be the hardest yet.

I. Forage for *Clinopodium menthifolium*, grown locally. Prepare and consume locally in accordance with your preferences. ✔

II. Conduct an Orientation spell with the Wharram Percy Pendulum. Use its direction as a guide. ✔

III. Complete the Ritualistic Restoration Cleansing in a pond, lake, or slow-moving river to prepare the body for the Reversal.

IV. Participate in a Full Moon Ceremony. Stay awake until the following sundown for maximum effect.

V. Commune with those who have passed on. They know more than any of us who remain in our mortal forms on Earth.

VI. Convince a skeptic of the existence of magic. Use the experience to fortify your powers to effectively produce the Reversal.

CHAPTER 24

Oliver

First thing in the morning, I was alone in the back of the shop, shelving new stock and rearranging a table display for October. Halloween was right around the corner, which meant business was about to pick up, and I had to decorate accordingly. Tourists loved Halloween. And tourists loved spending money. It was a win-win.

Minus how painful it was to decorate the damn place every year and deal with the customers dressed as the witches from *Hocus Pocus* asking me to take their photo in front of the window displays.

I was stacking every book I could find with a purple or orange spine in a haphazard pile on an end table surrounded by votive candles and miniature pumpkins when Willow knocked on the front door, rattling the "Closed" sign and demanding my attention.

"Good morning," I said, opening the door and motioning for her to come inside.

"I hope this is okay. You said I could come in early and I—"

"I meant it," I assured her. "And it's more than okay. On one condition." She widened her eyes, and I tried not to count the shades of brown and gold. "You help me with these bloody Halloween decorations."

A laugh escaped her in a rush of breath. "You made me nervous," she said.

"You always make me nervous," I countered, relishing the way surprise looked on her features. Her mouth a delicate O, her light eyebrows high on her forehead. If I regretted letting that bit of truth slip out, that expression was all I needed to change my mind.

"Lucky for you, I'm a pro at Halloween decorations."

"All the Americans are."

"Or I can just head back to my flat, and—" She hooked her thumb over her shoulder and took a step toward the door. I grabbed her hand, pulling her back toward me.

"I'm kidding," I said. "I would love your help, Willow. I like you in my shop."

She was almost right up against me, and I was certain she'd take a step back. Only she didn't. So I didn't, either. And we stood in the doorway of the shop at the crack of dawn, chest to chest, waiting for the other to make a move.

"Good," she said. "I like being in your shop."

"I'm glad you took me up on my offer."

"Needed to get out of the flat," she said.

"Ah, so it wasn't about me at all?" I teased, though I was desperate to know the answer. Because, selfishly, when I offered the shop as a safe haven, it was only partially about giving Willow a place to hide. The other part was about getting to have her here, all to myself.

"So what if it was?" she said, surprising us both and lifting her chin to meet my eyes. I'd expected banter. Expected some witty comeback. Not . . . the truth.

"I don't believe in witchcraft, but I'd say you're a mind reader," I said. The hitch in her breathing was too much for this hour. I wasn't sure if it was because of the light dig or because of my confession, but it sent me reeling. A single sharp inhale and I was already a goner. "Come in," I said, leading her out of the doorway and farther into the shop before I made a fool of myself.

She followed me through the stacks into the back room where we first met over an exploded lightbulb. It had only been a few months ago, but it seemed like we'd done more in those few months than I'd done in the past year.

I used to think I'd been comfortable in my life, but I was starting to realize that comfort might have been complacency. I'd gotten used to slow, easy routines, a low-maintenance lifestyle, two close friends, and my family just outside the city, and I didn't need much more than that. Or at least I thought I didn't, until Willow walked in the door.

But now as I watched her weave a string of lights around my stack of books, piling the end into a mason jar and stepping back to admire her handiwork, I couldn't imagine the hole she'd leave behind when she left.

"You're a natural," I said.

"Runs in the family." Her soft smile hid the edges of something that looked dangerously like embarrassment, and it cut through me like a dull knife in my shoulder blades. I didn't have to believe in witchcraft for it to be real for her. And it seemed like my disbelief was starting to make her feel bad about it, and that was the last thing I wanted.

"Tell me about them," I said.

"My family?"

"Mm-hmm."

We both busied ourselves untangling another string of lights, undoubtedly trying to keep from looking at each other while we had this conversation. I wanted to know, but that didn't mean I wasn't nervous for whatever came next.

"It's just us girls," she said. "My grandmother before she died, obviously, then my mother, my sister, Ivy, and me."

"All witches?"

"All witches."

I risked a glance at her and clocked a raised eyebrow. A challenge. "Do you, er, do you learn a lot from them?"

"I do," she said. "But apparently not enough. They're both much more talented than I am, and though they try not to show it, I know it frustrates them, having to constantly help me clean up my messes. I try not to burden them anymore, especially since I've moved out of the house, but even when they're annoyed, they still usually know the right thing to do. Neither of them would have ever found themselves in this position."

"Seems like you're doing okay, all things considered," I ventured. "You've done everything you've set out to do since you've been here, no?"

She sighed, and the sound burrowed under my skin. "I suppose so. Though I wouldn't be here in the first place if it wasn't for the disaster back at home, so."

"How'd it happen?" I asked. *What the hell am I doing?* Entertaining this conversation was so far out of my wheelhouse, but the more she spoke, the harder it was to stop myself. I wanted to know everything there was to know about her. Even if it wasn't real.

"You really want to know?" she asked, lowering the string of lights and looking right at me.

"Wouldn't have asked if I didn't."

"Even though you don't think it's true?"

"Doesn't matter what I think. What matters is what's true for you. And I'd like to hear the story, if you don't mind."

I, too, dropped the lights so that I could look at her properly. So I could make sure she saw I was earnest.

"It was humiliating," she started. "Vera and I were having an argument in my trailer because I didn't want to entertain the idea of doing a romance film instead of a drama, and in the heat of the moment she just . . . turned into a cat. And I know how it sounds. You don't have to say anything. But I don't know how else to explain it. One minute she was Vera, and the next she was a cat."

"Why didn't you want to do the romance?"

"What?"

"The romance. Why'd you say no?" There was so much to digest in what she'd said, but I couldn't move past this part. Maybe I was clinging to something familiar. Something that wasn't witchcraft. Or maybe I was clinging to the idea of Willow and romance in the same sentence. Hard to say.

"Oh, it's just, uh . . . it's not my thing."

"Romance movies or romance in general?"

"Both?" She laughed. "I mean, even the conversation about doing a romance turned my manager into a cat. So, doesn't bode well for filming the actual movie, does it?"

"What about this guy you're seeing? That's surely a romance, yeah?" Was I a masochist? Was that a new development in my personality at thirty-two years old?

She went back to the lights, and I wondered if I'd said the wrong thing. Or maybe the right thing, because every time we talked about him she seemed less and less invested.

"It's fine," she said, chewing on her lower lip. I waited for her to say more, but she didn't. *It's fine*. That's it? Her relationship was in early days and it was just *fine*? Maybe this guy really was a dick. "What about you?" she asked. "No romance?"

I watched as she staggered a few small pumpkins, then lit a votive with a decorative match from a glass case. She shook the match out, and smoke drifted from her hand into the space between us, at once heavy and light and making me wish there wasn't space between us at all. Was she asking because she was making polite conversation, or was she asking because she wanted to know?

"No romance," I confirmed, taking the match from her hand and dropping it into my back pocket to throw out later.

"What about that ex Lola mentioned?"

"Fuckin' Lola." I laughed, raking both hands through my hair. "She's digging, honestly. That ex is ancient history. I mentioned her once when I was drunk last year and Lola hasn't let it go."

"Why'd you break up?" she asked. I let out a whistle, not quite expecting that question and trying to figure out how to answer.

"Difference in beliefs, mostly," I said eventually, settling on the truth and trying not to cringe at her hard exhale. "She thought being in a relationship meant we should be together every second of every day. Same friends, same plans, same hobbies. You lose yourself pretty quickly like that, you know? Started to feel a bit suffocating after a while, but she wasn't interested in talking about it, so there wasn't much left to do but part ways."

"That must have been hard," she said, her brown eyes warm and soft in the morning light. "Dating in the industry is the exact opposite. No one ever sees each other, never has the same plans or is even in the same city. You get to keep yourself, but you lose the relationship."

"There's got to be a happy medium somewhere, don't you think?"

"In a perfect world."

"But not this one?"

"Remains to be seen." For a second, her smile was enough to convince me this might be a perfect world after all.

"Willow," I said, clenching my jaw while I mustered the courage to get the rest of the sentence out of my mouth. "Forgive me if I'm overstepping, but I have to ask. Is it serious with this bloke? The one you're seeing?"

She cast her gaze to the ceiling, taking a few breaths before she looked back at me. "It's . . . early days," she said again, a phrase that was becoming more meaningless every time I heard it.

"Early days that are going to turn to later days, or early days that are going to fizzle out before you get very far?"

"That's a loaded question, Hadley," she said, a smile playing on her pink lips.

"That isn't an answer, James."

"Why does it matter?"

"I have a hard time believing it isn't obvious why I'm asking." I stood from the stool I was perched on and took a few steps in her direction, hands in my pockets to mitigate temptation. She was too smart for me to have to spell it out. And I was too wired to say it eloquently. At this rate, I was at the risk of blurting. And I wasn't that kind of guy. The kind of guy who blurts.

"Oliver," she said.

"I'm listening."

She put the edge of her thumbnail between her teeth, and that look alone told me everything I needed to know.

"You wouldn't be asking if you didn't know the answer," she said.

Okay, so, same page. "Doesn't mean I don't want to hear you say it."

"You took the easy way out," she said, dropping her voice to a pitch I thought was meant to mimic mine. "*Isn't it obvious?*"

"Hardly the easy way. Just not keen on underestimating you, that's all. Don't want to be spelling something out for ya that you already know."

She rolled her eyes, and it drew me in even farther. Another step. "I wouldn't be here if it was serious," she said.

"Here in London?"

"Here in the shop."

This time she took a step, and time slowed. It was hardly eight o'clock in the morning, and my pulse was racing, my palms itching. Head spinning. Nothing ever happened to me. And I liked it that way. But now here I was, face-to-face with an A-list American celebrity in my shop before I even opened, dancing around things we couldn't quite say, for reasons we weren't willing to acknowledge.

But even without the words, we knew we were standing on the edge of the same cliff.

"Poor bugger," I said, my words entirely devoid of meaning.

"You're bad."

"You have no idea."

A knock at the shop door burst our bubble, a sharp needle to the trance we'd been lost in. "Is that a customer?" she asked, leaning back and squinting through the glass. Tempted as I was to study the shape of her body in that arc, I had to figure out who the hell was banging on the glass when the sign clearly said I was closed.

I pulled myself away from her, dragging my boots toward the door. Whoever was on the other side, I wasn't interested.

Even less so when I saw the camera looped around his neck.

"We're closed," I said from the other side of the glass, tapping on the massive sign that read . . . *Closed.*

"Aye, mate, just a minute of your time."

"Feel free to come back during business hours," I said, praying he would not come back during business hours.

"Will Willow James still be here during business hours?" he asked, and I froze. How the fuck did he know she was here?

"Not sure what you're on about," I said. "But I've got work to do, so if you'll kindly leave the shop and sort out your business elsewhere." I gestured down the street, clenching my teeth so hard I feared one might crack.

"Ah, come on. We've both got to make a living." He raised his camera and his eyebrows, and I wanted to smash both onto the sidewalk. "At least tell me what it is she's doing here."

"No one's here," I said, resisting the urge to turn around and check Willow was out of sight. "And whatever woman you're looking to photograph without her consent, I doubt she's interested."

"Fuck off, mate."

"Gladly."

We stared at each other through the glass for what felt like a decade before he finally took a step back. "You're a right wanker, you know that?"

"So I've been told."

"I know she's here, and someone will get a shot of her in town. Only a matter of time."

"Whatever gets you off my stoop," I said. It came out hoarse and combative, and I wondered if he could tell through the glass. Judging by the look he gave me as he shuffled away, I had a feeling he could.

I took a few deep breaths before I made my way through the shop to find Willow. I didn't want to scare her, but she should know she'd been spotted and people were looking for her. And in the bloody shop of all places. Somewhere that was supposed to be a safe hideout.

"Who was that?" she asked when I reached the back room. I dropped onto a stool, motioning for her to do the same.

"Paparazzi." I sighed, leaning forward with my elbows on my knees and my hands clasped to keep them from balling into fists. "I told him I had no idea what he was talking about and that there wasn't anyone here, which was enough to get him to leave, but he knew. He must have seen you come in this morning."

"Shit," she said. "I thought I was early enough, and with the sunglasses and the hats and the—" She cut herself off, pushing her long hair off her face and exhaling a long, slow breath.

"I'm sorry, Willow. I didn't—"

"Hey," she said, leaning forward to meet my eyes. "This isn't your fault. It just comes with the territory. But it has nothing to do with you. You've been so helpful."

"I should have always had you come in through the back. It was stupid to have you use the front door, and I should have known that."

"Oliver." The sound of my name in her mouth gave me goose bumps. "This isn't your fault," she said again, emphasizing every syllable. "Please don't beat yourself up about it. If it wasn't for you, someone probably would have approached me a long time ago."

"No one's going to approach you either way," I said. "They might know where you are, but they aren't getting close to you."

"I trust you." Those three words were all I needed to hear. "Besides, you said there was a back entrance?"

I wasn't the kind of guy whose face lit up, but I could feel it practically glowing. "You're coming back?"

"To the shop? Of course," she said, like it was obvious. "We'll just do a better job of hiding me."

I couldn't control what happened out in the city. I could protect her, but I couldn't stop people from noticing her entirely. From seeking her out and trying to make a few quid by splashing her across a front page somewhere.

But I could control what happened in the shop, and I'd be damned if anyone saw her here again.

@SamSeesCelebs: Willow James spotted in London bookshop. #WIWJ

@Love4Matcha_: What's she working on? Why hasn't anyone released a statement?

@CelineMachine: I heard she's dating Kit Hayes, but someone saw him in Erewhon this week. Why aren't they together? Did they break up?

CHAPTER 25

Willow

I was awake before my alarm, which made me think I hadn't really slept in the first place. Maybe because I was nervous about today. Or maybe because I couldn't stop thinking about Oliver. At all. For even a minute. No matter how hard I tried.

The sun wasn't even contemplating rising yet, and Vera and I were headed to Hampstead Heath for the Ritualistic Restoration Cleansing. Which I'd since learned needed to be completed in the dark and with as little clothing as possible. Nudity was preferred, but not required. For maximum contact with the water . . . or something like that. Because of course. What would my life be if anything was ever normal?

We opted for early in the morning instead of late at night to reduce the likelihood of being arrested for swimming in the ponds outside of guarded hours, and early morning in London in October was . . . freezing.

Bone-chillingly cold even on dry land with a coat on. It did not bode well for being in the pond in what felt like the world's tiniest swimsuit. Though Oliver assured me people swam in the ponds year-round, and so long as I had the proper recovery plan when I got out, I'd be just fine.

At the exact moment I thought of him, my phone buzzed with a text.

Oliver: See everyone at the Heath in 30. Do we have everything we need?

Lola: towels: check.

Minho: Hot tea ✔

Oliver: Grand. And I've got a couple heavy jumpers. Willow, you ready?

Me: Hardly. Have you been outside yet today?

Oliver: We'll have you warmed up in no time.

Little did he know, he'd been warming me up since the first time I set foot in the shop. At least now I'd have something else to blame my flushed cheeks on.

At this hour, Hampstead Heath was quiet. Tranquil. The swimming ponds and the changing meadows were empty, and a haunting wind curled through the trees.

"This would be creepy if it wasn't so chic," Vera said, climbing out of the carrier as I set her down. "But I have to admit, I do see why women have been bathing in these ponds for generations. Very Victorian. High class. Women in LA would eat this up."

"Easy for you to say when you aren't the one who actually has to get in there," I said.

"Have you forgotten I couldn't speak for a few days? Nothing's easy for me to say. I'm a cat, Willow."

"And yet, you seem to be yapping just fine."

"Just wait until Oliver gets here. If you think *this* is yapping . . ."

"Thank god he can't hear you," I said.

"I'd give him quite an earful if he could."

"My point exactly."

"I'm going to stretch my legs. I'll be back when it's time for the ritual."

"How will you know?"

"I can hear twice as well now, remember? And you're the only people in the whole park. I'll know." And with that, she scampered off beyond the tree line, leaving me alone in the cool quiet of the morning.

While it might have been nice to be alone for a moment, I needed the distraction of Vera more than anything else. This felt like part of the quest I could have done without the others, and the more I thought about it, the more nervous I was for them to show up. Did they really need to watch me take a freezing swim in a tiny bikini?

Maybe they'd occupy themselves with something else until I was done. Like Vera. Or like a sunrise walk in the park.

Either way, as I stood there looking at my reflection in the darkness of the water, I realized how much I'd changed.

Not a stitch of makeup, natural hair tumbling down my shoulders, unassuming black puffer coat. I could have been anybody. And it felt *good*.

For a second, it felt like that anybody could be someone who lived here. Away from the hustle of Hollywood, away from the never-ending social calendar and the constant demands and the toxicity of the industry. Someone who took morning swims in the Heath, who wandered the streets of Notting Hill in the fall, who had friends and plans and a life. A normal life.

Someone who had a relationship.

The kind that worked. The real kind.

My reverie was cut short by the sound of voices, familiar voices, cutting through the silence. Light bickering, low laughter, chattering teeth.

"Willow, is that you?" Lola whispered as they rounded a corner, squinting her eyes and leaning in a little.

"No, it's another insane person getting ready for a freezing cold swim at the crack of dawn. Of course it's me." The other two came into view, as did Vera, and I held my breath.

"Holy shit." Lola jumped when she clocked Vera at her feet. "Is that a black cat? That's bad luck, isn't it?"

"It's not bad luck," I said. "It's just . . . Vera."

"Vera?"

"My manager. The one who . . . uh . . . used to be a person."

Silence. Wide-eyed looks. Raised eyebrows. More silence.

"Someone please say something before I jump into the water and never come out," I said, but immediately changed my mind. "You know what, actually, nobody say anything at all. Just pretend she isn't here." Vera shot me a look I chose to ignore. "It's fine, just . . . forget I said anything."

"No, no," Min said, finally springing to life. "It's, er, it's nice to meet you, Vera." He looked down at her, and she looked up at him, both of them wearing matching bewildered expressions. Oliver cleared his throat, and I tried to ignore that, too.

"Does she speak?" Lola asked, cocking her head to the side.

"I . . . uh . . . I'm the only one who can understand her," I said.

"Bummer," Lola said. "She's gorgeous, by the way."

If cats could blush.

I looked up at Oliver, watching as he kicked a pebble into the pond and followed its path with his gaze, looking anywhere but at the scene unfolding in front of him. Another reminder he'd never believe in any of this, which should have been reason enough to stay away. But when he pushed a stray curl behind his ear and finally turned to face me, I forgot every reason entirely.

"What d'you say, Willow? Time for a ritual?"

✧

To SAY THE water was cold would be an understatement. To say it was freezing, even, wouldn't cut it. To say it felt like a million tiny knives cutting into my skin and stealing every ounce of air from my lungs . . . that was more like it.

"I can't do this," I said, stepping back up on the ladder and pulling my body out. "I can't. It's too cold."

"Isn't everyone in LA doing a cold plunge right now?" Lola asked. "I just watched a TikTok about it."

"In a spa," I said, teeth clacking. "With a sauna and a green juice and they only go in for a minute. I have to do a whole ritual in there!"

"Do you have a choice?" Minho asked. "I don't mean to be tough, but you kind of *have* to do it, right?"

Right. But that didn't make it any easier.

"Yeah, but what good am I if I die of hypothermia?"

"No one's dying," Oliver said, springing into action. "Min, Lo, give us a minute, will you?" What was he doing? The last thing I needed when I was trying to steady my breathing was Oliver Hadley in my space. But Min and Lo immediately backed off, retreating to a clearing under the trees with Vera, leaving me and Oliver alone at the edge of the pond.

"Breathe," he said, voice level.

"I'm trying."

"Try harder." I managed a few shaky inhales and exhales, but my lower body wasn't adjusting to the temperature. If anything, it was getting colder. "With me." He grabbed my face in both hands, locking our gazes. "Inhale," he said, making a show of taking a deep breath. "And exhale." My lungs emptied in one fast *whoosh*, and his lips curled into a slow smile. "Again."

I followed his instructions, syncing our breathing and trying not to crumble under the weight of his touch. "You can do this, Willow."

I shook my head, terrified to put the rest of my body back in the water.

"All right," he said, standing from where he was crouched and grabbing the hem of his sweater.

"What are you doing?"

"Getting in with you."

"Oliver, wh—"

"Don't argue."

Fortunately, watching him pull his sweater over his head to reveal his bare chest left me speechless, anyway. I studied the cut of the muscles that carved neat lines across his body, the gold Star of David pendant twinkling on the end of a thin chain, the smattering of dark hair that covered otherwise smooth skin, trailing down his stomach and into his jeans, which were . . . also coming off.

"Oliver," I said again.

"Willow." He slid off his boots, then his jeans, standing in front of me in only a pair of boxer briefs. "Move over."

"I can't."

"Why?"

"Because that would mean I'd have to put my whole body in."

"Sometimes the best thing to do is just go for it," he said, stretching his long arms above his head.

"Why do I get the feeling you aren't talking about swimming?"

"Because I'm not."

He splashed in beside me before I had a chance to respond. A perfect dive. When he resurfaced, he grabbed me by the waist and pulled me under.

My scream was muffled by the water, turning to a steady stream of bubbles as I came up for air. I turned in a frantic half circle to look for him, equally relieved and panicked to find him so close. A quick glance over his shoulder confirmed my suspicions: Minho and Lola were still giving us privacy, talking quietly with their heads bent together, far from where we were.

"Right, then." He smiled, pushing a soaking-wet lock of hair from my eyes and letting his hand linger on my jaw. "Are we ready to do the ritual?"

"Who's we?"

"*We* is you and me. I'm going to do the ritual with you."

"But you don't believe in it."

"I'm not the one who has to believe in it." He floated closer, and cold as I was, I could still feel the warmth of his body. He wasn't shivering at all. No chattering teeth. No pale lips. Just flushed cheeks and droplets of water sitting on his long lashes like diamonds. "Come on, Willow. We're freezing. And we have to just go for it, remember?"

Was I really going to let him into this? This cynical man who was undeniably bad for me? I was about to expose him to a Ritualistic Restoration Cleansing?

I knew the obvious answer was no, but I was unable to get my mouth to form the word. Maybe it was the cold. Or the shock. Either way, what came out of my mouth instead was "Okay."

"Yeah?"

"But I'm not telling you the words. Just . . . just follow my lead."

"Gladly."

Tempting as it was to try to get this over with as soon as possible, I needed to focus in order for it to work. I needed to lock in, center myself, and ignore the way Oliver was looking at me as if whatever came out of my mouth next was the most important thing he'd ever hear.

And I needed to ignore the way the pond was slowly starting to slosh up against the banks, waves forming with every glance, every brush of his skin against mine. I saw where this was going, and I didn't like it.

"So," I said, treading away to put some distance between us before a tsunami formed in the pond. "We float on our backs for as long as we can, eyes closed, letting the water wash over us however it wants. Ears, eyes, whatever. So long as you're floating with your arms out and your face toward the sky."

"Easy enough," he said, closing the distance once again. When I tried to back up more, the small waves nearly doubled in size. He didn't seem to notice, with our labored treading and the tension between us, but it was only a matter of time. "Then what?"

"Then I'm going to say the spell a few times—in my head, of course—until we slowly start to sink. Once our bodies are totally underwater, we hold for as long as possible, then take the biggest breath we can when we come back up."

"Then we're done?"

"Then we're done."

"Is the spell hard?"

"Not if I'm focused." Which I wasn't. Not even close.

"And are you?"

"Yes." *No.*

"Go on, then," he said, closing his eyes and floating onto his back. His fingertips brushed against me, and the waves rippled over both of us. *Breathe*, I reminded myself. *You have no choice. This has to work.*

I let my legs float to the surface so that Oliver and I were side by side, faces turned toward the early morning sky, dawn breaking in the silence. It would have been peaceful had the stakes not been so high and had my heart not been pounding out of my chest.

"Willow, relax," Oliver said, his deep voice following the current.

"I am relaxed."

"You are not."

"Are you sure *you're* not the mind reader?"

I turned my head just enough to see his smirk from the corner of my eye. It didn't help.

"You're easy to read," he said. "Very expressive. Which I'm sure is what makes you a good actor, yeah?"

"So they say." This time he cut his eyes to me, and it was my turn to offer a small smile. "Stop distracting me."

"Sorry, love." He leaned back again, closing his eyes. "Carry on."

Sure. No problem. I'll just carry on.

I shook out my shoulders and went back to floating, trying to ignore Oliver and the current where there absolutely should *not* have been a current. Both in the water and between us.

With my eyes closed and my arms stretched out, I gave the spell a try, repeating it like a mantra in my head.

Natural water,
Darkened sky,
Wash away
What's gone awry.

Cleanse my body,
Soul, and mind.
Leave what's negative
Behind.

Prepare me for
What's coming soon
Under the light
Of a shining moon.

I'll leave this water
Fresh and free
To conquer all
That's meant for me.

Only, the brush of my fingertips against Oliver's body halfway through ripped me from the moment. I tried floating farther away, but the waves were becoming problematic.

"Do you feel that?" he whispered. "Sorry, sorry. I don't mean to interrupt your concentration. It's just, does the water feel choppy to you?"

Shit.

"Does it?" I asked. He finally opened his eyes, bringing his body back upright.

"Yeah, look at it," he said. "There are proper waves in the pond." There were, indeed, waves in the pond. And the more I panicked, the more they picked up speed.

"You can get out," I said, "and I'll just wrap up the spell and be right behind you."

"That wasn't the deal. We're doing this together, remember?"

I couldn't exactly tell him he was the reason for the waves, especially when he likely already thought I was insane, but I needed to get him out of here if any of this was going to work.

"Just trust me," I said. The sun was starting to rise, and we were running out of time.

His reluctant sigh cut right through me, but I didn't have a choice. "I thought we agreed."

"Oliver," I snapped, harsher than I meant to. The glimpse of shock on his face was so brief, I wondered if I imagined it. "Please," I pleaded, softer.

"Fine," he said. "But I don't like this, Willow."

"I'll be fine. I just have to get through this before I get hypothermia and the pond overflows." He nodded, and I forced myself to refocus. At this rate, I was at equal risk of drowning as I was of freezing, and I needed to get this show on the road.

Come on, Willow. Concentrate. Like he isn't even here. It's just you, alone in the pond, casting an easy spell that's going to bring you one step closer to turning Vera back into a person. This isn't about you. You can do this because you have to do this.

I floated on my back one more time, my lungs full of air and my limbs limp, and I tried the spell again.

The water slowed, but my heart was still racing. *Come on.* I said it again, then again, until I felt myself sinking. I heard Oliver's sharp intake of breath just on the edge of the pond, and I forced myself to stay focused.

This isn't about him. Do not let him in.

Once my entire body was under, I held my breath in my lungs until it burned. *I can do this.* I kept sinking, letting the ritual work its magic. Letting it cleanse me so I could move on with the quest. Letting it restore me and my confidence in my power. Letting it *work*.

It had to work.

Underwater, under the spell, as I continued sinking, I lost my senses. I was weightless. At the mercy of the water and the spell and the stillness.

Until I wasn't.

I. Forage for *Clinopodium menthifolium*, grown locally. Prepare and consume locally in accordance with your preferences. ✔

II. Conduct an Orientation spell with the Wharram Percy Pendulum. Use its direction as a guide. ✔

III. Complete the Ritualistic Restoration Cleansing in a pond, lake, or slow-moving river to prepare the body for the Reversal. ✔

IV. Participate in a Full Moon Ceremony. Stay awake until the following sundown for maximum effect.

V. Commune with those who have passed on. They know more than any of us who remain in our mortal forms on Earth.

VI. Convince a skeptic of the existence of magic. Use the experience to fortify your powers to effectively produce the Reversal.

CHAPTER 26

Oliver

"Willow, can you hear me? Willow?" I shook her in my arms, desperate for her to open her eyes. "Come on."

"How long was she under?" Lola asked, looking on with Minho and Vera. Vera? The cat? I didn't know. Nor did I care.

"I wasn't timing her," I snapped. "She said to trust her and let her do her thing and I just . . . I figured she'd come up for air when she needed to."

"She knew what she was doing. Give her a second," Minho said.

"She's blue," I said. "Is she blue? She's fucking blue. Come on, Willow."

"Hey." Lola put her hand on my shoulder, but I shrugged it off. "She's—"

Before Lola could finish her sentence, Willow took a gasping breath. A watery, rasping breath that tumbled into a hacking cough before she could even open her eyes.

"Bloody hell." I sighed, holding her closer to me despite the coughing. "You're awake. You're alive."

"Are you sure?" she asked, her voice hoarse. "I feel like I'm dead."

"What happened in there?"

"How should I know?" She forced a laugh, and I'd never been so relieved to hear a single sound in my entire life. "I must have passed out. It must have been the cold. I can usually hold my breath for a long time, but I'm not usually swimming in ponds in freezing weather." She shuddered, and Minho appeared back at my side holding a pile of towels.

"Here." I wrapped the towels haphazardly around her body, trying to get her as warm as possible as fast as possible. Color was just barely coming back into her cheeks, but her lips were pale and I hated the way her teeth slammed together. "Min, can you get a tea on? D'you have that pot thing?"

"One step ahead of you."

"I'm fine," Willow wheezed. "You don't have to go through the trouble. Really. If I can just get back to the flat, I can take care of myself just fine."

"We know you *can*," I said. "Doesn't mean you should."

"Oliver, I'm serious."

"And you think I'm not?"

We stared at each other in a vaguely uncomfortable silence, the others looking on like they were watching a boxing match. *Try me, Willow.*

Eventually, she dropped her head against my chest, and I finally relaxed. "This is all so embarrassing," she mumbled, muffled by my jumper.

"What, would you rather be dead than embarrassed?" She coughed again, hard, when she tried to laugh, and the sound rattled around my chest, too. "Easy," I said.

"God, Willow, that was scary," Lola said, squatting next to us. "Are you sure you're all right? Do you want someone to come back to the flat with you? Any of us would be happy to."

"No—oh god, that's so generous," Willow started. "Thank you, but I could never—"

"I'll do it," I said before I even knew I was speaking. "I'll come stay with you." For a second, no one moved, and I wondered if I'd made a fool of myself. Who did I think I was, offering to stay in her flat with her? She was adamant she'd be able to take care of herself, and surely she had someone else she could—

"You would?"

"Without question." Apparently, speaking without thinking was my own superpower. "Say the word."

"He's a great nurse," Minho said. I wasn't sure whether I wanted to thank him or slap him. "Takes great care of you when you're drunk. Or in this case, when you've almost drowned in Hampstead Heath."

"Min's right," Lola said. "Once when I had surgery, he brought me ice cream in bed for a week."

"You had your wisdom teeth out. Hardly qualifies as surgery," I said, suddenly embarrassed by their effusive praise.

"Had you mentioned ice cream, I might have agreed a lot sooner." Willow smiled. It was tired, but it wasn't lacking any of her usual charm.

"I don't want to impose, but I do think you need looking after. And I'd like to be the one to do it, if you'd let me."

She glanced at the cat, and I tried not to notice. Were they communicating something? Did it matter?

"Only if you're sure."

"As sure as it gets."

"I have a nice living room," she said, "with plenty of space and everything. You'd hardly even know I was there."

"The point is to know you're there."

"I just mean I wouldn't be a bother. I'd be in my room, so you'd have your own space, and—"

"We can argue about it on the Tube," I said. "Feel like you can get out of here?"

She nodded, and the three of us helped her up, making sure she was steady on her feet before letting go. I kept my arm looped around her waist as we piled on the layers so that she didn't have to get on the Tube wrapped in every towel we owned. She could be wrapped in every jumper we owned, which would at least let her hang on to a bit more privacy.

With our pile of wet towels, Willow dressed like the Michelin Man, and the little black cat in tow, we made our way across the park in the direction of the station. The sun painted streaks of oranges and pinks across the hazy sky, but I didn't have the energy to notice. I didn't have the energy to do much of anything other than thank the universe Willow was okay and keep my arm around her waist, holding her tight. Keeping her upright. Keeping her warm. Keeping her close.

During the ride, she dropped her head onto my shoulder, and I wasn't sure if she was awake or asleep, and frankly, I didn't care. What mattered was she trusted me. I was a source of comfort to her, and I couldn't think of anything more rewarding.

Min and Lola got off at their respective stops, asking me to keep them posted on how she was doing and to let them know if we needed anything. I promised to do both, ultimately relieved when it was just me and Willow. And the cat.

"This is us," she mumbled when we got to the station, and I couldn't stop the pounding in my chest at the word. *Us.* I couldn't stop myself from imagining what it would be like to always share the same stop. To always be an *us*.

"Let's do it, then." I wrapped my arm back around her waist, grateful she wasn't too proud to use me for support. The train was crowded with rush hour commuters, and I had to bob and weave us off the carriage and out onto the street.

"Where's Vera?" Willow asked, suddenly snapping her head around to look for the cat.

"Relax," I said, hiking the carrier up higher on my other shoulder. "I've got her."

"You are a good flatmate," she said.

"I've not even been in the flat yet."

"Well, you're off to a good start."

I didn't use to be the kind of bloke who smiled to myself.

✧

HER FLAT WAS exactly what I had hoped for her. Peaceful, clean, secluded. She led me down a quiet side street and up a small flight of stairs to a glossy black front door, flanked by tall pillars and window boxes with ruby-red flowers.

I followed her to the second floor, keeping my hands braced at her hips in case she lost her balance. When she fumbled with the keys, I took them from her shaking hands and unlocked the door, ushering her inside.

"You should have a shower, if you fancy it," I said, heading into the kitchen to get her a large glass of water. "Might help to regulate the body temperature."

"And get the seaweed out of my hair."

"Not seaweed if it's in a pond, is it?"

"Now's an interesting time to argue," she said, and I could hear the smile in her voice. I handed her the water on my way to the bathroom, trying not to hold her gaze too long. I was barely keeping myself together as it was, and the last thing I needed was to look at her flushed face on my way to run the shower.

The bathroom counter was lined with candles, and I lit a few before turning the water pressure on full blast and letting the stream run warm. When I left the bathroom, I was surprised to find her already standing in the bedroom, peeling off the layers of jumpers we'd cloaked her in at the Heath.

"Oh, let me just—"

"Stay," she whispered, and time slowed. She moved through honey, continuing to peel off layer after layer, while I stood silent, trying to figure out what came next. She was down to that damn swimsuit and a pair of my sweatpants when she said, "Please."

I wouldn't have said no in any lifetime. Would have tried, maybe, to pretend I was a good guy. Tried to pretend I didn't want to get in the way of her thing with that bloke, tried to pretend I didn't want to keep her up, or didn't want to crowd her space, or didn't want to overstay my welcome.

But the moment that single syllable left her lips, I was helpless.

"I'll be right here when you get out," I said, my voice hardly more than a scratch in my throat. She smiled, satisfied, and disappeared into the bathroom without closing the door behind her.

I sat on her bed, letting my eyes wander around the room. It was impersonal, mostly, seeing as it was a rental, but there were glimpses of Willow in every corner: a pile of baseball hats, a stack of gold jewelry, more white trainers than I could count. I couldn't reconcile celebrity Willow with this Willow. The one who had a retainer on the nightstand and a fraying phone charger coiled beside the bed. The one I rescued from the pond this morning, who leaned her head on my shoulder on the Tube, who accepted help and asked me to stay. The one who was making herself a home here with my friends in my neighborhood. The one whom I wasn't sure how we'd say goodbye to when the time came.

My spiral was interrupted by a pair of yellow-green eyes peering around the edge of the doorway. A measured, knowing stare that said, *Watch yourself.* Cats always did have that weird way about them, didn't they? Like they knew something you didn't. Like they were watching you, judging you, even when you were simply minding your own business.

Which I was. Sort of.

I averted my gaze when she scampered out of the room, and that was when I caught Willow's eye. A stolen glance in the reflection of a foggy bathroom mirror. Her hands in her hair, a stream of water down her back, perfectly angled collar bones under the straps of her bikini that made me wish more than I was willing to admit that the mirror showed more. Her parted lips moved only slightly, just enough to mouth the word *hi*.

She wasn't embarrassed to be seen. She welcomed it.

Hi, I mouthed back, on pins and needles for what came next. I kept my eyes trained on her lips, which I likely would have done whether she was talking to me or not.

"Come here."

Would she ever stop surprising me?

"Me, or the cat?" I teased, fighting an embarrassing smile when she rolled her eyes. I stood up from the bed, taking slow, calculated steps toward the bathroom. Giving her plenty of time to change her mind.

With every step, more of her body was revealed in her reflection. Freckled shoulders, round breasts, the tempting, soft curve of her stomach. I couldn't believe I got to see her like this. What had I possibly done to get so lucky?

"You were soaking wet today, too," she said once I cleared the threshold. "Thought you might also want a shower."

Every word after "soaking wet" sounded like gibberish.

"I can, er, I can get in once you're out," I said. I didn't want to push my luck. I couldn't believe I was even in this bathroom in the first place. But she was right. I did desperately need a shower. The dry pair of clothes I'd taken for myself before the Tube ride was hardly a substitute for being clean, and I was desperate to wash the pond water from my hair.

"You don't have to wait," she said.

God, this woman.

She kept her eyes locked on mine as I undressed, not looking away even when the candles blew out one by one.

I left my clothes in a heap on the floor save for my boxer briefs, following her lead. If she was anything like I was, she was washing the swimsuit in the shower like I used to do after the beach, and my clothes could use the same.

I pulled the door open slowly, savoring the anticipation, before stepping in behind her and letting the steam engulf me.

CHAPTER 27

Willow

This was happening. The candles were out and the bathroom was dark and I was terrified disaster was about to strike, but this was happening. And if there was anything I could do to keep disaster at bay, now was the time to try. There were times for panicking, and being in the shower with Oliver Hadley at my back was not one of them.

"Look up," he said, and I resisted the urge to tease him for being bossy just in case it made him stop. I really, *really* didn't want him to stop. So I did as I was told and tilted my head toward the ceiling.

He gathered my hair in his hands, brushing it off my face in smooth strokes. It felt heavenly. Like my body had never known the horrors of this morning.

He slid his large hands from the top of my head down the sides of my neck, settling them on my shoulders and digging his thumbs into the space between the blades. The rhythm of his touch nearly brought me to my knees.

"Feel good?" he asked.

"You have no idea," I murmured, letting my eyes close and my head drop to his shoulder. His laugh was quiet, and I was grateful for the layer of clothing between us, no matter how thin it might have been. Without it, there was no telling what I'd have done in that state.

I tried not to shiver as he traced his hands down the sides of my waist, massaging the same slow circles into my lower back. His fingers curled around my hips, and I took half a step closer to him.

"Willow," he whispered in my ear, his lips just grazing the shell.

"I know," I said. Because I did. And because hearing him say everything I was thinking would have reduced me to ashes and washed me down the drain.

We were getting carried away. And I knew better. But it was too good to stop.

I squeezed my eyes closed, fighting the tingling sensation that was beginning in my fingers at the very thought of him letting go.

This might have been the most I'd ever wanted to get a handle on my magic in a situation like this, and that had to count for something, didn't it? I said a silent prayer to the universe that whatever cruel forces were working against me would let up and that I could channel the James women before me to have a single romantic encounter without catastrophe. *Please, let this one be it.*

And for a moment, it almost felt like my prayers were answered. Or like I'd actually managed to control my magic, instead of the other way around. The tingling stopped. The water cooled just enough to notice. Baby steps, but steps nonetheless. For a moment, it seemed like it might have been possible for me to actually have this.

Until Oliver released his hands from my lower back and wrapped both arms around my stomach, and it felt so good to be pressed against him I could feel it between my legs, and I started to lose it again.

The light fixture buzzed, hot steam billowed from the shower-head, and no matter how hard I tried, I couldn't get it back. I wanted to scream.

Instead, I laid my hands over his, sliding them off my body no matter how badly I didn't want to, and that was when the pipe blew.

A cracking explosion and a spray of water like a fire hose burst from beneath the sink, startling both of us from our trance.

"Bloody hell," Oliver said, uncurling his arms from me and jumping out of the shower. Like he'd never been there at all. "What's all this?"

I grabbed a towel from the rack and joined him at the sink, but I knew the answer to his question. I knew exactly what all this was.

Once again, I'd gotten caught in a moment and didn't get myself out fast enough.

But it didn't matter. Water was spraying all over the bathroom, and we had to do something about it.

"I've got it," Oliver said, dodging the spray and trying to duck under the sink. With his back to me, I tried to remember the spell my mom taught me and Ivy that time we overflowed the washing machine. It was on the tip of my tongue. Something about a wish? Or a dish?

"D'you have a wrench?" Oliver asked. *We're not going to need it in a second*, I refrained from adding aloud.

"Uh, let me look."

I slipped out of the bathroom and pretended to look for a wrench while I thought of the spell. *Come on, Willow. You know this.*

The bathroom was flooding more by the minute, and I already feared for my security deposit. It was such a silly spell. Like a nursery rhyme. We used to sing it when Mom made us do chores or when the garden hose turned freezing cold.

"Willow?"

"Just a minute!"

Think.

"It's a proper wash in here," Oliver called.

A wash.

I wish, I wish
There was a wash,
A wash that would wish,
A wish to wash,
And when that wash
Would then be dry,
We wouldn't even have to try!

I repeated it a few more times in my head to make sure I had it right before I slipped back into the bathroom as quietly as possible—which wasn't hard given the noise of the rushing water—and whispered the spell as earnestly as I could. Said it two, three times, watching in disbelief as the water slowed to a dribble. *Holy shit.*

Oliver whipped around from under the sink, bumping the back of his head on the way out. "What'd you do? Turn off the water?"

"Uh, yeah," I said, figuring his suggestion was a better lie than I'd have come up with. Only apparently I wasn't as convincing as I'd hoped, because he leaned back on the counter and crossed his arms like he didn't believe a word I said.

Fine. If he wanted the truth, I could give him that. And if he chose not to believe it, well, that was on him.

"It was a spell," I said with a sigh, trying not to notice the flick of his eyes toward the ceiling. "A simple one we used to do as kids.

A little rusty, but it still works," I said, trying to lighten the mood, which was a mistake.

"I don't understand," he said eventually, blowing out a measured breath.

"Are you trying to?" Silence. "Why can't you?"

"Why can't I believe?"

"Why can't you *try*?" I said. "Would that really be so hard? To consider that my experience is real?" I didn't expect my chin to wobble, but saying it out loud made me realize how frustrated I'd become.

"It's not that I don't think it's real for you," he said, and the words carved themselves into my chest. "It's just . . ." He ran both hands through his hair, undoubtedly looking for the right words to communicate whatever had been so stuck in his throat. "I used to. Sort of. As I kid, I was more open to thinking that kind of thing. But over time, as I grew up, it just . . . it stopped making sense. I started to see the logical explanation for everything I might have once thought was magic, and then eventually I couldn't believe I'd ever thought magic was real at all."

So it was possible. If Oliver believed once, couldn't he do it again?

"And you don't think you could ever change your mind? I mean, you changed it once before. Would it really be so hard to change it back?"

"Yes," he said through his teeth. Like he didn't want to say it. Like he might not have even believed it. "Because now I have the facts."

"And me using a spell to shut off the water wasn't fact enough for you?"

"You saw how it abruptly turned on," he said, his voice softer than a minute ago, like he was letting me down gently. "It could have turned off the same way."

"But I'm telling you it didn't."

Another deep breath. "It's hard, Willow. To go back on everything I've known. Things work a certain way. There are laws and rules that make the world make sense. And I just don't see how magic fits into that."

I didn't say anything for a while. Just tried to get my breathing under control. Tried not to cry. Tried not to believe he was like everyone else. "Right," I said eventually, because I was at a loss for anything else. "Well, now that I've recovered from this morning and the water is off, I'm sure you're dying to get home, so—"

"Willow—"

"No, no, it's fine, really." We were both still soaking wet, and I was ushering him to the door.

"Are you sure you'll be all right alone here?" he asked from the doorway, his concern written all over his face.

"She's hardly alone," Vera called from the other room.

"I'll be fine," I said, ignoring her. It probably sounded like nothing more than a meow to Oliver. I needed him out of my flat, and I didn't have time to explain any more magic to someone determined not to understand it.

"Do call me if you need anything, yeah?"

"Yeah."

"I mean it, Willow."

"Okay."

He nodded once, then disappeared out the door and down the stairs. I tried not to clock the reluctant set of his shoulders or the frustrated hand he raked through his damp hair, but I wasn't blind. And he wasn't the only one struggling.

When I turned back into the flat, Vera was sitting in the doorway.

"Don't," I said.

"I won't, but only because you've had a hell of a morning." She retreated into the flat, climbing onto the couch and settling on a stack of pillows in the corner. "But this isn't sustainable, Willow. You're going to have to sort it out one way or another. I can see how much you like each other and how much the magic is getting in the way."

"I thought you said I'd had a hell of a morning?"

"Trust me, there's a lot more I'd like to say. But for right now, all I'll say is you need to consider the next act of this story. It's going to be here before you know it. But I know you know that. So let's drop it and have a relaxing rest of the day. What do you say?"

"That sounds good," I said, and sighed. "The relaxing part, anyway." She was right. I knew that better than anyone, which meant we didn't have to talk about it now. Instead, we could mindlessly watch too many episodes of *Gossip Girl* with a bowl of popcorn between us and pretend everything was fine.

Though this was a lie I wasn't even sure I could tell myself. People didn't believe in magic all the time, but it never hurt this bad.

I was falling fast, which meant it was only a matter of time before I hit the ground.

✧

Over the next week or so, I busied myself with everything I could think of to resist the temptation of stopping by the shop. I ran, I read, I baked even though I didn't know how, I watched documentaries about religious cults and unsolved crimes and the deep sea, I called Ivy, I drank a lot of wine. None of it helped.

Through it all, my thoughts found their way back to Oliver. What he was doing, whether he was thinking of me. How much I wanted him to change his mind. How his hands felt on my body under the hot spray of the shower. How much it hurt that he didn't believe me. How much I could see it hurt him, too.

How he saved me.

When the night of the full moon finally rolled around, I found myself wishing I had more time. I wasn't ready to see him again, and yet, I was desperate to see him again. And conflicting emotions were notoriously problematic for magic's sake.

But we didn't have time to wait for the next full moon, so it was now or never.

Lola had found a full moon festival through her tattoo artist, so we were all prepared to head to Shoreditch tonight to check it out (save Vera, who wasn't at all interested in crowds). The instructions for the spell weren't specific regarding what kind of Full Moon Ceremony I participated in, so the Shoreditch Park Full Moon Festival felt just fine.

And best of all, it was a masquerade ball theme. Which meant I could let my guard down a little and actually try to enjoy it, safe behind the cover of my mask.

We'd agreed to meet at the Old Street Tube station at ten thirty, so I put the finishing touches on my look and prepared to head out. I left my hair down, another security blanket, letting the curtain of messy waves obscure my face. Hopefully, between the unassuming black dress and the oversize mask Lola had dropped off earlier this week, no one would recognize me and I would be safe to get the job done.

I grabbed yet another cold brew on my way to the train, preparing to be awake until sunset tomorrow. Which, if you asked me, felt highly unnecessary. But I wasn't one to question the spell's requirements, and I was willing to do whatever it took to get Vera back into her human body, so I had to get in the mood for an all-nighter. Fast.

The Tube roared east, and I kept my face buried in the copy of *The Picture of Dorian Gray* Oliver had been eyeing when he was at my flat, partially so no one would see me and partially because I couldn't put it down. I was usually more of a true crime girl, but something about Dorian's predicament, watching himself age in a portrait when in life he still felt young and beautiful, felt eerily similar to the experience of the modern celebrity. I felt for him in a way I didn't usually for rich white men in classic novels.

And Oliver had been eyeing it, so naturally I wanted something to talk to him about.

When I got off the train at the Old Street station, I didn't spot any of the others right away, which gave me time to finish the chapter I was on. I found a corner out of the way of foot traffic and leaned my shoulder against the wall, burying my face in the book while I waited.

"*The only way to get rid of a temptation is to yield to it.*" Oliver's voice cut through the buzz of the station, coming to me like a dream.

"What?" I asked, fighting the smile that was already stretching across my face. Apparently, I couldn't stay mad at him. Though I wasn't sure how badly I wanted to.

"Lord Henry," he said. "Say what you will about Oscar Wilde, but the bloke knew what he was talking about when he wrote that line."

His voice was rough, somewhere between want and restraint. I could tell even in the crowded station. The sound ran through me like a shot of tequila, and I was already craving another.

"Hi," I said, tucking the book under my arm and letting my eyes wander from his head to his toes. Navy wool coat, sport jacket, white button-down open at the collar to reveal the slightest bit of chest hair and the glint of his chain, tailored pants, and perfectly shined shoes. I took my time looking back up, though I couldn't deny the pull of his gaze.

"Hi," he said. "Before you say anything, I owe you an apology for the other day. I was rude, and you didn't deserve that. Belief systems aside, I should have tried to be more open and more respectful about what you were telling me, and I was the opposite, and I'm sorry."

I didn't realize I'd been waiting on those words until they washed over me like warm water. "Apology accepted." I sighed, relieved. "Thank you. And I'm sorry, too. I shouldn't have given you such a hard time."

"Say no more. I deserved it."

I wondered if this meant he was coming around to the idea of magic, but I knew better than to ask. I wanted this to be a nice night. I didn't want to risk ruining it with a disagreement. Instead, I decided to move on. Starting with the way he looked.

I held him at arm's length to get a better view, making no effort to hide my admiration.

"Like what you see, do ya?" he asked, his smile slow and indulgent.

"Can't complain," I said, though the reality was I more than *liked* what I saw. Was drooling over it, maybe. Paralyzed by it. Already memorizing every inch of it.

"If I look even half as good as you, I'll take it." He offered me his elbow, and I ducked my head so he couldn't see how hard I was blushing. It was already like our argument hadn't happened, and although I was certain it was bound to come back, I was relieved we didn't have to rehash it now.

And he must have felt the same, because he dropped his lips to my ear and whispered, "Seriously, Willow. I know I'm probably supposed to keep my hands to myself, but that dress is going to make it a proper challenge."

"You strike me as someone who likes a challenge," I said, keeping my eyes trained ahead. If this was how we were starting the night, I was hopeless to hold on to even a shred of control. It was slipping through my fingers like silk, and I was powerless to stop it.

"Lucky for you."

I glanced up at him, watching mischief dance in his eyes like flames. Shame on me for thinking staying up for two days was going to be the hardest part of this night.

Fortunately, Min and Lola came into view before he could say another word that threatened to turn me to liquid before the night even began.

"Look at you two," Min said, holding his arms out wide. "Clean up nice, don't ya?"

"Same to you," Oliver said, clapping him on the shoulder. "And you look fine, I guess," he said to Lola, laughing when she gave him the finger.

"You look beautiful, Willow," she said. "That mask really suits you."

"Thank you for dropping it off. It's already been a perfect disguise."

"Not to mention the air of mystery," Oliver said, dropping his voice low. There was no way we could keep this up all night. But I had a bad feeling we were going to try.

"All right, Lo. Give us the rundown," I said as we made our way out of the station. I needed to stay focused, to visualize the event and the goal. To stop visualizing the whole slew of other things I'd been visualizing since last week.

"Right, so the festival happens on every full moon, but the location changes and it isn't announced until the morning of. There are loads of vendors and artists and performances, some rituals, fire pits, music, dancing, drinks, the whole lot. It's a bit of cheeky fun, but you've gotta keep an open mind."

"Easy enough," I said.

"For you, maybe." Min laughed. "For this guy, who's to say?" He hooked a thumb at Oliver, who rolled his eyes.

"I'm very open-minded," Oliver protested.

"More now than you used to be," Lola said, and something like hope bubbled in my chest. It would have been vain to think any of that could have been because of me. But a girl could dream. "Last time we tried to get you to come to something like this, you told us to piss off."

"That's because it was an ancient crafts festival and I had other plans."

"With yourself, drinking whiskey on the couch and watching *Interstellar* for the millionth time."

"Those are still plans," he said. "And I'm here now, so."

"I'm just saying, I think we know why." She flicked her eyes to me, and I looked anywhere but back at her, too nervous to confirm or deny. Too nervous my hope would be written all over my face.

"D'you have the address?" Minho asked. "Or are we just aimlessly wandering Shoreditch." He always knew exactly when to change the subject. Bless him.

"You think I'd just drag you guys all the way out here with no idea where I'm going?"

"Yes," Oliver and Minho said at the same time, with the same level of emphasis.

"God, tough crowd," Lola said. "For your information, I do know where we're going. And if I'm right, which I sometimes am, it should be right . . . up . . . here!" She sounded surprised to have actually found the place, but we were all under some silent agreement to let her have this one.

We were standing on the outskirts of a park laden with tents so tightly packed together, it was hard to see beyond the perimeter. Neon lights and tiki torches lined every inch of the park, and somewhere a drumline was pounding out a tribal rhythm. The sound alone was intoxicating.

We watched groups of people in formal wear, ripped jeans, and what looked like bedazzled bathing suits pour in through the entrance, already dancing and cheering and holding drinks high above their masked heads. With the amount of energy this festival alone was going to take, I had no idea how I was supposed to stay up all night.

But one thing at a time.

"Are we ready?" I asked, relieved when Lola grabbed me by the hand and pulled me toward the gate. Her enthusiasm was infectious. Oliver and Minho followed close behind, equally wide-eyed and curious, and we were swallowed up by the festival as soon as we crossed the threshold.

Belly dancers swinging fireballs wove through the paths, alongside women on stilts with elaborate headdresses and hundreds of people wandering arm in arm from one booth to the next, spilling drinks and buying crystals and dancing to the ever-present drumbeat.

"Holy shit," Minho said. "Lo, did you know it was going to be like this?"

"They're all different," she said, "but they do all have the same kind of energy. Brilliant, isn't it?"

"It's definitely something," Oliver said, craning his neck back and forth to take it all in.

"Open mind, remember?" I said.

"For you," he said, "anything."

"What do I have to do to get that treatment?" Lola asked. "I've been asking you to do shit like this since uni. Willow just waltzes in—no offense, Willow—and now you're Gandalf the Grey?"

"There are so many things wrong with that sentence, I'm not even sure where to begin." Oliver shook his head, pinching the bridge of his nose. "And need I remind you of the experimental Danish music festival we went to last year? Or the time Min and I came to see you in that play . . . What was it called? *Crock of Bullshit?*"

"*Load of Lies*," she corrected him, and I bit my lip to stop from laughing. "Fine. Maybe you are supportive."

"Was that so hard?" he asked, nudging her with his shoulder.

"Keep him in check, will you?" she asked me. "He's exhausting."

I saluted her, ignoring Oliver when he threw his hands up in protest.

"Oh, relax," I said, linking my other arm through his and pulling him deeper inside the park. "The festival awaits."

CHAPTER 28

Oliver

I thought I knew what it meant to be overstimulated, but the festival taught me I hadn't even scratched the surface. Why was everything on fire? And why was there so much glitter?

And did the godforsaken drumming ever stop?

But one look at Willow and the glint in her eyes behind the mask reminded me why we were here, and that I promised to be open to the festival and all it had to offer. A promise that would be easy to keep if she kept up the doe-eyed look.

"Someone remind me what exactly we have to do here?" I asked.

"I think we're doing it," Willow said. "All the list said was to participate in the ceremony and stay awake until the following sundown, so . . . I guess this is it? Except none of you have to stay up. I can do that bit on my own."

"Are you insane?" Lola asked, taking the words right out of my mouth for what might have been the first time in our lives. "Of course we're going to stay up with you. We haven't pulled an all-nighter together since graduation. It'll be fun."

Willow looked to me for confirmation, and I gave her a firm nod. "What fun is staying up all night alone?"

The longer we stared at each other, the clearer it became we were thinking the same thing: staying up all night together was a recipe for disaster. Things were bound to unravel between now and tomorrow night. And we were pulling the loose thread.

We walked deeper into the festival, keeping tight to each other as we made our way through the maze and to the nearest bar. "Drinks?" Min asked, pointing at each of us and taking our orders. "Ol, give me a hand, will you?"

"Don't move," I said to Willow and Lola.

"Afraid I'm going to whisk her away?" Lo asked.

"Quite literally."

"You can relax, you know," she said. "She can take care of herself. If she gets whisked away, that's her decision."

"I know that," I said, rolling my eyes at Lola and turning my attention to Willow. "Please don't get whisked away. Even of your own volition. She looks nice, but she's insane."

"Guilty." Lola smiled.

"There will be no whisking," Willow assured me. "But there might be running if you guys don't get back here with drinks in the immediate future."

"You heard the woman," Lola said. "Off with you."

I found Minho at the bar and squeezed in beside him, signaling the bartender and keeping an eye on Lola and Willow on the other side of the crowd. Their heads were bent together and they were both smiling wicked smiles and I could only imagine what they were saying.

"You good?" Min asked, following my line of sight.

"Grand, yeah."

"Grand as in you don't want to talk about it, or grand as in actually grand because you're having a secret fling with a beautiful American celebrity?"

"No one's having a fling, mate."

"Maybe she can give you some acting lessons while you're having a fling," he said, "because you're shit at lying."

The bartender reappeared, and I drank nearly half my pint in one go.

"It's that obvious?" I asked.

"Nah, just haven't seen you this keen on a woman in a while. Kind of endearing, if I'm honest."

"Oh, piss off." I laughed. "It's nothing. Just a bit of chemistry, that's all. She's got some bloke back home and she's going to leave next month as soon as her thing is done, so."

"I don't see that bloke here," Min said. "And she's an actor. Can't she just hop on a private jet and fly back here anytime?"

"I'm not sure that's how it works," I said. "Even if it did, I doubt she'd want that. So I'm afraid it hardly makes sense to pursue this at all." *No matter how badly I want to.*

"But do you want to?"

"Do I want to what?"

"Pursue it. In a perfect world. Or even in this world. You're interested, yeah?"

Of course I was bloody interested. Anyone with eyes and ears and half a brain would be interested. And Min definitely knew that, so I wasn't sure why he needed to hear me say it. But the way he was looking at me with his brows raised and his pint halfway to his lips, I knew I'd have to say it anyway.

"Yeah, I'm interested. But it doesn't matter, really. Besides, there's the whole witch thing, which you know I think is shit, so."

"And yet, here you are." He smiled, and I didn't like where this was going. "At the full moon festival. Dressed in a mask and a sport jacket and preparing to stay up until tomorrow night even though you could be literally anywhere else."

"Doesn't mean I believe in it."

"Supporting something and believing in something aren't the same thing," he said. "Just keep an open mind, Ol. You don't have to believe in everything she believes in. You just have to support her. Try not to be a dick about it and this might work out for you." He raised his glass, and his smug smile made me want to slam my head into the bar.

"And what about the fact she's going back to LA, hmm? Can I find my way around believing in that?"

"Of course you can," he said, "by keeping an open mind. And not being a dick."

"Very funny."

"I'm serious."

"Won't matter if she runs away because we aren't back with a drink fast enough," I said, grabbing the other two glasses and nodding toward Lola and Willow. "Ready?"

"Are *you*?"

I rolled my eyes, and Min nudged my shoulder, following me through the crowd.

Not that I'd ever say it, but he did sort of have a point. Was it possible I could look past the witch thing? Chalk it up to two different belief systems? It would be like dating someone who wasn't Jewish. Or who thought milk belonged in tea.

Not that we were dating. Or even could be.

I was getting way too far ahead of myself and needed to reel it in before it was too late.

"It's about time," she said as we approached, taking the proffered gin and tonic from my hand.

"Missed me?"

"Terribly." She smiled around her straw, and I almost collapsed into the dirt.

"Gross," Lola said, ruining what might have been a nice moment, if a little sarcastic.

"Ignore her," I said. "She may wear a lot of things well, but jealousy isn't one of them."

"You lost me after 'she may wear a lot of things well,'" she said, and Willow laughed. A relaxed, melodic laugh that made me grateful Lola was here, even if she drove me insane. If she could get that uninhibited laugh out of Willow, she was welcome around anytime.

"So, what's the plan?" Min asked, ever the leader. Without him, we'd likely still be stuck on the isle. If we even made it that far.

"There's a meditation later we could try," Lola said, flipping through a brochure she must have grabbed when we walked in. I reminded myself to keep an open mind. "And a moon water workshop. And a lantern walk through the park—that might be nice."

"Where to first?" I asked, trying to throw myself into it before I could run in the opposite direction.

"Moon water, for sure," Lola said, and Willow nodded in agreement. I hadn't the foggiest what made that the obvious choice, but who was I to argue?

The workshop was being held in an open part of the park, which I quickly learned was so the water could absorb the moonlight without being obscured by a tent. We listened as the woman running the workshop, Aurora, explained the importance of moon water rituals, reminding us of the divine femininity of the moon goddesses.

She read some poetry or spells or something about the water acting as a catalyst for the moon's power, before distributing vessels filled with water and instructing us to place our meaningful objects inside. It seemed like everyone else had come prepared with all sorts of things to put in the water: herbs, dried fruit, crystals. The four of us looked around, somewhere between bewildered and self-conscious about our lack of preparation.

"What the hell are we supposed to put in there?" Minho asked, holding the water up to the moonlight and peering through the glass.

"Whatever this is?" Lola asked, pulling up a small weed and dropping it into her glass.

"So meaningful," Min said.

"Do you have any better ideas?"

"I have a lavender perfume?" Willow said, riffling through her bag. "Maybe a spritz of that?"

That bloody lavender perfume. I hadn't been able to stop thinking about it since the first time I got close to her, and now I was supposed to actually bottle it? Maybe I wouldn't trash the moon water as soon as we left here after all.

"Now it just . . . sits and waits?" I asked, and she nodded.

"Gets charged by the moon."

"Then what do we do with it?"

"Sometimes you can drink it, but I hardly think with the perfume and the weeds any of us plan on doing that," she said, and laughed. "But you can water plants with it, clean with it, whatever. You just have to, uh, put an intention into it for it to work. You don't have to say it out loud or anything. Or I guess you don't have to say it at all. But if you wanted to, you could think of something you want, and the water would sort of help you achieve it."

I hated the way her sentences sounded like questions even though she knew exactly what she was talking about. She was softening her beliefs for me, which made me an arsehole. And I needed to snap out of it. Fast.

"Right, then. I can just think of something and it'll go into the water?"

She smiled, and I stopped caring if I sounded like an idiot. "Yep," she confirmed. "Just close your eyes when you do it. And make sure you really mean it."

"And it can be anything I want?"

"That's the beauty of it. You can ask for healing, clarity, growth, whatever."

"Can we ask for love?" Lola asked.

"You don't want love," Min said. "You'd rather ask for a good shag."

"I don't have to ask for that." She wiggled her eyebrows, and Minho pretended to gag himself.

"Don't ruin the moment," I said, and they both snapped their heads to me, as surprised as I was.

"Yes, sir," Minho said. "Let's set our intentions, then." He and Lola immediately closed their eyes, leaving Willow and me to linger a moment longer. The way she was smiling at me, soft and hopeful, I thought I'd never close my eyes again.

Go on, then, I mouthed.

You first, she mouthed back, her gentle smile turning into a full grin.

I knew exactly what to ask for.

CHAPTER 29
Willow

The festival was going even better than I'd hoped. We'd done the moon water workshop, meditated, listened to a sound bath, watched a fire show, drunk cocktails with names we couldn't pronounce and herbs sticking out the top, and danced along to the relentless drummers. If all I had to do was participate, I was doing a hell of a job.

"Reckon we should take that lantern walk?" Oliver asked, stretching his long arms above his head. "Getting a little batty just wandering through this part of the park over and over. Ready for a change of scenery."

"A walk sounds nice," I agreed, hoping I didn't sound as eager as I felt.

"You guys go ahead," Lola said. "I need to rest my feet. Min, come with me."

"But the lantern—"

"Min," she hissed, and he got the message. There was no question they were leaving us alone on purpose, and I couldn't bring myself to care. At this point in the night, a little peace and quiet might not be the worst thing. And if that meant time alone with Oliver, well, I wasn't complaining.

Oliver only laughed and shook his head, and I followed his lead in the direction of the path.

"Don't do anything I wouldn't do," Lola called over her shoulder as they walked back toward the center of the festival.

"There isn't much you wouldn't do," he said.

"That's the point."

"She's too cheeky for her own good, that one," he whispered to me, guiding me toward the path with a steady hand on my lower back. "A break from her might actually give us a second to hear ourselves think."

"And what are you thinking about?" I asked, emboldened by the night and the moon and the fact that nothing catastrophic had happened yet. And it wasn't exactly like the night was young. It might have actually been possible all my magic had been channeled into the moon rituals, and I wouldn't explode anything just because Oliver was close to me.

"You," he answered easily, falling into step beside me as we made our way. At this hour, a gentle quiet blanketed this part of the park, and the paper lanterns lining the path cast Oliver in a warm yellow glow. He looked just as magical as anything else we'd done so far, and it made it hard to focus.

"What about me?"

"Well, first of all, you look freezing." He shrugged off his wool coat and wrapped it around my shoulders, and I didn't argue. It was the middle of the night in November, and I was not dressed appropriately for the weather. I looked great, but it came at a price. A hefty one. "And second of all, you look beautiful."

The back of his hand brushed across the back of mine, and my goose bumps had nothing to do with the temperature.

"Thank you," I said. "You don't look so bad yourself." He adjusted his lapels, and I had a brief flash of wanting to grab them and rip his jacket off. A searing, haunting vision of what it would look like to give in to temptation and see what happened next.

"What are *you* thinking about?" he asked, one eyebrow raised like he could read my mind.

"I, uh . . . you," I said, and laughed, unable to think of a lie. And it wasn't like he had to know the *whole* truth.

"Ah, something we have in common." He smiled. "I'm grateful you brought me here, Willow."

"Really?"

"Yeah, not just to the festival but out of the shop and out of my comfort zone. I can get a little complacent when things are easy, and it's been nice to be reminded of what else is out here in the city."

I wasn't expecting that, and it took me a minute to calibrate. This whole time, I thought this adventure had been primarily an obligation for him. Something that started as work and might have turned into more, but never crossed the line of responsibility. He planned to use his industry knowledge to help me find what I needed, planned to help keep me out of the public eye, and planned to let his friends in on a little quest. I never considered it might be benefiting him, too.

"Careful," I teased. "Keep talking like that and I might think you actually like witchcraft."

"It isn't the witchcraft I like."

When I turned to face him, he was already looking at me. Pushing the mask gently off my face so he could see me clearly, tucking me hair behind my ears and letting his hands linger on the side of my neck.

"Oliver." The lantern light flickered across his face, illuminating the hope in his eyes. The searching, pleading expression that I was certain matched my own.

"Tell me you've been feeling what I've been feeling," he said. "I know it doesn't make sense, and you've got that bloke and you're going home, but at least give me this. If you're feeling even a fraction of what I am, tell me the truth." I exhaled, long and slow, and he threaded his fingers through my hair. "Put me out of my misery," he said, but his expression was anything but miserable. Even behind the mask, he was optimistic. Longing.

So I did what he asked.

In a moment of weakness, chaos, desperation, lust—I put him out of his misery.

I leaned forward and pressed my lips to his, throwing my arms around his neck and leaning into him. His surprise quickly disappeared, and his kiss was just as hungry as mine. More so, even.

He dropped his hands to my waist, walking me back a few steps until I was leaning against a nearby tree draped in lanterns, which hung over us like spotlights. When he pushed against me as he deepened the kiss, I felt every inch of him in a way that made me desperate to get out of the woods and back into my flat. Back into that moment in the shower. Anywhere but here.

He tilted my head back by my hair, pressing kisses against my neck and mumbling into my skin. "I've been thinking of nothing but this for months," he said. "Every day . . . and every night." A kiss behind my ear. At the hollow of my throat.

I laced my fingers through the curls at the nape of his neck, relishing the low sound that escaped his throat when I pulled. "Now I'll be thinking of nothing but *this* for months," I whispered, bringing his lips back to mine. He tasted like beer and cinnamon and the best worst decision I'd made in as long as I could remember.

When he hiked my leg up around his hip to press harder into me, I let the hem of my dress fall to my waist so I could feel the heat of his hand on my thigh. I could feel how hard he was even through his pants, and it was making me desperate. I ground against him, and he broke away and sucked a breath through his teeth.

"Fuck." He exhaled, long and slow, pressing his hands against the tree behind me and dropping his forehead to mine.

"We shouldn't have started this here," I said, looking around at the sound of rustling in the leaves and trying not to cringe at the state of us in such a precarious position.

"No," he agreed. "We definitely shouldn't have. But that doesn't mean we can't end it somewhere else, does it?" Another kiss to my neck, my jaw, my throat.

"If you keep kissing me like that, we're not going to have much of a choice," I said.

"That's the plan."

I pulled back to look at him just in time to catch the devious grin spreading across his face, turning his whole vibe from innocent librarian to filthy professor, and I couldn't get out of the woods fast enough.

✧

THE WHOLE RIDE back to my flat, I waited for the lightning strike. Waited for the train car to explode, for a delay that would leave us trapped for hours on end, for a serial killer or someone with a speaker to get on and ruin our moment. I waited for whatever catastrophe was bound to follow, however my magic was going to backfire, whatever drama was going to unfold because I was doing something romantic. Or at the very least, highly sexual.

And yet, nothing came.

The train didn't explode, the skies didn't open up on the walk back to the flat, my keys didn't disappear. Vera was even out on a late-night prowl around the neighborhood, judging by the open cat door and her tendency to snoop at this hour. Things were . . . working out.

I should have known better than to think it would last.

But I was greedy, so I let Oliver in anyway.

I thought it was only in the movies when people went back to kissing before the door even closed behind them, but when Oliver pushed me up against the wall the second we crossed the threshold, I was reminded there's a reason people say life imitates art.

Thank god Vera wasn't in the flat, because things were escalating at a dizzying pace. It was like we pressed fast-forward on every desire from the last few months and tried to rip through them all at once. Hot, open-mouthed kisses, handfuls of hair, skin on skin.

He ran his hands over my ass and scooped me up off the ground, and my legs wrapped around his waist as he carried me in the direction of my bedroom.

"How do you know where you're going?"

"It's a flat, Willow, not a maze."

He kissed me again before I could respond, which was probably for the best. At this rate, I wasn't sure I'd ever be able to form a coherent sentence again as long as I lived. So much for my acting career. Unless someone wanted to cast me as a character who only said, *Yes, more, please, Oliver*, I was useless.

I pushed his jacket off his shoulders, finally giving in to my vision of undressing him. I'd seen him without his clothes before, but nothing compared to being the one to take them off. He hiked my dress higher over my ass as I undid his buttons, both of us fumbling to get closer to each other.

"Your skin feels incredible," he mumbled against my mouth, sinking his fingers into my hips. "You're even better than I imagined."

"Oh, you imagined me?"

"You have no idea."

He dropped me onto the bed, watching with heavy eyes as I undid his belt and pushed his pants to the floor. "You drive me insane," he whispered.

"That makes two of us."

I melted at the sight of his slow smile. He leaned over me until I was on my back, then planted both hands on either side of my head and brought his lips back to mine. His kisses were slower, teasing, and I couldn't stop myself from arching into him. Close wasn't close enough. I needed more.

"Can I take this off?" he asked, slipping a strap of my dress from my shoulder and kissing the newly exposed skin.

"Please."

At that single syllable, Oliver began to peel my dress down my body, tracing his lips over my jaw, my collarbone, the edge of my bra, the curve of my waist, my hip bones. No one had ever taken his time with me like that before. Like he was studying me. Memorizing me.

The same way I would do to him, because we both knew this couldn't last. If we wanted another night like this, it would have to be in memory. Not that I could ever forget this.

It was my turn to watch as he dropped my dress to the floor and traced a path back up my leg, over my hips, before settling on the swell of my breast. Heat bloomed low in my stomach as he swept his thumb over my nipple, teasing me through the lace.

"This is beautiful," he said, dragging his fingertips over the outline of my bra. A very expensive bra. One I was thrilled was getting the appreciation it deserved. "You look so good in this, I almost don't want to take it off." He kissed the edge, right where the lace met my skin.

"Please take it off."

Before the words were even out of my mouth, he unclipped the back and added the bra to our pile of clothes on the floor, bringing his lips back to my skin. He sucked my nipple into his mouth, swirling his tongue in a slow pattern that made me arch my back like a contortionist. *More.*

I reached down between us to trace the outline of him through his underwear, savoring the way he moaned into my collarbone.

"I can't focus with your hands on me," he breathed.

"What exactly do you have to focus on?"

"You," he said. "Getting this right. Making this last." I nearly gasped at the graze of his teeth. "Making you come." He switched to my other nipple, and the shock of his mouth made me squirm.

"Oliver," I whined. I was all for taking our time, but this was excruciating. I wanted to touch him. All of him. And I wanted him to touch me. And I was done waiting. "Touch me."

"Impatient?"

"We've been waiting months, have we not?"

"Ah, so you admit you've been feeling what I have?"

"Is now the time for this conversation?" I reached back between us, running my hand over the length of him, watching as he closed his eyes and dropped his head to my chest.

"You're cruel." He raised his head and flashed a wicked grin, and I knew we were finally done waiting.

He sat up just enough to hook his fingers in both sides of my panties, pulling them down the length of my legs and flinging them to the side, pile of clothes be damned. And just when I thought we were done taking things slow, he knelt down and pushed my knees to the side, taking an extra second to stare at me. Wide open.

And the longer he looked, the more confident I felt. His eyes were glassy, lids heavy, pupils blown wide. Lips parted just enough to take deep, shaky breaths. When he dragged his eyes up my body to meet my own, I saw a reverence there I wasn't expecting.

"You're gorgeous, Willow." A kiss to the inside of my knee. "A kind of gorgeous that makes it hard to believe any of this is even real." A kiss to my thigh.

I laced my fingers through his hair, murmuring my gratitude and holding my breath for whatever came next. When I could find the words again, I would tell him he was gorgeous, too. His dark curls and his translucent eyes and the sharp angles of his jaw that I was desperate to hold in my hands with him inside me.

But for now, he would have to settle for my incoherent rambling and the moans I couldn't conceal.

He traced his thumb over my opening, his other hand splayed across my stomach, holding me to the bed. I hoped he could feel how wet I was already. I wanted him to know what he was doing to me.

When he changed his angle, pressed his thumb to my clit and slipped two long fingers inside of me, I dropped my head back and gave up on looking at him. All I could do was close my eyes and give in to the sensation. Let it wash over me in waves.

"Bloody hell," he whispered, more to himself than to me, as he split me open with two fingers. I raked my nails over his scalp, gasping lightly when I felt the warmth of his mouth in place of his thumb.

"My god," I said, and he murmured in agreement. With every slow circle of his tongue, I felt myself careening closer to the edge. Hurtling toward a cliff with no way of slowing down. Not that I wanted to.

At the exact moment I opened my mouth to tell him I was close, he was one step ahead of me. "Let go," he said against me, hoarse and needy. Exactly what I needed to hear to do exactly that. "Come for me, Willow."

Stars exploded in my eyes as my orgasm crashed over me, prolonged by the way he moaned against me. Like he was feeling my pleasure just as much as I was.

Before I could even come back to earth, we were face-to-face, breathing heavily and kissing desperately, and I was blindly reaching for his briefs, pulling them down and finally holding him in my hands. He sucked in a breath through his teeth as I began to stroke him, relishing how he felt. Warm, heavy, hard.

"I want you inside of me," I whispered. Something about being with him like this made me bold. Made it easy to speak my mind. Tell him exactly what I wanted and trust he wanted it, too. Without my having to ask, he found a condom in his wallet in the back pocket of his pants and rolled it on. If there was anything more erotic than actually touching him, it was watching him touch himself.

His chest heaved with every labored breath, and his big hands stroked his cock in a slow rhythm as he traced my lower lip with his thumb. When he slipped his finger inside my mouth and I sucked on it, whatever last shred of restraint he was holding on to snapped.

And Oliver Hadley unchecked was its own kind of magic.

He scooped me off the bed and into his arms, sitting on the edge with me on his lap. Even with our foreheads touching, I could see his eyes were wild.

"I've wanted this for so long," he said against my lips.

"So have I," I confessed. I kissed the hinge of his jaw, inhaling the warm scent of his cologne in the space behind his ear. Masculine. Spicy. Intoxicating.

I braced my hands on his broad shoulders, and with one arm around my back and the other hand holding me tightly by the hip, he lowered me onto him.

"Oh my god," I breathed, letting my head roll back on my shoulders. He kissed the base of my throat, grabbing my hair at the nape of my neck and pushing deeper into me. I began to rock, grinding against him faster and harder with every expletive mumbled through his clenched teeth.

"Willow," he groaned, "fuck." In one quick motion, he stood up and flipped me over, laying me on the bed. I understood without him having to say anything. He needed to be the one in control.

I wrapped my arms around him and studied the way the muscles in his shoulders moved under my hands, the coldness of his chain against my chest, the dimples in his lower back, the way his rib cage expanded with every breath. The moans coming from my mouth were desperate, loud, passionate in a way I didn't even know I was capable of.

In all my life, I don't think I'd ever wanted anyone this much.

"God, you feel so good," he said, grabbing my hip to give himself more leverage. I watched the space where our bodies met, where he pushed in and out of me, where my clit rubbed against him so perfectly I was sure I'd come again before he did.

"Yes," I said. "Just like that." I was so wet, I could feel myself dripping. "Right there."

"God damn it," he grunted. "Willow, I'm going to come with you." His movements were erratic, his voice rough. "I can't—"

"Oliver," I said against the shell of his ear, "please."

The sound that came out of his mouth and the last few hard thrusts were exactly what put me over the edge, the two of us tumbling together down an elusive rabbit hole I hadn't believed actually existed. Divine timing. Our mutual unraveling. The pulsing in and around each other that I wanted to last forever.

"That was—"

"I know."

When we finally untangled from each other to share a knowing smile, the only other thing I knew for certain was that nothing this good could last forever. I'd only hoped it could have at least lasted longer than the night.

I. Forage for *Clinopodium menthifolium*, grown locally. Prepare and consume locally in accordance with your preferences. ✔

II. Conduct an Orientation spell with the Wharram Percy Pendulum. Use its direction as a guide. ✔

III. Complete the Ritualistic Restoration Cleansing in a pond, lake, or slow-moving river to prepare the body for the Reversal. ✔

IV. Participate in a Full Moon Ceremony. Stay awake until the following sundown for maximum effect. ✔

V. Commune with those who have passed on. They know more than any of us who remain in our mortal forms on Earth.

VI. Convince a skeptic of the existence of magic. Use the experience to fortify your powers to effectively produce the Reversal.

CHAPTER 30
Oliver

I'd dreamt of Willow quite a bit since she'd arrived. I'd had more than my fair share of fantasies. More than a few late nights with visions of her in the shower, undressing for bed, showing up at my flat . . .

And not a single one held a candle to the real thing. Even as a bookshop owner, I didn't have the imagination required to conjure something so beautiful.

The flush of her cheeks, the way she said my name, her full lips and her full chest and her full ass, each a work of art in their own right. She was magnetic. I could live a thousand lifetimes and still not be able to get enough of her.

"I can hear you thinking," she whispered from where she lay on my chest. "What's going on in there?"

"I don't want this night to end," I answered honestly.

"Good thing it doesn't have to." I could hear her smile. "In case you've forgotten, we have to stay awake until tomorrow. Or to-night. I have no idea what time it is."

She stretched over me to reach her phone on the nightstand, and the light illuminated her face just in time for me to see her expression change completely. A full 180. Elated to confused to angry in a matter of seconds.

"What is it?" I asked, sitting up underneath her arm. "What's wrong?"

"Someone saw me." She spoke slowly, scrolling through what looked like hundreds of notifications. "Saw *us*."

"What?"

"In the woods. Kissing. Someone saw us."

She turned her phone screen so I could see it, and I tried to keep my expression neutral. Tried not to add fuel to the fire. But there we were, only slightly blurry, kissing on the lantern path.

"My god, Willow, I am so sorry."

"This isn't your fault."

"I was supposed to protect you." I got out of bed and ran my hands through my hair, trying to make sense of how I got so lost that I let this happen. "And instead I was the one who took your mask off. And I was the one who wasn't on the lookout for anyone else."

"And I was the one who kissed you," she said. "I'm not your responsibility, Oliver. Even if you've put that on yourself. I knew the risks, and I too chose to ignore them."

"That rustle in the leaves—"

"I know."

"I should have done something." *Why didn't I do something? How could I have been the one to let this happen?*

Before I could spiral any further, we heard the same rustling again. Only this time it wasn't from the video on Willow's phone. It was from outside the window.

"That couldn't—"

"There's no way—"

"They're here?" I jumped out of bed to push back the curtain just enough so that I could see outside, and I regretted it immediately. "Don't move," I said.

"Of course they followed us," she groaned, flopping back onto the bed. "Please don't go out there."

"Why not? Someone needs to tell them to get the hell out of your garden."

"Yeah, and if it's you, your face will be all over the tabloids tomorrow. Next to my face."

"Nervous that other bloke will see?" I teased, though I wasn't entirely sure I was joking. Could that have been the real reason she didn't want anyone to see us together?

"What bloke?" she asked, scrolling her phone again, undoubtedly reading something unpleasant judging by the look on her face.

"That bloke you were seeing . . ."

"Oh, right, er, that bloke." When she looked up at me, I saw the truth written all over her face.

"There never was a bloke, was there?" Everything was unraveling. Coming apart one string at a time to the chorus of paparazzi outside. And it was too late to stop it.

"Does that matter right now?" she asked, gesturing outside. "We've got paparazzi outside the house, Oliver. We're trapped in here until they leave."

"Perfect," I said. "That'll give you plenty of time to tell me why you lied about the guy."

She heaved a frustrated sigh, and I wondered if she was frustrated that she'd lied in the first place or frustrated I'd found her out.

"Does it even matter at all?" she said. "It definitely didn't stop us from doing whatever we wanted, obviously." She gestured to the unmade bed and the pile of most of our clothes still on the floor. "Even though that was the whole point of the lie in the first place."

"The whole point of the lie was what? To keep us apart?"

"Yes," she groaned, "and while I'd love to explain myself, I'd love it even more if the paparazzi wasn't outside my door."

Before either of us could say another word, there was a pounding on the door. Loud, persistent, more than one set of knuckles.

"Willow! Come out and give us a statement, love!"

"Miss James, just a few questions!"

"Are they serious?" I asked. "They're at the door?"

"Who's the bloke, Willow?"

"We'd love to see the both of ya!"

"They are definitely serious," she said. "This is what they do."

"And you have to live like this?"

"I'm sure now you can understand my need for privacy."

Anger pricked the back of my neck like a thousand tiny needles. Didn't they realize she was a human being? How could they treat someone this way? How could I have let this happen?

"Miss James, what about Kit Hayes?"

I narrowed my eyes at the exact moment Willow widened hers. "I thought there was no Kit?"

"There isn't."

"So why are the reporters asking about him?"

"I don't know, Oliver," she snapped, and I realized now was not the time for this conversation.

"Are you having an affair?"

"Who's the dark-haired gentleman?"

"Is this why you've run off to London?"

"An affair?" she said. "Jesus Christ."

"And you've no idea why they think this?"

"Don't you think I'd have told you if I did?"

"I don't know what to think," I said. "About any of this. But I do know if we're going to think at all, they need to get the fuck out of the garden."

Before she could stop me, I closed the bedroom door behind me and stormed toward the front. I knew it was probably better not to provoke them, but I couldn't let this carry on. I had too much momentum to slow down. Even with Willow calling to me from her bedroom.

When I flung the door open, I was met with blinding camera flashes and incoherent shouting.

"Sir, over here!"

"Are you and Miss James having an affair?"

"Where's Kit Hayes?"

"You have about thirty seconds to get the fuck out of the garden before the police arrive," I lied. "So if no one wants a trespassing arrest, I suggest you leg it. Now."

One by one, they dragged their sorry arses from the garden, muttering to one another and spewing obscenities in my direction as they left. When they finally all cleared out and I turned back around, I saw Willow standing in her doorway. Arms crossed, wearing my shirt, leaning on the doorjamb like a bloody painting.

"I hope you're prepared to be all over the media," she said. "Shirtless. Shouting at paparazzi to get the fuck out of the garden."

"Are you mad?"

"Grateful," she said. "And maybe a little mad. I would have liked to have handled it without a scene, so our night wouldn't end up all over the internet. But I am glad they're gone."

"I'm sorry, Willow. I just couldn't sit around while they harassed you like that."

"Now they're going to be harassing *you*, too," she said.

"Hell if I care." And it was the truth. I only cared about Willow. They could say whatever they wanted about me. I doubted I'd even see it in the first place. "They can say whatever they want about me. But they can't be banging on your door and shouting accusations and thinking that's okay."

"It never stops," she said. "They're gone now, and I'm grateful for that, but now they know where I am. They know who you are. Or at the very least that you're someone I was kissing in the middle of the night in the woods at a full moon festival. How am I going to explain any of this?"

"Don't you have a team for that?"

"She's a cat!" Willow threw her hands in the air and collapsed back onto the bed. "Which I know you don't believe, so you probably think I'm an idiot, but I'm serious, Oliver. And now I have to navigate this mess on top of that mess. And I'm not blaming you. I know I also created this. But we could have done without the shirtless shouting at the crack of dawn."

"I don't think you're an idiot."

"Doesn't matter much anyway, does it?"

"What's that mean?"

"If the media now knows where I am and thinks I'm having an affair, it's not like we can be running around the city together, can we? I don't even know why they think I'm with Kit in the first place. Who knows what other false information they have, and who knows how much worse I can make it by being seen all over the city with you."

They say when you're at rock bottom, the only place to go is up. But no one ever says when you're on top of the world, the only place to go is down.

The swing from the highest high to whatever this was right now was so dramatic, it was hard to wrap my head around. We'd finally spent the night together, finally gave in to the building tension of the last several months, only to have to cut ties in the blink of an eye?

I paced the length of her bedroom, lacing my fingers behind my head and trying to steady myself.

"But why did you tell me you were seeing him in the first place?" I asked. Maybe if I had all the facts, it would be easier to make sense of this.

"I thought it would make it easier to put some distance between us. It was Vera's idea."

"Vera . . . the cat?"

"The manager."

"Who's the cat?"

"Oliver."

"Sorry. I'm just trying to understand."

"Are you? Because from here it sounds like you're passing judgment."

None of this was coming out right. Or all of it was coming out exactly as I meant it and I needed to get myself in check. I was passing judgment. And if I actually cared about this woman, which I did, deeply, then I needed to lose the attitude.

"I'm sorry," I said, sinking onto the edge of the bed beside her. "It's just . . . it's all a lot right now." I took a deep breath and tried again. "Why, exactly, did you want to put distance between us?"

"God, how do I say this without sounding insane?" she said, mostly to herself. "Things happen with my magic when I start feeling something for someone." She clapped her hands together, turning to face me. She meant business. And I needed to listen. "And I didn't want either of us to have to experience that. Especially because I knew you'd try to explain those things away with logic, and I'd know they were because of my magic, and I didn't know how we'd get past that."

"How did you know it was going to happen?"

"Because it always happens. It started happening immediately. The light in the shop. The sparks in the subway. The pipe in the bathroom."

"Come on, Willow. Those were just freak incidents. You can't beat yourself up over that, can you?"

"See? This is exactly what I was afraid of. It's easy to say that, and I'm sure from the outside that's how it looks, but you have to trust me when I say they weren't."

"Then how do you explain last night?" I asked. "Nothing caught fire. Nothing exploded. Aside from the paparazzi, which hardly seems like a freak incident, nothing catastrophic has happened. And correct me if I'm wrong, but it seemed like there was a whole lot of feeling from where I stood."

"You're not wrong."

"Then how do you explain it?"

"I don't know!"

Her outburst reverberated around us until it turned to silence. Even her echo sounded like it was going to cry.

"Hey," I said, reaching out to her and trying not to wince when she pulled away.

"I don't have answers," she said. "I don't know how to explain any of this. When we first met in the shop and I said I had bad genetics, this is what I was talking about. Everyone in my family is a brilliant witch, and I'm a wreck. I didn't want to have to lie to you, but I thought it was the only way to protect either of us. To keep us from getting to this point. What a bust that was." She rolled her eyes at herself, pulling my heartstrings in the process. I didn't know if I was mad or frustrated or embarrassed or disappointed, but what I did know was that I hated seeing her so hard on herself.

"So I thought it would just be easier for us both if you thought I was involved with someone," she continued, "but then when you asked me if it was serious and I had every opportunity to run with it, I couldn't bring myself to do it. So I let it slip away, but someone else must have heard something anyway because now I'm Hollywood's newest adulterer."

"I swear I didn't say anything," I said, holding my hands up.

"Of course you didn't." She laughed, just barely. "You weren't even sure who I was when I first walked into the shop. I doubt you're running off and leaking anything to Page Six."

"It wasn't Lo or Minho, either," I said. "I know they're a little batty, but they wouldn't do something like this."

"No, no, I'm not worried it was them. I like to think they've become friends by now and that they wouldn't sell me out. Who knows who it was. Hell, maybe it was Kit, even. He'd been on Vera's side trying to get me to do a film with him before I left, so maybe that was his way of getting my attention. But none of that changes the mess we're in."

"Can't you just set it straight with the media?"

"If only it was that easy," she said, and sighed. "If there was a way to just 'set something straight' with the media, there would be no celebrity gossip at all. There might not even be celebrities."

"So . . . what?" I asked. "That's it, then?" I couldn't believe we'd finally gotten here and now she was slipping through my fingers like sand. As soon as I saw the wobble in her lip, I knew I had my answer.

"I . . . I don't know what else to do," she said. "I think I just got too comfortable. With you, in the city, with the quest. I lost sight of the fact I was supposed to be out of the public eye, you know? Forgot I was supposed to be hiding and instead just settled into a life here. One I knew was never really mine. And I got sloppy and made mistakes, and now I need to figure out how to fix this. How to get my name out of the headlines and how to end the rumors about Kit and how to get a video of me in the woods with a leg wrapped around your waist off the internet." The reminder was a knife in my chest. Sharp, hot, destructive. "And if I'm going to do that, I can't keep running around the city with you like I belong here. I have to figure this out on my own."

"But what about the quest?" I was grasping at anything I could to keep her close to me. Even with all the lying, I couldn't bring myself to be as mad as I should have been. I was hurt, sure. Frustrated, definitely. But I couldn't hold on to my anger. Especially not when she was looking at me like it hurt her even more to say these words than it hurt me to hear them.

"I only have two more things," she said. "One is 'commune with the dead,' which is hardly a group activity, anyway, especially for someone who doesn't believe in magic. And the other is to convince a skeptic, and, well . . . I'll just have to figure that one out on my own. For all I know, that's going to be impossible, and all of this will have been for nothing."

"Is that what you think? This was all for nothing?" There was no way she could say none of this meant anything to her, was there? After the night we had? I'd always prided myself on being intuitive, but had I read this all wrong?

"I came here to reverse the spell," she said. "And if I can't do that, then . . ."

"Right."

She couldn't even finish the sentence, and I didn't want her to.

I knew how it ended. I should have known how all of this ended. When she tried to put distance between us, I should have let her.

"I'm sorry, Oliver."

"Me too."

With little left to say and the paparazzi gone from the garden, I supposed it was finally my cue to leave. "You'll be okay staying up until sundown?" She nodded. "And you'll be okay with the rest of the quest?" She crossed her fingers, but still said nothing. "We're still here to help, Willow. At least call Min and Lola. They won't get you in trouble with the press, will they? Maybe they can help you finish."

"I'll be fine," she said, but neither of us believed a word. "If I need anything else from the shop, maybe I'll come by before I head back to LA."

"I'd like that."

Her soft, sad smile was the last thing I saw before I slipped from her front door and into the dull light of the early morning. The start of a day I wished hadn't come.

@CelebrityWeeklyLA: Willow James confirmed in London. See post for more.

@SilverLakeUnderground: Love in London: Willow James Spotted in Embrace with Unidentified Man at Full Moon Festival.

@LylaWithAY: Willow James kissing pics are HOT. Anyone know who that is? And if he has a brother? #AskingForAFriend

@UnluckyInLove4390: Not surprised Willow James is cheating on Kit Hayes. This is what happens when women let fame get to their heads.

@GraySkiesForever: Where is Willow James staying? Could have sworn I saw her in my neighborhood. Anyone know if she's in West London? #WhereIsWillowJames

@SonjaFilms: Willow James mystery kisser IDENTIFIED. Article in bio for everything we know about her Swedish billionaire lover and their secret honeymoon.

CHAPTER 31

Willow

So much of this trip seemed hard to believe. The places I'd seen, the things I'd done, the ways I'd tested my magic. The rhythm I'd slipped into. But what was hardest to believe was Oliver. And how quickly I'd both had and lost him.

When he said nothing catastrophic had happened the night we slept together, he was only right in terms of the magic. Everything else seemed like it qualified.

But he *was* right in terms of the magic. Nothing exploded, or caught on fire, or caused a scene. And whatever that meant . . . I hadn't the slightest clue. Nor did I have the brain capacity to try to figure it out.

Priority number one was finishing the quest and turning Vera back into a person. Priority number two was clearing my name with the media and getting the story out of the papers. And priority number three, well, maybe that was figuring out what the hell happened that night. And why it hurt so bad to watch Oliver leave.

Lucky for me, the next step of the quest was exactly what I needed to get myself together. If anyone could mend my broken heart and whip me back into shape at the same time, it was Granny Annie.

Communing with the dead was something she taught Ivy and me when we were in high school and lost a close mutual friend one summer. It wasn't a hard spell, but since it wasn't something to be taken lightly, we spent weeks preparing. We shared memories of Nicola, made a scrapbook of old pictures, listened to music she liked, thought about what we'd say to her if we were able to cast the spell and got a chance to say goodbye. It was emotional, and without Granny Annie to walk us through it, I wasn't sure we'd have made it at all.

But I could hear her voice now as clearly as I could then, reminding Ivy that none of us can escape death, so the best thing to do is honor it. To honor those gone before their time, to keep their memory alive only in ways they would have wanted.

So when we finally connected with Nicola one late summer night nearly a year after she died, we said our goodbyes with a dance party in the backyard, like we used to do when she was alive. We put on a playlist she made when she and Ivy were getting ready for prom, and we danced in the moonlight surrounded by her spirit before we finally parted ways for good.

And since I'd spent the past year since Granny Annie died compiling all our old memories, helping Mom clean her house and sorting her things, keeping and cherishing the ones she'd always wanted me to have, wishing I could talk to her one more time, I'd hardly had to prepare for the spell at all. I only had to lower my inhibitions and open myself to her influence, find a place she would have loved to cast the spell, and invite her in.

I could have done this at any time since she passed, but she'd explicitly instructed us not to right away. She said if we brought her back too soon, she wouldn't get a chance to settle in wherever she was and we wouldn't adjust to life without her.

But now, since she was the one who essentially directed me to this quest in the first place, I had a feeling she wouldn't mind. She was probably properly settled by now, and I doubted she'd complain about an invitation to Notting Hill.

This version of the spell meant we could feel the spirit of someone who had passed only if they accepted our calling, and while they could hear us, we couldn't hear them. We could feel their presence, but they couldn't say a word. Granny Annie said it worked better this way because they'd already said all they were meant to in this lifetime, and their presence alone would guide us toward what we needed to hear. Even if we were the ones who had to say it.

So, after weeks of essentially hiding in the flat and feeling sorry for myself despite Vera's attempts to snap me out of it, I threw on a floor-length puffer coat, a knit balaclava I found near the door, and my trusty oversize sunnies, filled a thermos with steaming-hot coffee, and headed to Kensington Gardens at dawn.

Instead of taking the Tube, I set out on foot, planning to spend the walk mentally preparing to be with her again. In some ways, I'd known I'd be with her since I first found the instructions for the spell, but it was easy to put it out of my mind to focus on what else was at hand. But now, in the cold silence of the morning, I had to face it.

And even on the walk, at a time I should have felt my most alone, not a single part of me felt lonely. For the first time in months, I didn't feel heavy or daunted or lost.

It was like she was already there.

The flower boxes on the pastel row houses that were so full when I arrived were frosted over, taken inside, changing with the seasons. Brass door knockers were covered with wreaths, string lights wrapped around the pillars; streetlights were adorned with twinkling snowflakes.

It was a sister city to the one I arrived in five months ago. While some neighborhoods were ramping up in preparation for the holidays, others were slowing down, cozying up for the winter, and I was grateful Notting Hill was somewhere in between. Frankly, *I* was somewhere in between.

Part of me was ready to hightail it back to LA at full speed and leave this entire mess behind me, while the other part of me was reluctant to leave the life I'd settled into here. The long walks, the quiet social calendar, the easy routine. My days looked nothing at all like they did at home, and had I not been momentarily heartbroken, it was possible I wouldn't have wanted to go back at all.

It wasn't like I could stay here. Vera would drag me back to LA kicking and screaming if she had to. And I *wanted* to go back, didn't I? I had a life and a career that wouldn't wait for me forever.

But getting this time to myself? Focusing on making sense of my magic and testing its limits? It might have been born from a massive mistake, but the learning experience was more necessary than I'd realized.

And even just admitting that felt like growth.

I couldn't wallow in being a bad witch anymore. At thirty years old, it was a choice. If I was still a bad witch, it was because I wasn't trying hard enough to be a good one. I wasn't learning, or practicing, or pushing myself to be better.

And while I'd been making strides since I'd been here, I had to make the full leap if any of this was going to be worth it. I had to decide I was good.

By the time I arrived at Kensington Gardens, the sun was on

her way up, painting the garden with soft, butter-yellow fingers. I couldn't see anyone in either direction once I slipped through the gates, so I spread out my picnic blanket and settled under the biggest tree I could find.

With my back up against the trunk and my legs stretched out in front of me, I took a few deep, steadying breaths. In the midst of the chaos, I was getting an opportunity to connect with Granny Annie. And beyond the spell, that required my full attention. This wasn't something I was going to miss because I was hung up on drama I'd created.

This was an opportunity so few people were lucky enough to have, and as Granny taught us when we were young, the real magic was in the connection, not in the spell itself. And I'd be damned if I ever forgot a piece of her advice.

So, with her brooch in my hand and my eyes closed, I started the spell.

Spirit, spirit, hear my call.
Come back to me once and for all.
Grant us this one last try
To show our love and say goodbye.

And like clockwork, she first appeared with the wind through the leaves. Whether I'd done a decent job on the spell or she was watching and helping me out, I couldn't be sure, and I wasn't sure it mattered. What mattered was the wind that swirled around me where I sat, rustling only around the trunk of the tree.

I squeezed the brooch tighter, planting the palm of my other hand firmly against the cold ground, willing her to give me another sign.

The wind whistled a gentle melody, like a lullaby, before lifting my hair off my shoulders, out of where it was tucked beneath my hood, and letting it float around my head like a halo. I had to stifle a laugh as the wisps tickled my cheeks, knowing she was with me. Even as a slow tear slid down my face, my hair continued to swirl, the wind continued to sing its song, and the stillness of the morning now buzzed with unmistakable energy.

"Hi, Granny," I whispered, smiling at the bird that fluttered across my path. It had no business being in London in the winter, but I had a feeling I knew why it was here. "Please forgive me for doing this spell. I have to turn Vera back into a person, and of course you're the only one I want to commune with. And I'm sure you know by now that Vera's a cat, since you could always sense when I was in trouble even if you couldn't see me, and now I feel like you can see me all the time, so I'm sure none of this is a shock to you."

The bird came back and landed on a low branch right above my head, quieting its wings and looking down at me. I knew I was rambling, but I also knew she didn't mind. She was always the best listener. The kind that never made you feel like you had to say anything at all.

"Anyway, I've messed up. And I don't just mean turning Vera into a cat. I've messed up in a lot of ways." The sunrise bled across the horizon, and I listened to the bird flap its wings once more. Even if I wasn't talking to Granny, sitting on that hill still would have felt like I was hardly on earth at all.

"I haven't been giving my magic the attention it deserves," I confessed. "And I'm sorry about that. I'm sure you're disappointed. I am, too. I've been making excuses, letting acting distract me, prioritizing that part of myself because I was ashamed of this one. Not ashamed of being a witch, but ashamed I was never as good at it as you and Mom and Ivy. But since I've been on this quest, testing the limits of my powers and pushing myself, I've realized I could have been doing this all along. Hell, had I not hidden from it my whole life, it probably wouldn't have ended up always causing such a scene."

Slowly, so slowly I thought I might have been imagining it, snow began to fall. Soft, gentle flakes I couldn't even feel with my palms turned toward the sky. But I could see them, white and puffy and impossibly delicate, floating to the ground.

"I know now that it needs nurturing. It needs practice and care and trust and a million other important things I haven't been giving it because I've been afraid. I shouldn't have let it be on the back burner. But you should know I don't plan to do that anymore. I'm going to honor our family and do the right thing and stop complaining that Ivy is better than I am at everything."

The bird made a soft sound, which I hoped was a laugh.

"And I messed up with Oliver," I said, almost more to myself than to Granny Annie. When I didn't say anything else for a while, the snow began to fall harder. Fat flakes collecting in my hair, on my eyelashes, the toes of my boots.

Even though I hadn't lived here long, I knew it almost never snowed in London.

"I assumed it wouldn't work out because nothing ever works out, but I didn't even give it a chance. I told lies to protect myself. I held him at arm's length and still somehow had him right in the cross fire. And now I'm the face of a cheating scandal for a relationship I was never even a part of." A sharp wind whipped my hair across my face, stinging my eyes. "Okay, okay, you're right. It isn't the rumors I'm upset about. I know better than that. It's that I used them to drive a wedge between us. And for what? So no one would get hurt?" The wind softened, and my hair settled. "So much for that idea."

I closed my eyes and held my face to the sky, letting the snowflakes mingle with the tears on my cheeks. Granny always said if you were going to cry, it was best to do it outside. There was little that fresh air and Mother Nature couldn't heal.

"It doesn't make sense, Granny," I continued. "I hope this isn't awkward to tell you, because if you actually do know everything, then I guess you already know, but we slept together, and nothing malfunctioned. I mean *nothing*. Well, other than whatever we'd been dancing around for the past five months. But nothing exploded or caught on fire or anything. How do you explain that? Every other time I've even gotten close to someone, Oliver included, something has gone awry. And now, after we'd gotten as close as we possibly could have, nothing. I don't know what to make of that. I've turned it over in my mind a thousand times, and I'm at a loss."

The wind whistled another tune through the trees, but I wasn't sure what to make of that, either. So I kept talking, wondering if it would make sense the more I spoke it into existence.

"And if nothing catastrophic happened that once, does it mean we might be so lucky again? Or does it mean the next time catastrophe might hit twice as hard?"

Silence. *Come on, Granny. I can't figure this part out on my own.*

"I know you'd say it was worth the risk, but if it hurts this badly now, how badly is it going to hurt if we try and fail again? And does it even matter? The solstice is only three weeks away, which means all I have left to do is convince a skeptic of the existence of magic and then I can perform the spell. And the only skeptic I know at the moment is Oliver, and I think I'd be hard-pressed to convince him to do anything. Especially believe in magic. So I'm not sure where to go from here on that front, either."

The bird made another sound, and I opened my eyes to find it looking right back at me.

"I know I just said I was working on honing my magic, but this feels beyond a spell or a manifestation or a little moon water. But I can't have come this far for nothing."

I let my head fall back against the trunk, reeling from the physical pain radiating from my chest at how much I missed her. How much I could feel her with me now. How much I would have given anything to hear her voice.

Had it really been five months since I last listened to that voicemail? Since I last heard her husky laugh, her familiar timbre telling me—

I am the magic.

It didn't have to be a spell or a manifestation or a little moon water. She'd been telling me this all my life, and most of the time I'd been too stubborn to listen. The same way I hadn't even remembered she'd told me to find Coven & Codex until I went back and listened to the voicemail again.

I am the magic.

"You're not saying I can change his mind without a spell, are you?" The bird fluttered out of the tree and landed right in front of me, stern eyes and tight wings. "Surely that's a little conceited, even for us James women." This time, the bird didn't laugh. It only took a step closer.

"What if the magic is gone?" I asked, so quietly I could hardly even hear myself. Afraid to say the words loud enough that the universe might hear them. "What if I burned right through every ounce of magic we had together?"

There was the wind again. Cold, biting.

"Okay, I get it," I said, laughing through my tears. "You never know until you try, right?" She'd always said that when we were nervous to try spells as kids, and she was always right. Even when we failed, we didn't know until we tried.

It had been so long since I'd felt anything so deeply, and I let the waves of emotion roll over me, squeezing my chest and tingling my toes and reminding me I was alive and I had a big heart and that feeling and loving and trying were what the whole thing was all about.

"Thank you, Granny," I said. "For everything."

The bird flapped its wings hard, signaling an imminent takeoff, and I knew it was Granny telling me not to bother. She already knew.

"I love you," I whispered. "A bushel and a peck."

Even though she wasn't there to finish, to whisper back, "And a hug around the neck," I felt it all the time. Felt it in the sunrise and the snow and the warmth in my heart.

"And before I'm done communing with the dead," I said as I got to my feet, wondering if any other spirits could hear me, "if you're out there, Granduncle Arthur, might I just say leaving Coven and Codex to Oliver was the best decision you could have made. Thank you for all you've done for me and my family and for Oliver. I'll try my best to make it worth it."

I. Forage for *Clinopodium menthifolium*, grown locally. Prepare and consume locally in accordance with your preferences. ✔

II. Conduct an Orientation spell with the Wharram Percy Pendulum. Use its direction as a guide. ✔

III. Complete the Ritualistic Restoration Cleansing in a pond, lake, or slow-moving river to prepare the body for the Reversal. ✔

IV. Participate in a Full Moon Ceremony. Stay awake until the following sundown for maximum effect. ✔

V. Commune with those who have passed on. They know more than any of us who remain in our mortal forms on Earth. ✔

VI. Convince a skeptic of the existence of magic. Use the experience to fortify your powers to effectively produce the Reversal.

CHAPTER 32

Oliver

You still haven't heard from her?" Lola asked, swiveling in my office chair and sipping a latte like we were in my living room and not at work.

"Don't you think I'd have told you if I'd heard from her?" I said. I knew she was also upset Willow had shut us out of the quest, but I didn't have the energy to manage anyone else's emotions around that. I was frustrated and confused enough on my own.

But Lola had brought me lunch, so I couldn't kick her out just yet.

"Do women usually throw you out right after a shag?" she asked.

"For the millionth time, Lo, you know that's not what this was."

"Aye, sorry, I was only joking." She held her hands up in surrender, and only then did I realize I'd snapped.

I scrubbed my hands over my face and through my hair, trying to regain my composure. I'd been such a wreck the past few days, just holed up in the shop with my phone in my flat so I wouldn't be tempted to check it. I was really leaning into the whole grumpy bookshop owner vibe, only I wasn't sure if it was bringing in business or turning it away.

"I'm sorry." I sighed, collapsing into a chair across from her. Wesley had everything under control out front, and it would probably do me some good to take a break to eat. Lola slid a chicken shawarma wrap across my desk in my direction, watching as I peeled back the paper and took a bite. "This is delicious," I said with my mouth full, even though I knew it would drive her crazy.

"Figured I owed it to ya," she said. "Remember when Anika dumped me and you brought me wonton soup?"

"Willow didn't dump me," I said, going in for another bite. I hadn't realized I was starving.

"Then why have you been acting like you've been dumped?"

"I haven't."

"Ol."

"What?"

"You've been sulking around for a week. Min told me you haven't been running, and the shop has never looked so clean. Did you dust the vents?" She squinted at the ceiling to make a point, and I rolled my eyes. "And you skipped pub quiz. On horror film night."

"I had a headache," I said, knowing neither of us believed my lame excuse. If either of them complained of a headache and tried to get out of pub quiz on horror film night, I'd have told them to pop a few paracetamol and get their arse on the Tube.

"It's okay to be upset about this, you know," she said, unwrapping her own sandwich and giving me a break from the eye contact. "I'm upset about this. So is Min. We all got attached to her, and it sucks when you get attached to people and they leave. Why is it such a big deal to admit that?"

"It isn't a big deal," I argued. "I just don't think there's much to say. I should have known better than to get attached in the first place, so really I had only myself to blame. And I'm sorry you and Min got dragged into this mess."

"Are you kidding? This is the most exciting thing we've done all year."

"Didn't you guys go to Glastonbury?"

"Exactly."

"Well, in that case, I'm sorry it ended this way."

"How do we know it's over?"

"Apart from her telling me she had to finish the quest on her own? Because that felt pretty obvious to me."

"You're such a pessimist," she said.

"Weren't you just telling me it was okay to be upset?"

"Upset, yes, but not negative. Isn't the last thing she has to do convince a skeptic?"

"Yes, and?"

"*And* last I checked, you're pretty damn skeptical."

"Lo, if you're implying she's coming back into our lives to try to convince me magic is real, you've officially lost the plot. And besides, even if she did, I can't say she'd have much luck."

"You're exhausting," she said, dropping her fork directly into the hummus. "You work in a bloody magic bookshop, Oliver. Wouldn't it be so much easier to just embrace it?"

"I'm not having a hard time, last I checked," I said. "It's not like I'm resisting it. I'm just being practical. There's a scientific explanation for everything, even the anomalies. People don't actually have powers. It's all confirmation bias."

"If you're going to try to win Willow back, you better not let her hear you saying that."

"I'm not trying to win her back." Right?

"Well, you should be," Lola said, dragging a piece of pita through the baba ghanoush. I held my breath, watching her bring it to her mouth and praying she didn't drop any on my desk. "Because if you've been this much of an arse about the magic the whole time and she *still* shagged you, you've got a good thing going."

"Lola—"

"I know, I know. I'm taking the piss. But I do mean you should try to win her back. She was obviously into you, Ol, and I haven't seen you that into anyone since—"

"I know."

"I'm only giving you a hard time because I want you to be happy. And I don't think your differences in beliefs should be a dealbreaker. Though I do think you should keep more of an open mind. Magic doesn't have to just look like waving a wand and saying a magic word and turning a princess into a frog, you know."

I didn't want her to be right. Everything would have been so much easier if she wasn't right.

And she usually wasn't. Her advice was usually chaotic at best, destructive at worst, and she'd be the first to admit it. But this wasn't one of those times.

I knew "magic" wasn't waving a wand and saying a magic word. I was a cynic, not an idiot. And if I'd learned anything from Willow and from my years in the shop, it was that there were a million types of "magic" and a million types of "witches."

I knew there was always logical reasoning, and I chose to see that.

And I'd been comfortable with that. Until now.

Not once in thirty-two years had I asked myself what would happen if I made another choice. Why I was so attached to logic in the first place and what would happen if I abandoned it.

"You don't think it's too late?" I asked Lola. It probably was, in which case I wouldn't actually need to entertain the idea after all.

"You're bloody Oliver Hadley!" she said, slamming the desk with the palm of her hand.

"I have no idea what that means."

"It's never too late. You know better than that."

"Do I?"

"Unless you're not the man I thought you were."

"And what man is that?"

"The kind of man who knows what he wants," she said. "Ever since I met you, you've always been particular. In a charming way, if a little weird." She popped a French fry into her mouth, and I waited with raised eyebrows.

"Thank you?"

"You've never been indecisive, or insecure, or doubtful." Now she was chewing with her mouth full, waving fries around as she spoke. "And for someone so obsessed with logic—"

"I'm not *obsessed*."

"—you'd think you'd have realized by now that it's a perfectly viable outcome she's more than likely to give you a second chance."

"You've been spending too much time with Min."

She rolled her eyes. Brushed salt off her hands onto my desk chair. "Because you've been sulking," she said. "And I'd like for everything to get back to normal. Willow included."

"I thought this was about my happiness," I said. "You've a selfish hidden agenda now, do you?"

"Two things can be true," she said with a smile. "Come on, Ol. Are you really going to let the last few months go to waste because of some stupid celebrity gossip?"

"Need I remind you it was her idea to end things because of the celebrity gossip?"

"You said yourself it didn't seem like she wanted to." That much *was* true. She hadn't even bothered to hide it.

She was an actor. She could have faked it if she wanted to. Pretended she believed it was the right thing to do and left it at that.

But she didn't. She let me see how much it hurt her to break things off right when they were getting good. How much it hurt her to go it alone when she'd gotten so comfortable in our little world.

"You don't have to say I'm right out loud if that makes you feel any better," Lola said.

"Cheeky sod."

"Guilty."

"Thanks, Lo," I said. "For the sandwich, I mean."

"Ha. Ha."

"I never should have underestimated the power of a good Lola Martinez pep talk."

"That's Dr. Martinez to you."

"It most certainly is not."

"Piss off, then." She laughed, finally getting up from my desk chair but leaving her mess behind. She stopped beside my chair to rest her hand on my shoulder, and I leaned my head on her wrist. "Remember, nothing changes if nothing changes. If you want her, you've got to go get her. Maybe it can be your turn to teach *her* a thing or two about magic."

✧

If Min and I pointed out every time Lola was insane, we'd have done nothing but point out that Lola was insane. Which was why it was so hard for me to get my head around the fact that this time, she was actually making sense.

Or we were *both* insane. Which was probably more likely.

I spent the days following our lunch lost in thought instead of lost in misery, and it was a nice change of pace, though my customers probably couldn't tell the difference. To them, I was still quiet, still pensive, still more engrossed in inventory and organization and responding to the emails I'd let pile up than I was in helping them figure out how to cook their food faster or grow their plants taller or start a fire with a snap of their fingers or whatever nonsense they were attempting.

The days were long and slow, but I liked them that way. It gave me the opportunity to really think about what I wanted. To look at the shop with a new perspective, to try to understand why I was so attached to logic, to make sense of what was next.

And most of my questions had the same answer: Willow James.

Save the logic, obviously.

But above all else, she was what I wanted. And she was what came next. Whether that was with happiness or heartbreak remained to be seen, but I owed it to us both (and Lola, unfortunately) to try.

Admitting I wanted Willow, however, was the easy part.

It was understanding my resistance to magic—challenging it, even—that kept me up at night. And in a fog during the day. And in a state of quiet chaos and painful existentialism every minute in between. The cliché of grumpy bookshop owner opened its arms even wider, and I walked right into them.

So, I did exactly what I would have been expected to do, given the persona and that, and I poured a few fingers of whiskey, then a few more, then settled in an armchair in front of my fireplace, where I planned to sit for the rest of the night until I figured out a plan.

It wasn't fair to Willow for me to go chasing after her while still being so cynical about such a huge part of her identity, so I needed to sort that out before I did anything else. And I needed to figure out what the hell was going on with that Kip Whatever, but I needed to focus on one thing at a time.

The fire roared in front of me, the only light and sound in my tiny flat. I never felt like it was particularly safe to have an active wood-burning fireplace in a flat, but Uncle Arthur seemed to use it for his whole life and he didn't burn the place down, so I figured I could indulge. With my heels on the bridge edge, I let the flames warm my feet and the whiskey warm the rest of me, savoring the bitterness of it on my tongue.

Trying not to remember the sweetness of Willow by comparison.

I'd gotten so lost in her that night, I wasn't sure I'd ever be able to find my way back out. Lost in her scent, in the feel of her skin, in the sound of my name in her mouth. Lost in the feeling of finally connecting with someone, wanting someone, feeling wanted in return. The thoughts alone were so intoxicating, I felt my stomach clench at the memory.

I was fucked.

So fucked, in fact, I found myself *wanting* to believe in magic. Wishing that disconnect didn't stand between us like a bloody monolith.

How did Uncle Arthur do it? And how did he do it while he was brothers with Grandad?

As whimsical as Uncle Arthur was, Grandad was the opposite. And my dad took after him. Stern, cold, formal. Everything someone who believed in magic was not. And I was told *their* dad was even worse. So for Uncle Arthur to believe even despite that, so much so that he opened the shop, was an act of immense bravery. More bravery than I had, that was for sure.

If only I'd asked him more questions when he was alive. If only

I had the courage to continue believing the way he had, instead of letting Grandad and Dad get under my skin. Letting them convince me I was "too old" or "too clever" to believe in magic. Then maybe I would have known what Uncle Arthur would have done.

Maybe I was the one who needed to commune with the dead.

Holy shit. I need to commune with the dead.

I shot back the rest of my whiskey in one burning gulp, then ran downstairs and into the shop to find Uncle Arthur's ledger. The ledger I'd completely forgotten about after I took over, stashed under the desk with his other personal effects that had been left behind, things I figured I'd pass along to another family member at some point. The ledger that was more like a diary than any kind of business operation.

No matter how many nights I spent closing the shop alone, no matter how many times I left something down here and had to run back long after the city had gone to sleep, I'd never gotten used to how unsettling this place was in the dark. It wasn't that I minded, necessarily. Just that I'd noticed.

It was then the building really acted its age. The pipes whined, the lights flickered, the floorboards creaked as the place settled, dust drifted from books and shelves onto the floor even when I wasn't walking past. Uncle Arthur always said there was so much life within these walls, and times like these I knew exactly what he meant.

And for him, his *entire* life was within these walls. Coven & Codex was everything to him, and if I let myself dwell on how it wasn't everything to *me*, the guilt would eat me alive.

As a gay man during his time, he relied heavily on this community for acceptance and understanding, especially because he got neither from his family. So he made a family of his own. Back then, the customers weren't tourists or secondary school kids looking to get out of the house and cause trouble. They were real, proper believers. People who didn't judge or ask questions or exclude anyone because of their beliefs. They were people who wanted a world that was better than the one they were living in, so they took matters into their own hands.

Uncle Arthur would have been ashamed of me had he seen how far I'd drifted from those values. How much I'd fallen into my father's trap and left any shred of magic—sorcery or otherwise—behind.

I loved the shop. It was a part of me, and I couldn't imagine a life without it. But I didn't believe in the shop the way he had—didn't believe in anything the way he had, to be fair—and this might have been exactly the wake-up call I needed to change that.

The ledger was dusty from years of sitting beneath the till, and I brushed the cover clean to discover Uncle Arthur's initials engraved in the corner. Class.

I cracked it open, smoothing my hands over the worn pages covered in his chicken scratch. It always was the creative types who had the worst penmanship, wasn't it?

My eyes skimmed the contents of the first few pages, which appeared to be the only part of the ledger in which he actually attempted to log anything remotely related to the business. By the looks of it, this was where he kept track of the unique volumes he was searching for and where he found them. There were contacts for people I assumed to be other sellers in the industry, illegible titles with strikethroughs and stamps that read "out of print."

The more pages I turned, the more it dissolved into mayhem. Phone numbers scribbled in corners with notes like *La Douce, Friday 11p*. A smudge of lipstick, cigarette ashes, pressed flowers, and gin labels. Like the ledger somehow became at once a business log and a living scrapbook. It made me wonder about the people who'd been inside these walls. Whether they all believed in magic or just simply believed in the community.

Though for Uncle Arthur, it wouldn't have mattered. Believing in anything would have been enough.

I poured another whiskey from my secret stash beneath the counter and slowed down, taking the time to try to decipher his scribbling. To find something that might make sense to me. Might make sense of my circumstances. Of what I wanted. Of what I didn't want to want.

The notes that weren't in his handwriting were even harder to read, but they felt important. Notes from the others who came and went through the shop. Honestly, I hadn't seen the shop mean that much to anyone in a long time. Until Willow, anyway.

Most of his notes were plans, and the subsequent notes about the plans. Like: *Soho tonite. Meeting S for late dinner.*

And then three days later: *S still here. No signs of leaving. Not asking, either. Chuffed for the company.*

Or: *Reading at National Gallery with P.*

Update: Reading was mediocre. P was delightful.

Or: *Tarot at Jo's.*

Don't remember the cards, but her partner makes a lovely spritz. Must ask for recipe. Or invite myself back for another one of hers.

The more I skimmed, the more I found his entries were more about people than magic or the city, every time. And no one loved magic or London more than Uncle Arthur. But still, he seemed to love the people more.

Somewhere in the summer of 1960, an inky scribble caught my eye. I hadn't known what I was looking for, but that changed the moment I found it.

Met quite a fine American today. Anise. Lovely thing. Single mum. Hope she will return.

I scanned the next few pages, suddenly desperate for more information. That couldn't have been Willow's gran, could it? Surely there were plenty of single American mums visiting the shop. With plant names.

It seemed weeks went by without another mention, and just when I started to get discouraged, I found her again.

Anise is back. I've invited her for tea.

I turned page after page, following their story like a gripping thriller.

Reminder: find the collector's edition of Healing and Hygge. *Surprise her with it when she comes back.*

A curious woman. Wee bit odd. Asks many questions. Cupboards open and close of their own volition when she's near.

Curtains caught fire above the radiator today when she was in the back room chatting to a bloke. I suspect she was the culprit.

Wants Volume II. Call Fergus.

Back for tea. This time with her daughter. Another lovely thing.

Wants to introduce me to a friend in America. I've no desire to go to America.

Came with me to Jo's for a dinner party. Seemed to have turned the punch to gelatin at the exact moment I heard her turning down a date with a handsome fella because she was meant to go back to America. Like I said: a bit odd.

Plans to return home. I do suspect she'll take the magic with her. Good for the linens, bad for the soul.

Maybe her daughter will return on her own once she's grown. If I'm here, I'll welcome her for tea. Perhaps she, too, will be magic.

I closed the ledger, afraid what might happen to the pounding in my chest if I continued. It had to have been Willow's gran. There wasn't a doubt in my mind.

And while I didn't think Uncle Arthur ever did meet Willow's mum again, I had the sense I'd finally have the chance to make him proud. To do something we both wanted. He might not have been here, but the least I could do was invite the granddaughter for tea on his behalf.

Because the granddaughter was more magic than the whole lot put together.

And if Anise's magic had misfired because she *rejected* a man's advances, I had a feeling I knew exactly what had happened with me and Willow the night of the full moon festival.

CHAPTER 33
Willow

Oliver Hadley: fancy a tea?

After weeks apart, all I could do was stare at the text like it might spontaneously combust. We hadn't spoken since the night of the full moon festival, and I couldn't tell if these three words were a threat or an olive branch.

Did I fancy a tea?

I supposed the question was more like, *could* I fancy a tea? Of course I *did*. I wanted nothing more than to pretend the last few weeks never happened, to slip back into the life I'd only been trying on for size, to make it real and tangible and mine, even if it was only temporary.

But I knew it wasn't fair, to either of us, so the right thing to do would have been to politely decline, produce the spell, leave London altogether, and disappear back into the depths of Hollywood.

But if I was good at doing the right thing, I probably wouldn't have been in this mess to begin with, so . . . I entertained the idea of fancying a tea. I did have to convince a skeptic, after all, and while I wasn't sure Oliver Hadley could be convinced of a damn thing, he *was* the only skeptic I knew, so it was worth a shot.

The clock was ticking, and if I didn't convince someone magic was real before the solstice tomorrow . . . I shuddered at the thought.

Fortunately, since I hadn't left the flat much, the paparazzi didn't have a whole lot to report on. They continued circulating the photos from that night, along with the story about Kit, both of which Vera was working as hard as she possibly could (considering she didn't have thumbs) to get taken down. She kept telling me to stay focused on the spell and she'd stay focused on the media, which made sense, all things considered, but I wasn't happy about it.

Even less happy when I told her Oliver texted me and she told me we needed to talk.

"What's going on?" I asked, gently lowering myself onto a barstool next to where she sat on the counter.

"I have to tell you something, but I don't want you to freak out."

"You know I'm already freaking out, right?"

"Then I might as well rip off the Band-Aid." She sighed. "I was the one who told the media about Kit."

"You . . . what?" I'd heard her perfectly fine, but I needed to hear her again to understand. And maybe even again after that.

"It was right when we got here," she said. "And we decided we were going to pretend you were seeing him so you wouldn't have to worry about Oliver and you could focus on the spell and—"

"And you deliberately put me in the center of a scandal?" I asked. "Isn't your job to do the opposite?"

"I had no idea it was going to become a scandal," she said. "Thought it was just a bit of celebrity gossip. I even left the tip anonymously so no one thought it came from a member of your team. And no one had done much of anything with the information at first, anyway, so I didn't think it was a big deal. It only became a big deal when they tracked you down and saw you with Oliver. Which I had nothing to do with, I promise. I'd never compromise your safety. I just figured it might help you stick to the story and maybe even interest you in—"

"This was all a scheme?" I stood up from the stool, needing distance between us. Needing something to do with my body. "Be honest, V. Was it to protect me or Oliver at all, or was it just to get me to agree to your stupid romance idea? To play into the rumors and get a movie out of it? Have you forgotten this is the exact argument that landed us here in the first place?"

"It was wrong," she said. "I made the wrong call. I know that. And I'm sorry, Willow."

I was silent. I wanted those words to settle. I wanted to feel them. I wanted *her* to feel them.

"I should have gone back on the story once I realized you and Oliver were getting more serious. But I thought you were being careful, so I didn't expect any of *this*."

"Are you blaming me?"

"Of course not," she said. "The rumor was my fault in the first place. But you did let your guard down, Willow, which I thought we were going to avoid."

"God forbid I try to have a normal-person moment for one second."

"That's the thing," she said. "You aren't a normal person. So if you want to be kissing in the woods, you have to expect the worst."

"Then maybe I want to actually *be* a normal person," I said, without having realized I even had that thought until the words were out of my mouth. It felt like a line. Very *It's not my dream, Dad. It's yours.* But the more it hung in the air between us, the truer it felt.

I didn't want to always expect the worst. What kind of life was that?

And it wasn't that I wasn't grateful for my career. I knew how lucky I was to have had the opportunities I'd had, to be in a position where I could choose to take a step back if I wanted to. That wasn't lost on me.

It was just that I was missing out on everything *else*. The lazy days, long walks, pub quizzes, day trips, sitting around a friend's flat with nowhere to go and no one to see. Kissing a damn boy and not having it plastered all over the internet.

"You don't mean that," Vera said, widening her eyes when I didn't answer right away. "Do you?"

"I don't know. This was obviously the first time I've said it out loud, and it's a lot to think about. But I don't want to take it back, I know that much."

"All because of this guy? Willow—"

"Not because of this guy," I said, growing increasingly frustrated. "Because of my inability to even pursue anything with a guy without a camera in my face. Because of my inability to explore my magic or learn a damn thing about myself because I don't have a minute to breathe back home and this whole part of me has to stay a secret. I'm missing out on a social life *and* a personal life."

"Let's not get carried away, here. You have quite the social life."

"Not with anyone I care about," I countered. "It's just parties and galas and appearances and award shows and premieres and shit. When was the last time I just sat in a pub?"

"Do you even like pubs?"

"I love pubs! But I wouldn't have known that if I hadn't had the opportunity to go to one."

"I'm glad my misfortune is so convenient for you."

"You know that's not what I mean," I said. "I just mean the opportunity to not be Willow James for five minutes. To be far from home and to blend in and just exist in a city where I'm not filming or attending some event or getting ready to go to another city."

The more I talked about it, the more I gained momentum. The idea was slowly becoming less of an interest and more of a necessity. I couldn't keep doing what I was doing. I needed to start prioritizing myself and my magic, and that wasn't going to happen in Hollywood. Hell, I wasn't even sure that was going to happen in LA.

"So, what? You're just done acting? You don't have to do a romance, Willow, if that's what this is about."

"It's not about the romance. It's about *me*." Why was it so hard for everyone to see that? "Actors take breaks all the time. Would it really be such a big deal?"

"It would be if you wanted to get back into the industry after you were done being a 'normal person.'"

"What if I didn't?"

"Willow, be serious."

"I am being serious. Maybe I'd like being a normal person."

"And if you came to your senses and hated it?"

"That would be for me to figure out, wouldn't it?"

She stared at me, a piercing stare with her green marble eyes, and I stared back, unafraid of whatever she was about to say. It was becoming increasingly apparent a break was definitely in order, and in that case, I *did* fancy a tea.

What I did not fancy was arguing with Vera about my future. She might have known what was best for me as an actor, but that didn't mean she knew what was best for me as a person.

"I'm sorry," she said eventually, shaking her head like she was snapping herself out of whatever mood she was in. "I know I'm being hard on you. And I know that's something I have to work on. I've been thinking about that a lot over the last few months. All I've ever known is that life, and I'm projecting that onto you, aren't I?"

"I'm sure we're projecting onto each other." I sighed, sitting back down.

"Maybe a break for you is good. Maybe that'll mean a break for me, too."

"You won't pick up another client to replace me? I know people in the industry who would kill for you as a manager. I'm sure you could have someone new in a heartbeat."

"I don't doubt that," she said, and winked. It was unnerving on her cat face no matter how normal it would have been on her human face. "I haven't wanted to admit it, but this has been nice for me, too. Minus the cat thing, obviously. But the time off. It's not as boring as I thought it'd be. Turns out podcasts and audiobooks and walks around the neighborhood aren't such a bad way to pass the time. I'm sure I'll be bored to death before I know it, but for now, it hasn't been so miserable."

It was more of a relief than I could have anticipated to hear her say those words. And for her to sound like she actually meant them. Every moment of the last six months had been riddled with an undercurrent of guilt, and to hear Vera say she actually saw value in this experience made me feel slightly less awful for what had happened. Not a lot, but enough to release my shoulders from my ears for a few minutes.

"And I'm going to make it right with the press," she said. "I've emailed our lawyer to confirm he's gotten all major entertainment news outlets to scrub the photos and videos, and I've already spread the word about your relationship with Kit being nothing but a rumor. Seems to have done his career some good in the meantime, but without you even in the city, I doubt he'll be hanging on to that story."

"Thank you," I said. Mad as I was that she was the one to tip off the press in the first place, I was glad she was making it right.

"You're really going to walk away?"

"I'm not sure I have much of a choice," I said. "I need to put myself first. My magic, my personal life, everything I've been missing out on."

"And what about Oliver? What does this mean for you two?"

"I hope I'm about to find out."

✧

Oliver's flat door was unlocked when I arrived, and he'd instructed me to just let myself in. Lush kitchen smells wafted down the staircase, making me all the more eager to see what the night had in store.

I had no idea where any of this was going or what any of it meant, and even as I climbed the stairs, I still hadn't the slightest clue what to say. All I knew was I owed him an apology, and if there was even a chance he might believe magic was real, I needed to know. The solstice was tomorrow, and I was running out of time.

"Willow?" he called at the sound of my footsteps. "That you?"

"Who else would it be?" I asked. "Did you invite someone else for tea?"

"Thought Kit Hayes might like a cuppa." I froze halfway up the stairs, relieved when I heard the sound of his laugh. "Too soon?"

"Entirely."

When I made it up the stairs and rounded the corner into the kitchen, I froze for the second time. Oliver had a dish towel slung over his shoulder, one hand on his hip, and the other stirring a pot of what looked to be a curry on the stove. He wore a navy sweater and a pair of dark jeans, both of which made his eyes seem even clearer than usual when he turned to look at me. A dark curl hung in the center of his forehead, and I briefly forgot the reason I was here. Frankly, it would have been a miracle if I could have remembered my own name.

"Hi," I said, suddenly feeling painfully awkward and unsure of what to do with myself.

"Hi," he returned. "Please, come in. Make yourself comfortable." He brushed off his hands on the towel and pulled out a kitchen chair, gesturing for me to sit. I handed off the bottle of wine I'd brought—it felt weird showing up empty-handed, especially since I was beginning to learn *tea* actually meant dinner—and he accepted with a wary smile. We were both uncertain, but we were trying.

His flat was exactly what I'd have expected, had I allowed myself to daydream about it. Warm, cozy. Sophisticated. Dark wood furniture and a small selection of vintage-looking art. Books piled on every surface, windowsills included. Heavy throw blankets draped over the back of the couch, a tattered ottoman, a TV that looked like it was collecting dust. He mentioned he didn't spend much time here and that most of his time was spent in the shop, but aside from the television, it looked pleasantly lived-in. I wondered how much had been left over from his uncle Arthur.

"I hope vindaloo is okay," he said, returning his attention briefly to the stove. "I remembered a while ago you said you'd been eating a lot of Indian takeaway, so I figured I'd hedge my bets."

"You hedged right," I said. He turned down the heat and popped the cork on the wine, pouring us two generous glasses.

"It's a good job we've got something stronger than tea," he said. "Reckon we'll need it."

I hummed in agreement for lack of a better response, taking a long swig after hesitantly clinking our glasses together.

"I didn't know you could cook," I said eventually, enamored by the ease with which he moved around the kitchen.

"Every day's a school day," he said, and smiled. "There's a lot you don't know about me, Willow."

"Care to share with the class?"

"You still want to learn?" He raised a thick eyebrow, and I felt the pull of guilt in my stomach.

I sighed, taking another swig and trying to control my breathing. "I'm sorry," I said. "For how I treated you that night. For how I've treated you this whole time, honestly. The mixed signals, the meltdown over the paparazzi, kicking you out in the middle of the night. That wasn't fair, and I . . . I'm sorry."

It came out faster and more frantic than I'd intended, but it was out there, and that was what mattered. I watched as he took a deep, measured breath, dragged out another kitchen chair with his foot, and dropped down into it without breaking eye contact.

"Thank you," he said. "I'm sorry, too. For causing a scene. And for being judgmental about the magic. I was also unfair, and I apologize."

"Thanks," I echoed. Relieved as I was neither of us was holding a grudge, I couldn't ignore that something still felt vaguely sad about this conversation. Like it was a goodbye in addition to being an apology. Which, in a sense, I supposed it might have been.

We both knew the solstice was tomorrow, and if I was able to effectively reverse the spell, I'd have no real reason to stay in London. And besides, just because we had one night together where nothing went awry—magic-wise, anyway—it didn't mean we'd be so lucky again. I knew how much of a risk this was. What I didn't know was if it would be worth it.

Before either of us said another word, he reached out slowly, gently, and tucked a stray lock of hair behind my ear. "I know it might not have been the right thing to do," he whispered, "but I don't regret it for a second, Willow." He ran his thumb and index finger down my jaw, tilting my chin so I was looking directly at him.

We were quickly picking up where we left off, and I wasn't sure I could keep up.

It wasn't that I didn't want to. It was just that I came here to apologize, to see if he'd changed his tune on the magic. Not to fall back into bed, no matter how tempting it was.

And believe me, it was tempting. The warmth of his flat, the dish towel over his shoulder, his large, rough hand cupping my face. The ticking of his watch near my ear an ominous countdown. To the solstice or to our mutual destruction, I couldn't be sure.

"Oliver," I whispered, searching for the right words. Afraid to talk too loud and ruin the moment.

His kitchen was the eye of a hurricane. Outside this moment, there were 101 things for me to worry about. Vera. The spell. My career. Figuring out how to get back in touch with my magic. How to get back in touch with *myself*. And I knew none of that would be made easier by sleeping with Oliver again.

"We can't," I said, even quieter than before. I rested my hand on his wrist, planning to return it to his lap, but I couldn't bring myself to move. My protest lived only in those two words. The lights flickered, but neither of us blinked.

"Because of the press?" he asked. "Because last I checked, love, they aren't exactly in the flat with us."

I laughed, feeling my face heat like it always did when he called me "love." That accent would be the death of me.

"Because of *me*," I said. "I need to get my head on straight, and being with you does the opposite. I need to focus on my magic, figuring out what I want, finishing the spell, and then there's the fact that being with you makes my magic go haywire, and now is *not* the time for my magic to go haywire."

"Speaking of which"—he smiled, and I held my breath—"I think I might have some ideas why that's happening."

"You . . . what?" For the second time tonight, someone was saying words to me, in plain English, slowly and carefully, and I could not understand a word.

"I went through Uncle Arthur's ledger, which was really more of a diary, and I think I might know what's really happening with your magic."

If I thought my head was spinning before, it was nothing compared to now. He was thinking about my magic? He had *ideas* about my magic?

"Oliver, I'm going to need you to slow down," I said, trying to wrap my head around what was happening here. It felt huge. Monumental. And if I was going to remember it properly, I wanted to at the very least understand it. "Are you saying what I think you're saying?"

He nodded, slow and meaningful. "I am."

Two words that might very well have changed the course of my entire life.

"If you think you know what's going on with my magic, does that mean—"

"I believe in your magic, Willow." I couldn't speak. Couldn't do anything but stare back at him, lips parted, eyes wide, skin burning under his touch. "And I've been wrong this whole time to doubt it."

"What changed your mind?" I whispered.

"I just had to change my perception of magic in the first place," he said. "Uncle Arthur helped me with that. I had to realize it was a belief system just like any other, and I didn't need tangible proof for it to be true. And that really the magic is in people all along, I think."

"What do you mean?"

"What I mean," he said, leaning in so close I could feel his breath on my lips, "is that I've known magic is real since the first time I saw you."

CHAPTER 34

Oliver

Willow's kiss was unexpected, but it only took a fraction of a second for me to adjust. To wrap my arms around her, pull her into me, and kiss her in a way I hoped communicated everything I felt. *You've been the proof magic exists this entire time. I'm sorry I didn't recognize it sooner. Please don't leave.*

I pulled her up from her chair and walked her backward until we reached the wall, cushioning her head with my hand and nearly collapsing when she moaned gently into my mouth. Whatever reservations we had, whatever she believed her magic was going to do, whatever uncertain future lay ahead, none of it mattered.

All that mattered was right now. The feel of her body against mine, the night that stretched out ahead of us, the chance to show her how I felt. To find out if she'd been feeling the same.

We didn't need to finish our conversation. Maybe someday, but based on the way she kissed me, it seemed safe to assume the chaos of the full moon festival was water under the bridge. Right now, with her hands in my hair and her tongue in my mouth, she didn't appear worried about the spell at all. If she heard what I said—which it definitely seemed like she did—then she would know she'd completed the list. All she had left to do was the spell itself.

And since she couldn't do it until tomorrow, that meant there was nothing more to be done tonight. We could give ourselves over to *this* spell, the one we seemed to fall under every time we were together, and we could enjoy it. No strings, no stress. Just each other and quiet moans and candlelight.

I hiked her leg up over my hip the way I had in the woods, only this time there was no risk of paparazzi. Just the two of us and the divine privacy of my flat. She pulled me closer, and my head was spinning. Already lined up against her, I could hardly catch my breath, and we hadn't even made it out of the kitchen. Hadn't removed a stitch of clothing. *Bloody hell.*

She tugged at the bottom of my jumper, her fingers a cold shock against my skin. I released her leg only so my hands were free for her to pull it over my head, then quickly scooped her back into my arms, trying not to laugh at her gasp.

I planned to walk her down the hallway to the bedroom the same way I had in her flat, but with her arse in my hands and her lips on my neck, I couldn't bring myself to move. Instead, I lowered her right onto my kitchen table, relishing the way her eyes flew open in surprise before her gaze turned wicked.

She wanted this just as much as I did, and the bedroom just wasn't close enough. "Are you sure?" she asked as I laid her down, kissing a line over her jaw and down her throat.

"You've no idea," I mumbled into her skin, tasting every inch of what was exposed. It wasn't enough. I pushed her pullover off her shoulders, holding her by her lower back as she slid her arms out. "All of it," I said, running my hands over her ribs, bunching her T-shirt over my wrists until I could slide it over her head. "I want to see every inch of you."

She arched her back so I could unhook her bra, a black, lacy thing that cupped her so perfectly I was almost sad to see it go. Until her breasts were free and I forgot about her bra altogether.

Her curves haunted me. From the time I saw her in the shower, I was unable to forget the shape of her body. Her thick thighs, her soft stomach, her breasts that fit perfectly in my hands. The smattering of freckles over her collarbone. The dip of her waist. The taste of her.

With her jeans thrown over my shoulder, I was free to admire how she looked in nothing but a pair of panties, the same black lace as her bra, before I slid those off, too. Only instead of tossing them blindly over my shoulder with the rest of her clothes, I folded them neatly into my back pocket. Something that sexy shouldn't be thrown on the floor of my flat.

Before I could fully appreciate her nakedness on my kitchen table, she pulled me closer by my belt, undoing the buckle with deft fingers. "You're not the only one who wants to stare," she whispered, pushing my jeans and my briefs down my legs at the same time. I was already painfully hard, and it felt good to be free of any constraints.

"I don't think I could ever get enough of you," she said, taking her time dragging her eyes back up to my own. "I know this is only the second time we've done this, but—"

"I know," I said, leaning over her with one hand on either side of her body and kissing her hard. "I know."

And I did. This could have been the thousandth time we'd done this and it wouldn't have even been close to enough. I wanted every single piece of her. Every moan, every whisper, every inch of skin, every second of pleasure. I wanted to know exactly what brought her to the edge and what she liked when she was alone.

"Show me how you touch yourself," I whispered, realizing I had the chance to find out.

"Only if you promise to do the same," she said, already dropping her hand between her legs.

Saints alive. This woman was going to be the death of me.

I watched with heavy-lidded eyes that undoubtedly matched hers, glassy and wanting. She rubbed herself in slow circles, and I matched her pace, already eager for my hand to be replaced with hers.

"You drive me crazy," I said, trying like hell to keep my eyes open so I didn't miss a second of this. "I could come just watching you like this."

She increased her pressure and speed at the sound of my words, and if I continued to match her pace, I would be finished before we even started.

"Touch me," she said.

Who was I to disobey?

I closed the gap between us, running my fingers over the length of her and moaning in appreciation. I couldn't help it. She was so wet, I was desperate to be inside her, but I knew I had to be patient. I wanted to make this last as long as possible.

I slipped two fingers inside, kissing her throat when she dropped her head back on a sharp inhale. When I settled into a slow pattern, feeling her pulse around me, she grabbed my wrist and whispered "more" into my ear.

As soon as I added a third finger, she sank her teeth into my shoulder, grinding against me. I wrapped my arm around her lower back, pulling her closer, cupping her clit with the palm of my hand to give her more of what she was looking for. More friction. More pressure. More of us.

"Please," she breathed, ragged and shaky. She didn't have to say any more. I curled my fingers toward me, pressing against her walls in the rhythm of her hips, holding on to every ounce of restraint I had as she came apart around me.

"Take me to bed," she mumbled when she came back down to earth. "I want all of you."

✨

LYING ON MY bed, naked, with her auburn waves around her head in a halo, she was an angel. Otherworldly. I'd never before had a reason to use the word *ethereal*, but there was a first for everything, I supposed.

"Why are you looking at me like that?" she asked, sitting up on her elbows, giving me an even better view of her face.

"I've just discovered magic exists, Willow. Give me a minute."

Steadying my breathing was even harder when she was smiling at me. But this wasn't about me. This was about her. Pleasuring her. Worshipping her. Giving her everything she wanted.

"Come here," she whispered after a minute. "Let me feel you."

I rested my hands on either side of her head, inhaling through my teeth when she put her hands on my chest. Holding my breath when she slid them down my stomach and wrapped them around me.

"Sit back," she said, and I nearly turned to dust just at the thought of where this was going. I leaned back on my hands, watching intently as she took me in her mouth.

"Fuck, Willow."

She hummed around me, getting into a rhythm that already had me dangerously close to the edge. I wrapped my left hand around her hair, holding it off her face and winding it around my wrist. She whimpered, and I had to pull her away before it was too late.

"I need to be inside of you," I said. "I need to be in control."

"I'm all yours," she said. How I wished that were true.

I flipped her over onto her hands and knees, pressing a line of kisses down her spine as I rolled on a condom, then worked her with my fingers. She was nearly dripping by the time I pushed into her, both of us letting out a groan that was entirely unholy.

"God," she exhaled. "Oliver."

I let my hands roam over her breasts, the curve of her waist, her arse as it pushed back against me. She felt so good, I was seeing stars. I reached around to feel the soft skin of her stomach, holding her tighter against me when she sat up and dropped her head to my shoulder.

When she reached back and wrapped her hand around my neck, lacing her fingers tightly through my hair, I lowered my hand to touch her, whispering praise into her ear over the sound of her moans.

She fit perfectly against me, and as we moved in a steady rhythm, her nails on my scalp, my fingers against her clit, my cock inside her, I nearly went blind.

"Oliver, I'm going to—"

She didn't even finish the sentence before her words turned to screams, dragging me into her orbit. I was only a second behind, one arm tightly around her, the other hand still against her clit, letting her pleasure drive mine. It was the hardest I've ever come in my entire life. And I already wanted to do it again.

When we finally collapsed side by side on the bed, the duvet twisted in a heap at the bottom, I watched the rise and fall of her chest as her breathing returned to normal, wondering when mine would do the same.

I had an arm draped over her stomach, partly because I couldn't resist touching her and partly because my limbs were all too heavy to move.

She rolled over under the weight of it, pinning me with her golden-brown eyes. "You're going to have to let me go eventually," she said, and laughed.

The problem was, I didn't think I could.

CHAPTER 35
Willow

The sun slanted through Oliver's curtains, throwing a bar of light across his bare chest and casting the rest of him in shadow. He looked like a sculpture. An ancient god.

"I can feel you staring," he said, a slow smile spreading across his face before he even opened his eyes.

"Could do it all day," I said. At this point, there was no use in being anything but honest.

"Then it's a good job it's the longest day of the year."

Holy shit. It was morning. Which meant it was the solstice.

I was out of bed and throwing my clothes on before I could even get my head on straight, crashing into the dresser as I shoved my legs into my jeans. No panties. Those were long gone. All day I'd feel the reminder of the night before in more ways than one.

But I needed to focus.

Everything I'd done in the past six months led up to this day, and I couldn't afford to lose it to a daydream.

"Slow down," Oliver said, sitting up and pushing his hair from his eyes. I couldn't look at him. Couldn't risk a second of distraction. Couldn't risk my magic failing me today. "Willow, hey."

He reached out and grabbed my wrist, spinning me to face him. "You're okay. You know what you're doing. You've prepared for this, you've done everything you needed to do. You're ready."

"Have I?" I asked. We both knew what I was really asking. *Did you mean what you said last night? Have I* actually *convinced a skeptic magic is real? Have I proven myself?*

"Sit down," he said.

"I don't have time."

"Please." His eyes were so soft, I had no choice but to listen. I sat, letting him hold my hands in his lap. "I meant what I said last night. Every word."

"You just changed your mind about magic? Real magic? After all this time?"

"I was looking at it all wrong." He shook his head, like he was ashamed of himself. "I wasn't open-minded, and it took a little communing with the dead of my own to see that. But I need you to know I get it now. And most importantly, I believe in you."

He was so straightforward, it was hard to believe any of this was real.

"Why are you looking at me like you don't believe me?" he asked.

"Because it seems too good to be true," I said. "You just . . . changed your mind."

"*You* changed my mind."

I couldn't do this now. My mind was becoming cloudier by the minute, and I needed as clear a head as possible for the spell. Today wasn't about me. Or Oliver. It was about Vera. And the more he talked, the more I could feel myself teetering on the edge of a very dangerous cliff. If he believed in me, if he knew magic was real, and that was no longer standing as a barrier between us . . . did that mean a future could actually be possible?

I knew better than to get my hopes up, and I had to remind myself to stay grounded like a mantra. I couldn't stay here. I had to get home to Vera before my magic spiraled completely out of control.

"I have to go," I said.

"Willow, come on."

"I'm not saying we aren't going to talk about this. I'm just saying we aren't going to talk about this right now." That familiar, foreboding tingling returned to my toes, and I knew exactly what happened next. Some catastrophic reminder of why I couldn't have this, couldn't make this work, and I didn't have time for that today.

"I'll come with you," he said, throwing off the covers and pulling on a nearby shirt. "For support."

"I have to do this on my own," I said, grateful we were no longer looking at each other. It was all too much, and I couldn't bear to add his disappointment to the lump of emotions stuck in my throat.

This moment felt dangerously close to the moment I kicked him out of my flat, the moment we said painful goodbyes after an otherwise perfect night together, and I had no interest in reliving it. But if I prolonged this at all, let my emotions get in the way and let my feelings for him bubble to the surface, I didn't stand a chance of completing the spell.

"I'm sorry," I said, turning to look at him only when I had my hand on the doorknob. Hating that this was the second time we were ending a night this way.

"I don't want to keep doing this, Willow."

"I know," I said, feeling a shock through my fingers as I pulled open the door. "Neither do I."

"So let's stop."

I leaned my forehead against the door, trying and failing to figure out what to say to make this better.

"You know what, you're right," he said suddenly. "This isn't a conversation for right now. But will you promise me it *is* a conversation? I can't have you walk out of this flat and never see you again, Willow. I can't have you complete this spell and disappear back to LA like this never happened. And I don't think you can, either."

He had no idea.

"It *is* a conversation," I conceded, feeling the tingling subside just enough for me to actually get a grip on the doorknob. "Just, please, I have to—"

"Go," he said. "I'm rooting for you, Willow. I know you can do this."

That made one of us.

I thanked him and ran down the stairs before I could fall into his arms and beg him to come with me. If the magic was going to work, I needed to be as far from Oliver as possible.

"Vera?" I called as I threw our front door open, looking frantically around the flat. "Vera? I'm sorry I was out all night and I'm late now but it's finally the solstice and—"

"It's time?"

"It's time," I confirmed, balling my hands into fists so she couldn't see them shaking. I should have known that with those marble eyes of hers, she saw everything.

"Relax, Willow," she said, jumping off the counter to sit at my feet. "I can't have you freaking out about this."

She was right. I put her in this position in the first place, and it was my responsibility to get her out. That meant I didn't get to panic, didn't get to freak out. Didn't get to fail.

It was now or never.

Well, now or next year, but we'd both really like it to be now.

"I'm assuming you were out last night convincing a skeptic?" she asked, raising a delicate brow.

I nodded. "It's all taken care of." She deserved to know I was ready to do the spell, but I was far from ready to disclose anything else.

"Why are you saying it like you're Tony Soprano?"

"Because I don't want to talk about it," I said. "If I talk about it, the magic will go to shit. Do you want the magic to go to shit?"

She put a paw over her mouth, and I thanked her.

"So it's time, then," I said again, unsure how to begin.

"Indeed it is."

"Do we just . . . do it right here in the living room?" I asked, suddenly realizing I had no real idea how the spell was actually going to go.

"You're the witch," Vera said. "Does feel like as good a spot as any, though, doesn't it? If you did it the first time in a trailer, the living room is probably fine."

"You're right," I said, shaking out my shoulders and trying to rack my brain for whatever else I might have been overlooking. "Are you going to be naked when you turn back into a person?" I asked. "Do you want me to, uh, have some clothes ready?"

"They disappeared when I turned into a cat, didn't they? So I'm hoping they'll reappear when I turn back? Might be a touch overdressed for the living room, but that never hurt anyone."

"What if they don't?"

"Willow, stop stalling. You have to trust yourself," she said, undoubtedly sensing my mood. She was an excellent mind reader. Or we just spent entirely too much time together in high-pressure situations. Hard to say. "This is no different than the first shot of a film or the first few steps onto a red carpet. You're putting yourself out there, putting your work on display, putting yourself in a situation that you *could* fail, and trusting that you won't. You need to get into that mindset. This is your art just as much as acting. You have to take the leap."

"You're good. You should go into management or something."

"Willow, I swear—"

"I know, I know," I said, feeling my shoulders come down from my ears as her words settled in. She always knew exactly how to talk me down.

"You're prepared for this. More prepared than I've ever seen you be for anything, quite frankly." *Fair point.* "But it's all going to go to waste if you can't pony up and get it done. So hop to it. I'd like to be back in my human form before the Golden Globes, if you don't mind."

"Right," I said. "Okay, I guess there's no time like the present. Are you ready?"

"Been ready for six months."

"Right," I said again. There was nothing left to say except the spell. So I dug deep, and I did what I had to do.

In the past six months, I'd done everything on the list and more. I'd tested the boundaries of my magic, I'd cleansed, I'd talked to Granny Annie, I'd proved the existence of magic, for god's sake. Well, in one way or another. But I hardly thought it mattered now. What mattered was that Vera was right. I *was* ready. The only thing left to do was let it rip.

I took a deep breath and said the chant as loud and proud as I could.

Time turner, turn back time.
Reverse this spell that was not mine.
Undo the damage
I have done
And take us back to square one.

And nothing happened. A light fixture swayed, a strong gust of wind rattled the windows, and Vera remained a cat.

"Are you sure you did it right?" she asked.

"How would I know? I don't even know how I did it in the first place!"

"Take a deep breath," she said, "then try again. Maybe you just need to warm up."

I did as I was told, trying desperately not to let my emotions into the driver's seat. After a long inhale and a slow, steadying exhale, I said the chant again.

I focused on every word.

I didn't let myself think about Oliver. About his definition of magic. About how he was the last piece of the spell.

And still . . . nothing happened.

"Okay, let's not panic," Vera said, watching as I panicked. I was pacing the floor with both hands in my hair, mumbling the spell to myself and trying to figure out where I was going wrong. Trying to keep the tears at bay.

"I've done everything I was supposed to do," I said, hearing my voice crack but unable to get it back under control. "I found the leaves and drank the gross tea, I used the damn pendulum, I nearly died in the freezing pond, I stayed up for two days, I talked to Granny, I proved magic exists to someone who didn't believe in it—what more could I have done? I mean, seriously. What else is there?" I was becoming more unhinged with every word that came out of my mouth, but I didn't care. I needed to know what I was missing. "Of all times for my magic not to work, why now? I'm focused, I'm prepared, I'm—"

A gentle knock on the door interrupted my rant, and Vera and I stared at each other with equally shocked expressions.

"Are you expecting company?" she asked.

"Definitely not. Are you?"

She gave me a look that said, *Really?* Which was fair.

"Are you going to get it?"

"Right now?" I asked. "Who the hell could it be right now?"

"Willow, it's me." His voice drifted through the door like smoke, and my heart squeezed in my chest. "I know you said you wanted to do this alone, but I didn't get a chance to tell you last night what I think I've learned about your magic, and I think, well, I don't know, but I think it might help."

I'd completely forgotten about that. One kiss and every brain cell left my body, including the ones carrying the bit of information about Oliver thinking he had some insight into my magic, which he didn't even believe in until yesterday. What the hell was going on?

"How did you know to come here right now?" I asked, still on the other side of the door.

"Gut feeling," he said. "Can't explain it."

"You know what we call that in this house?" I asked.

"I reckon I might have an idea." I could hear the smile in his voice. In all the times I'd heard him talk about magic before last night, all I could hear was a scowl. And edge. The sharp blade of disbelief. But now? He was soft. Compassionate.

For a second, I considered the possibility he'd actually be able to help me. Until I realized the absurdity of it all a second later.

"Let me in, Willow." We both knew he wasn't just talking about the physical closed door between us. And that was the exact reason I couldn't.

"I can't," I whispered, up against the door and wishing I could run to him on the other side. "Being with you, you know it makes my magic—"

"It's not being with me that's the problem," he said. "That's the thing. It's *resisting* it."

It's . . . what?

"Oliver, respectfully, I've been dealing with this my whole life, and resisting is definitely not the problem. It's the only thing that's kept my magic under control. Well . . . more or less."

"Think about it," he said, and I could hear him getting more animated. "Every time something has gone awry, it's because you've been pushing me away. When you pushed me away in the Underground and the Tube showered us in sparks, when you pulled my hands off of you in the shower and the pipe blew, when you tried to slam the door in my face and your hair caught on fire. Your magic misfired because you were pushing me away.

"And then think about the first time we slept together. When we finally gave in. And there was no catastrophe. And again last night, you let your guard down, and nothing happened, did it? No fires, no explosions, no power outages. Nothing."

I slid down the door until I was sitting, afraid I might collapse if I didn't. That couldn't be true. There was no way I'd had it backward for thirty years of my life. All this time, and pushing people *away* was the problem?

"And didn't you say the spell on your manager went wrong when you were in an argument about doing a romance film? When you were quite literally resisting romance? Willow, it all makes sense."

"But how did you—"

"Uncle Arthur's ledger," he said. "He knew your gran, Willow. And the same thing happened to her. Her magic went haywire when she was talking to a man in the shop, and I wasn't sure at first if that was connected, but then Uncle Arthur wrote she turned punch to gelatin at a party when she was telling a bloke she couldn't go on a date because she had to return to America and it just, it all just clicked."

"He wrote about Granny?" I asked, feeling my chin start to wobble. Anyone who knew Granny was the luckiest person in the world. And to hear stories about her from an outsider? Stories about her magic working just like mine? It was like she was giving me a gift.

"He did," he said. "And he said the loveliest things about her. I can tell how much you take after her." I swiped a tear from my cheek, unable to hold them in any longer. "And I reckon she'd have more faith than anyone that you could do this spell, Willow. With me as a close second, of course." I laughed through my tears, wondering if any of this really could be true. "I think it's worth a try, don't you?" he asked.

"Letting you in?" I asked.

"Letting me in," he confirmed.

I stood up and flicked the lock, prepared first to just let him into the flat. One thing at a time. I opened the door to find him leaning on the doorjamb, his hair a mess, his shirt wrinkled. Like he'd bolted out of the house the second he realized I needed him.

"Hi," he said.

"Hi."

"Are you ready to try again?" It was such a loaded question, I felt it wrap around me like fog. Like I could almost reach out and touch it.

"What if it doesn't work?" I asked, my own voice smaller than I'd ever heard it.

"If you don't trust me, trust your gran," he said. "She'd tell to you go for it, wouldn't she? Worries be damned?"

I laughed again, unable to resist the mental image of Granny Annie cheering me and Ivy on as we learned spells as kids. Jumping up and down with her arms in the air, even if we failed.

"So I just have to—"

"Stop resisting," he finished. "Give in to it, Willow."

For the sake of my magic, and for the sake of my happiness, I did. I kissed him like we were the only two people in the whole city, laughing against his lips as Vera groaned, relishing the newfound lightness that came with acceptance.

"Do it," he said, pulling away and turning his back to give me privacy. "Do it now."

Before we lost the moment, I turned to Vera and chanted the spell one more time.

Time turner, turn back time.
Reverse this spell that was not mine.
Undo the damage
I have done
And take us back to square one.

And just like last summer, there was a flash of a light and a swirl of smoke, and then a woman stood before me.

"Good god, must that be so aggressive?" She coughed a few times and brushed dust from her clothes, shaking out her shoulders and pushing her hair from her eyes.

"Holy shit," I cried. "I've done it! Vera, you're back!"

"Indeed I am." She smiled. "Well done, Willow."

I sank to my knees, unable to believe I'd actually done it. That after the last six months, the uncertainty, the stress, the heartache, the challenges, the victories, the growth, the roller coaster, I'd really done it.

And Oliver was *right.*

"You must be Oliver," Vera said, extending her hand. Thin, manicured fingers instead of a paw.

"Pleasure," he said, giving her hand a firm shake.

I couldn't believe this scene. Even as it unfolded before me, I couldn't believe it was actually happening. Couldn't believe I'd done something right. Not until Oliver lowered himself to the floor in front of me and grabbed me by the shoulders.

"You've done it." He smiled, and every nerve ending in my body lit up.

"Is now the time you say *I told you so?*" I asked, wiping a happy tear from my eye.

"No, Willow," he said. "Now's the time I say I love you."

I. Forage for *Clinopodium menthifolium*, grown locally. Prepare and consume locally in accordance with your preferences. ✔

II. Conduct an Orientation spell with the Wharram Percy Pendulum. Use its direction as a guide. ✔

III. Complete the Ritualistic Restoration Cleansing in a pond, lake, or slow-moving river to prepare the body for the Reversal. ✔

IV. Participate in a Full Moon Ceremony. Stay awake until the following sundown for maximum effect. ✔

V. Commune with those who have passed on. They know more than any of us who remain in our mortal forms on Earth. ✔

VI. Convince a skeptic of the existence of magic. Use the experience to fortify your powers to effectively produce the Reversal. ✔

EPILOGUE
Oliver

The summer solstice was right around the corner, and every inch of London was alive. The parks were green, filled with families on picnic blankets and lovers under trees and dogs running off lead; the pubs were overflowing long before the workday was over, and the sun beat down between bouts of lashing rain.

And Willow was still here.

Six months later—and probably even six minutes later—I could admit it might have been premature telling Willow I loved her. I could have blamed it on the heat of the moment, the adrenaline, how badly I wanted her to stay, but the truth was, she made me brave. Watching her open herself up to me, to the possibility of something more, watching her relearn the limits of her magic, do things she was afraid of, try and try again, it gave me the courage I needed to tell her how I felt, even if too soon. It was true, and that was all that mattered.

And when she said it back, well, that didn't hurt, either.

It took some time for her to work out what came next for her career, a lot of phone calls and emails and tears of all kinds, but after she confessed to feeling the same way, I had a bottomless well of patience. I'd have waited years, lifetimes, for her, and I knew how spoiled I was when she stayed.

She wasn't ending her acting career, but she seemed impossibly relieved to be taking a much-needed hiatus. A break to sort herself out, focus on her magic, give herself time to grow in other ways.

Human Vera—who was lovely, if utterly terrifying—ended up taking on a smaller client part-time, allowing her some of the freedom she'd grown to love in her months as a cat. Willow seemed happy for her about that decision, so I imagined it was the right one. And the less guilt Willow had about the break in her career, the better.

"Ol, are you almost ready?" she asked, stumbling as she slid her shoe onto her foot in the doorway. "Lola is going to kill us if we're late."

"Lola's always late," I said, catching her and pulling her in for a kiss. She smiled against my lips before melting into me, moaning gently into my mouth when I wrapped her ponytail around my wrist.

"Oliver," she protested, but the way she said my name only made me want her more. "The full moon festival waits for no one," she said.

"It goes all night," I mumbled against her. "It waits for everyone."

"Keep arguing and—"

"And what?" I teased. "You'll turn me into a cat?" She froze, mouth open in mock horror. "Too soon?"

"Too soon is your specialty." She smiled, and it lit up her whole face. Hell, it lit up the whole flat. The full moon couldn't hold a candle to her.

"You're right," I said. "And in that case, we better get our arses to the festival before I do something crazy like ask you to move in with me."

She gasped. "Oliver—" she started, but her mouth turned from an O to a smile before I could say another word.

"Come on." I pulled her by the hand toward the door, letting the question tag along for the night like a welcome third wheel. Maybe with enough moon water she'd say yes. "The full moon festival waits for no one."

ACKNOWLEDGMENTS

This project was the loveliest surprise, and my gratitude for those who helped me get it here is immeasurable.

To my agent, Hannah Todd. Thank you for providing me with this opportunity and encouraging me to get outside my comfort zone to pursue it. Every call with you means something fun and exciting, and this project was no different!

To my editor, Shannon Plackis. It was such a joy working together, and without your eagle eye, I have no idea where this story would be. (Just kidding. I know exactly where it would be: riddled with plot holes and magic-related inconsistencies.) You asked the hard questions about Willow, Oliver, and how they exist in the world, and the story is so much stronger as a result.

To the rest of the incredibly dedicated, highly talented, detail-oriented team at HarperCollins. Your efforts are the reason I get to have this incredible career, and I am eternally grateful for the time, energy, and attention you give to these stories.

To my friends. My very close few. You know who you are. Thank you for listening to me talk incessantly about "the Witch Book" for the difficult few months it took to put this story together. And thank you for offering every ounce of sci-fi, fantasy, or witch-related knowledge you have. Trust it all made it into this story in one way or another. (Special shout-out to Davis, for forcing me to write even when we were in Ireland and on flights and drinking in the backyard and all the times I didn't want to write. You might be the reason I hit this deadline.)

To my coworkers. Thank you for lending me your names and for your endless support. If you're sick of listening to me talk about my writing every Monday morning during Huddle, you never show it, and for that, I am grateful. Being surrounded by strong, inspiring women makes it that much easier to write strong, inspiring women.

To my mom. Thank you for forcing me to stick to my daily word count goals even when I complained, for reminding me that I Am a Writer and I *get* to do this, for encouraging me to try new things and push the boundaries of my writing. For helping me decorate my new office so I have a little creative haven. For giving me the kind of life advice that inspires my wise old ladies. For taking me on my first trip to London.

To my dad and Kristen. Thank you for getting excited about all things witchy and checking in on my progress, begging to read an early copy. It's so much easier to write with someone excited in your corner.

To my siblings, Jake Rosone, Steph Rosone, and Daniel "The Swamp Dog" Rosone. There are no louder, prouder supporters of my work (even if you're vaguely threatening). If you've made it this far in this one, hopefully you skipped the sex parts. (Sorry.)

And to Adam. You're in every word I write. My sparks, my late nights, my compass, my highest highs. My proof that magic exists.

ABOUT THE AUTHOR

Alexandra Paige is a novelist and a marketing copywriter. Her debut novel was *Weekends with You*. She currently writes in an apartment she shares with her boyfriend in a cozy New Jersey suburb or in the coffee shop down the street, though her stories are always taking her elsewhere. She has a BA from Moravian University and an MFA from Lindenwood University.